To Vincent & Áine

A STORY OF THE
BODKIN MURDERS
By

Paul B Mcnulty

A Club Lighthouse Publishing Book

ISBN: 978-1512111545

Cover Rendition: T.L. Davison

For further information contact:

editor@clublighthousepublishing.com

**A Club Lighthouse Historical Romance Edition
Published In Canada**

DEDICATION

To *Treasa, Dara, Nora and Meabh*

ACKNOWLEDGEMENTS

I wish to thank my son, Dara, who reviewed a 50,000-word draft written in the month of November 2010 as part of the National Novel Writing Month. I am indebted to the members of a writers group, The Corner Table, who reviewed drafts of individual chapters and Elaine P Kennedy who structurally edited and copy edited my manuscript.

I also acknowledge the assistance of Dr A J Claffey, Tuam, Co Galway; Frank Canavan, Belclare, Co Galway; John Courtney, Kilconly, Tuam; Frank Higgins, Carrowbeg North, Belclare and Ger Hoade, Carrowbeg House, Carrowbeg North, Belclare both of whom suggested locations for the now destroyed Carrowbaun (fictionalised as Liscarrow) House as being near Polldarragh, Belclare or near a cattle crush close to the Bird Hide, Pollaturk, Belclare; Sean Murphy, for expert advice on family history; Patricia O'Reilly, who introduced me to creative writing; and members of my extended family.

Proposed pedigree of the Bodkins of Carrowbeg and Liscarrow,
Belclare, Tuam, County Galway, Ireland.

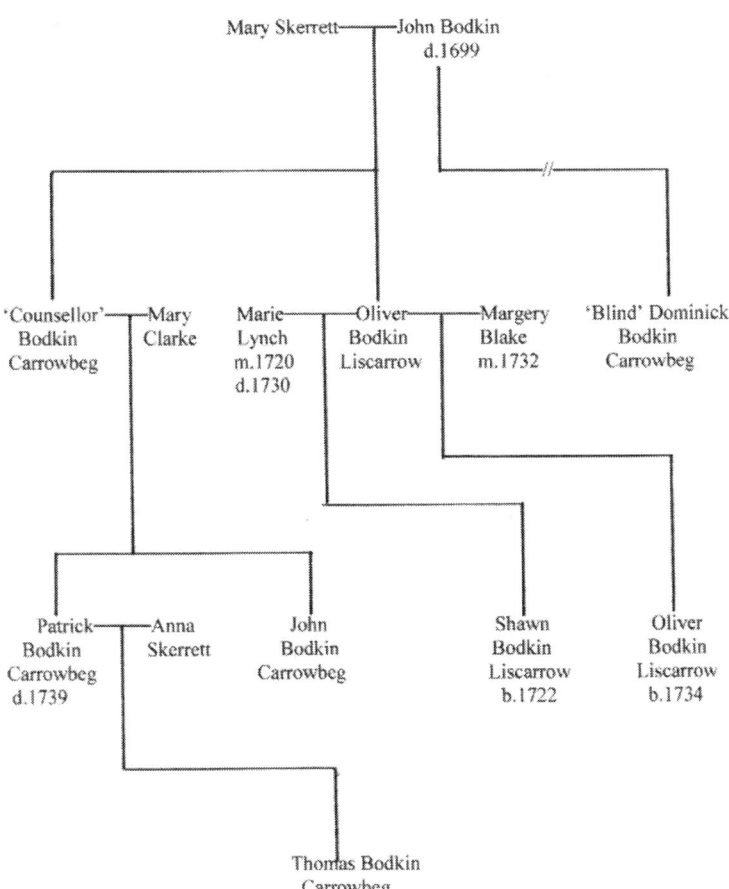

CHAPTER 1

Liscarrow House,
September 1741

AS JOHN BODKIN WALKED through the door, the smell of stale blood assailed his nostrils, nauseating him. The blood was everywhere in the hallway: spattered on the carpet, on the great clock and on the hanging mirror. He scarcely recognized his family home.

A shiver ran up his spine as the agent, James Joyce, gestured towards two crumpled bodies at the end of the dimly-lit hallway.

John stared at the slit throats of the dead bodies. It took a few moments before his brain registered what his eyes were seeing. *Good Lord! Surely, those are not the bodies of the butler and the housekeeper?* A cold sweat washed over him and his gorge rose. He dashed out into the fresh air. Placing his hands against the wall of stone, he fought to retain the contents of his stomach.

When he had regained control, John saw three out-servants leaning over the body of a dog in the farmyard.

"What happened?" John asked.

"Someone came in the night and slit his throat." The agent shook his head. "The same happened to the other guard dog."

"Robbers?" John asked.

"Nothing seems to have been taken from the house." Joyce's voice quivered.

"Where is Uncle Oliver?" Surely, his uncle would know what had occurred.

Joyce paled. "You should not go upstairs."

John trembled. "I must see him." He re-entered the house that he knew so well and followed Joyce, stopping at the entrance to the bedroom of the Master of Liscarrow.

"Please do not enter," Joyce pleaded.

John steadied himself. He turned the knob and slowly pushed the door open. Oliver Bodkin lay in the bed, high on the pillows, his eyes and mouth opened wide. Blood had congealed on his throat. His heavily pregnant wife, Margery, lay beside him, her throat slit also.

"I don't believe this!" John cried. *It cannot be true. I must be dreaming.* How could such an outrage have occurred in the quiet village of Belclare? He felt the strong arm of Joyce around his shoulder.

"A terrible day, Mr John."

John walked towards the window feeling dazed. For a moment, he thought he had caught a glimpse of his loveable cousin, little Oliver, riding a pony in the garden. How he had enjoyed teaching him to ride while the child's mother had looked on.

"Where is little Oliver?"

Tears welled in the eyes of the agent as he glanced downwards to the side of the bed that John had just passed by.

"No. No!" John shouted. Little Oliver was dead, a bloodied axe lay beside his mutilated body. John could take no more. He ran out of the house. This time he felt like puking but his stomach was empty.

There he remained for some time as he tried to make sense of the gruesome slaughter. He forced himself to return and walked through the ground floor. Apart from the desecrated hallway, the reception rooms were in a pristine state. There was no sign of robbery. The silver plate sat gleaming and untouched on the sideboard of the dining room.

John walked upstairs again. All the bedrooms were undisturbed apart from that of Oliver and the visitor's room.

"You should not go in there, Mr John," Joyce repeated. "Marcus Lynch, a visitor from Galway, lies murdered in that chamber."

"The poor man—he was just here for the Galway Races. Is that the whole of it?"

"I fear not. This way, sir." John followed Joyce to the rear of the house, through the deserted kitchen, and through the farmyard to the servants' quarters.

"I suspect the murderers started here," Joyce said, opening the door of the sleeping area. Four servants, one a maid, lay dead on their straw pallets; each one's throat had been slit.

"Ten people murdered in one night," John said incredulously. "What madness is this, Mr Joyce?"

The agent, who wore a dark jacket, beige breeches and black boots, shook his head in apparent despair.

* * * * *

JOHN RETURNED TO THE farmyard to find that Shawn Bodkin had arrived. The sight of his cousin in bloodstained clothes recalled the commotion he had heard earlier that morning in the house they shared at nearby Carrowbeg. He had woken up with a throbbing headache even though he had drank little at their Saturday-night carousing. In addition to

2

Shawn, those gatherings involved their uncle Dominick Bodkin, the shepherd Shane Hogan, and the Whiteboy, Roger Kelly, the agrarian rebel. When Hogan and Kelly were present, John was obliged to make himself scarce to facilitate their confidential discussions. He knew that their deliberations revolved around the disinheritance of Shawn Bodkin by his father, Oliver, at Liscarrow.

On this occasion, he had heard more shouting and roaring than ever before, at such a late hour. Then there was a period of quiet, followed by the banging of doors. Through his bedroom window, John heard Dominick and Hogan slurring their words in the farmyard. Shawn roared at them through the opened window of an adjoining bedroom; then came the whinnying of horses and the clattering of hooves as both rode away before sunrise.

John was mystified as to why Dominick and Shane had ridden away without Shawn; and where was Roger Kelly? He slept fitfully and woke up at about nine of the clock. Dashing his face with cold water, he walked downstairs where the housemaid was cleaning up after the rowdy gathering.

"Good morning, Julia," John greeted her.

"Good morning, sir!" she replied, sighing. "The mess is worse than usual. That red mark will never come out."

While John looked absentmindedly at the stained settee, he thought he heard a sound at the far end of the house. "Did you hear something?"

"I'll check it out, sir."

As Julia walked down the corridor of the long stone house, John was distracted on hearing a loud knocking at the front door.

A breathless messenger rushed in. "A terrible thing has happened at Liscarrow!"

"What?" John asked.

"Mr Joyce said to come at once; he'll tell you then."

* * * * *

THAT IS HOW JOHN Bodkin, now aged twenty-one, had ended up at Liscarrow on Sunday morning, 20 September 1741. He stared at his cousin Shawn Bodkin, who threw his arms around him and wept.

"What happened?" asked Shawn unsteadily.

John smelled the alcohol from Shawn's breath and retreated in disgust from contact with his red-stained jacket. "Your family has been brutally murdered."

"No!" cried Shawn, covering his face. "Who could have done such a thing?"

By now, Lord Athenry had arrived on his black mare. The local Justice of the Peace walked into the house, followed by Shawn.

John suspected that his cousin was involved in the killings because of his bloodied clothes and his known determination to recover his inheritance; but why had he not run away with Dominick and Hogan? Shawn appeared to be in a dazed state without any apparent realization of what had occurred.

When Athenry emerged from the house, his face was drained of colour. He held a grim-faced Shawn by the arm and sent him away with two yeoman soldiers. The Justice of the Peace called John aside. "This is the worst atrocity I have ever seen. I have arrested Shawn Bodkin on suspicion of murder."

John was aware that Athenry was in possession of a letter from Shawn threatening his father and demanding the reinstatement of his inheritance.

Athenry's cold blue eyes glanced at the red stain on John's jacket, transferred to him when Shawn had embraced him. "I must arrest you also on suspicion of murder."

"No!" John shouted. "I was summoned here only an hour ago."

Athenry looked deep into his eyes. "That remains to be seen."

John looked in stupefaction at his jacket. "I don't understand," he said. "Shawn held on to me when he arrived. That's how it got stained."

"I shall speak to you later today in the Bridewell."

John was seething with rage when he was hauled away to join Shawn in a holding cell in the nearby town of Tuam. Alone there, he looked angrily at his cousin. "Where did you get that stain on your jacket?"

"Mind your own business!" Shawn had sobered up.

"Why did Dominick and Hogan ride away?" John paced the floor restlessly.

Shawn grabbed him by the neck and hissed, "I told you to mind your own business."

"How could you be so evil?" John pushed Shawn away. "Killing an innocent seven-year-old boy to recover your inheritance!"

"What about the inheritance you gained when Patrick died?" Shawn smiled grimly.

"That was a natural death, as you well know." John could not control the rush of colour to his cheeks as he recalled the night that his elder brother, Patrick, had died. Only he and his betrothed, Catherine Bermingham, the daughter of Lord Athenry, knew the full story of what happened on that night.

"I did not kill little Oliver!" Shawn's eyes darkened.

"But you planned it, you scoundrel." John raised his fist, which he dearly wished to smash into his cousin's smug face.

With his back to the wall, Shawn slid down on to the earthen floor. When his cousin remained silent, John began to prepare himself for interrogation by Athenry. He appreciated that Catherine's father needed to arrest as many potential suspects as possible to allay the inevitable anger of the relatives of the deceased. News of the massacre would spread rapidly throughout the community and further afield.

Athenry was right about one thing: John had heard snatches of conversation about the need to recover Shawn's inheritance. However, he had never suspected that it would be regained by murdering Shawn's half-brother, little Oliver, the new heir.

Catherine would be baffled when she heard of his arrest by her own father. John suspected that Athenry was unimpressed by his modest credentials as a fiancé. However, the aristocrat would hardly allow such a prejudice to cloud his judgment on a case that would bring him to national attention.

Shawn had now slipped on to his back and was snoring peacefully, much to John's relief.

On his return, the warder said, "Lord Athenry wishes to speak to Mr John Bodkin in the keeper's office."

John rose, dusted himself down and followed the warder into a sparsely furnished room. A portrait of George II appeared to stare benignly down at him. Athenry beckoned him to sit down on the opposite side of a bare table.

"I have reviewed your situation," he spoke slowly. "I have concluded that you were not directly involved in the heinous crime, although you may have had some foreknowledge of it."

"I had nothing to do with it," replied John tersely, feeling that Athenry had more to say.

"You may be of greater value as a witness for the prosecution than as a suspect."

So this was the way of it! The old codger will release me if I testify for the prosecution. John nodded perfunctorily.

"Your parents will arrive in Tuam from Dublin this afternoon. I expect you to be there at four of the clock to greet them. They will already be aware of what has happened. I shall join you there and travel with you to Liscarrow so that your father can identify the bodies."

John heaved a sigh of relief. He remained in his chair as Athenry stared at him again with those unblinking eyes of authority. Presuming that he was free to leave, he rose slowly and departed. As he walked the pavements of the town of Tuam, he sucked in the billowing air to refresh his lungs after the stench of the Bridewell. Entering The Thomas Bagworth Inn, he sat alone in a quiet spot and ordered a brandy. He needed time to make sense of the morning's events.

* * * * *

WHEN JOHN REPORTED TO the stagecoach stop at the appointed time, he saw the Bermingham carriage waiting there. He walked by to announce his presence without looking-in. If Catherine had travelled with Athenry, she would have signalled to him. How he longed to meet her to discuss the horrid tragedy. He wished that she could be by his side when his parents arrived.

And arrive they did at four of the clock, ashen-faced as they disembarked. Mary Bodkin rushed towards him and threw herself sobbing into his arms. Counsellor-at-law Bodkin wrapped his arms around both of them as tears formed in his eyes. They stood like that for a time, sobbing inconsolably, until Athenry approached.

They disengaged to allow him to pay his respects, first to Mrs Bodkin and then to his long-time friend and associate, Counsellor Bodkin. Local people stopped to observe the grieving family and cross themselves with a blessing—news of the heinous crime had spread rapidly. John could see that his parents were in a state of shock as Athenry escorted them into his carriage.

They were soon on the road to the village of Belclare, four miles west of Tuam. They travelled in silence until Athenry removed the top of his hamper.

"I have a flask of ale, a naggin of brandy and some food in case you are hungry or thirsty."

"I have no appetite, Lord Athenry," Mary said.

"I shall have a small drop of brandy, thank you," Counsellor Bodkin added.

Athenry passed the liquor to John's father who unscrewed the naggin and held it to his lips. "Where are we going?"

"To Liscarrow," Athenry replied.

"To identify the bodies." Bodkin sighed. "Who could have committed such a dastardly deed?"

"Shawn has already been arrested," John said.

"Good grief! My own nephew." Bodkin shook his head in disbelief.

"Uncle Dominick and Shane Hogan have run away." John said, looking out the window. He heard little birds chirping as they flew hither and thither. Apart from passers-by blessing themselves, apparent normality surrounded them as they proceeded towards their destination of horror.

Liscarrow, with two storeys and a basement, was a finer house than Carrowbeg. The landscaped surround of shrubs and trees was in sharp contrast to the unkempt appearance of his father's house. On their arrival, the out-servants approached his parents, doffing their caps and muttering, "Sorry for your troubles."

Removing his tricorn hat, the agent addressed Counsellor and Mrs Bodkin, "On behalf of the tenants and workers of Liscarrow, please accept our sympathies. May the Lord have mercy on the souls of the departed."

"Thank you, Mr Joyce," replied Bodkin.

"The womenfolk have cleaned up the drawing room, with Lord Athenry's permission. He has locked that room pending identification of the …" Joyce's voice tailed away, his brow furrowed. He added, "The women are anxious to clean the house for the wake."

John nodded in agreement.

His mother retched upon seeing the bloodstained floor in the hallway.

"Mama, you should stay in the carriage; Papa too. I can identify the bodies."

"John is right, Mary," replied Bodkin. "But I need to see what has happened."

A stale smell hung in the air and an eerie silence still prevailed. Even the great hall clock was silent. John resisted the temptation to wind it up because it could bring bad luck. Red spatters on the furniture and carpets of the hallway, and throughout the two disturbed bedchambers, contrasted sharply with the pristine condition of the other areas in the house.

Athenry bore a large iron key as he approached the drawing room. When he turned the key, the door groaned on its hinges. Moving into the oak-panelled room, John saw the three Bodkin victims laid out side by side on marble-topped tables. The undertaker had preserved the bodies as best he could. The light from flickering candles revealed the brutal nature of the murders.

"My God!" cried Bodkin. "My poor brother, Oliver, the kindest man in the world—who could have done this?"

John saw a thin white bandage running across the throat of Oliver's neck reminding him of the slit throats of the guard dogs. The undertaker had similarly bandaged his pregnant wife, Margery. Most poignant was the fully bandaged neck of little Oliver, only seven years old.

After official identification of the victims, Athenry took his leave. John caught his father as he stumbled. He brought him to the drawing room and sat with him. When his father had recovered, they kneeled and prayed to the Almighty in their hour of need.

After an interval, John told Joyce that the waking could commence. Wooden benches lay around the walls of the drawing room. The out-servants carried bottles of brandy, whiskey and port, jugs of ale, wooden cups and glasses on to a sideboard. Dishes of cold ham, salads and bread soon weighed down another sideboard, together with crockery, plates and napkins, kindly donated by friends of the family.

Dean Bruce arrived with the local vicar and cried out with his booming voice on seeing the bodies. He sat with the Bodkins for a long period, silently drinking a glass or two of brandy. His presence was some consolation, as was the arrival of their closest friends, standing by them in their hour of need. John wondered why the Blakes of Oranmore had not come to mourn their daughter, Margery, the wife of the late Oliver Bodkin.

This was not a time for celebration. There would be no wild drinking or bawdy songs. Of conversation, there was little: only the occasional sound of shuffling feet and the clearing of throats. John listened to the keening of the Catholic servants, grieving their murdered friends. They also wailed in lamentation for little Oliver whom they had adored. The solemnity of the occasion helped John to mourn his lost relatives.

Gradually, over time, the visitors dispersed. Most of the food remained un-eaten. The servants waited a while and then walked home to their cabins. Finally, John left with his parents as Joyce locked up, having left three candles lit in the window of the drawing room.

On arrival home at Carrowbeg, Counsellor Bodkin sighed while reclining on the settee now covered with a blanket. "I need a brandy. How can we sleep tonight?" Shaking his head, he continued, "What shall we do tomorrow?"

"What do we need to do?" John asked as the footman served the golden liquor.

"I must visit Margery's relatives in Oranmore, and those of Marcus Lynch of Galway, as well as the bereaved parents of the servants."

"I shall go with you, my dear," Mary said.

"I will alert the groom," John added, poking the smouldering embers of the fire of wood.

CHAPTER 2

CATHERINE BERMINGHAM WAS FURIOUS that her father, Lord Athenry, had not allowed her to attend the Bodkin wake at Liscarrow, knowing that John would be upset at her absence. Now nineteen, she was on the road with her chaperone, Matilda Blake, travelling further away from her beloved. She understood why Miss Blake needed to grieve for her sister, Margery Bodkin, but felt uncomfortable at intruding into the private domain of the Blakes.

On arrival at Oranmore, she was pleasantly surprised to find the Bodkins sitting in the drawing room with the Blakes. She gazed straight at John, whose brown eyes warmed her very soul.

"Welcome to our home, Miss Catherine," Colonel Blake said.

After Catherine curtsied, Blake continued, "It is regrettable that we have to meet under such tragic circumstances."

"Thank you, Colonel Blake. Please accept my sympathies on your great loss." The reference to the tragedy brought tears to her eyes. Before sitting down, she said, "Would you excuse me, please, for a few moments?"

When Miss Blake nodded, Catherine prayed that John would follow her, needing to speak to him alone, if only for a few moments. After attending to her toilette, she waited in the hallway until she saw the knob of the drawing-room door turning. She hid in the library but left the door ajar. Peering through the crevice at the door hinge, she saw that it was John leaving the room. She opened the door and beckoned him towards her.

"Oh, John, this is so terrible." She flung herself into his arms.

"I know, my darling." John held her tight.

"Papa said he arrested you." Catherine blushed. "I could not credit my ears."

"Only temporarily, it was purely procedural."

"Hem!" *Procedural* was not how she would have described her father's actions. *I know only too well how little my father thinks of my fiancé.* "We must talk later; we had better return before Miss Blake thinks my absence overlong."

Back in the drawing-room, Catherine saw a tear roll down the ruddy cheek of the colonel.

"How could this massacre have occurred?" Blake asked standing in front of the blazing fire. "I have heard rumours of a family feud—was that behind it?"

"We do not know for certain." Counsellor Bodkin frowned. He tightened his grip on his wife's hand. "I regret to say that my brother,

Dominick, and my nephew, Shawn, have been arrested on suspicion of murder."

Catherine held her breath. Did the Blakes know that her father had also arrested John even though he had been released shortly afterwards? Her beloved shifted in his seat. She could almost feel his distress.

Her meandering thoughts aligned with the words of the colonel when he said, "Margery did not get on with her stepson, Shawn Bodkin. She said he had tried to poison her. We thought she had imagined it, at first."

"Shawn broke his father's heart. He went astray in Dublin," Bodkin responded. "He failed in his study of the law and grew bitter. Now he may pay the ultimate price."

Catherine shivered when she heard those words, *ultimate price*. It brought her back to the night more than two years ago when John's elder brother, Patrick, had died. Her father had pronounced his death as natural after consulting with the coroner. She knew differently, but now was not the time to think of this.

Blake said, "I understand that Shawn resented his disinheritance in favour of little Oliver."

"That is correct," Bodkin replied.

Catherine was surprised at the frankness of the exchanges. She was anxious to talk to John at greater length. He would be able to tell her the full story of his arrest by her father and his subsequent release.

Clasping his blackthorn stick, the Colonel said, "Is it true that he was …?" His voice tailed away.

Bodkin responded, "Little Oliver's wound was heavily bandaged; a bloodied axe was found nearby."

Catherine felt sick as Blake said, "Once I heard … I could not persuade my wife to attend the wake."

"Papa would not allow me to attend either," Catherine added mournfully.

Feeling uncomfortable in the tense atmosphere, Catherine looked around the oak-panelled room. Her gaze fell on the smiling face of little Oliver in the portrait she herself had painted just last summer. John's engagement gift of a painting kit that included brushes and natural pigments had delighted her. She felt so proud that she had developed her art sufficiently to capture John's cousin on canvas while the poor boy was still alive.

"We must not intrude on your grief any longer," Bodkin said. "Please excuse us."

Catherine could sense the frostiness emanating from Colonel Blake. The origin of the combative nature of the late Margery became clear: she had surely been her father's daughter.

Summoning up her resolve, Catherine said, "Counsellor Bodkin, may I travel with you, please?"

Bodkin glanced at Matilda Blake who nodded in agreement.

As they traversed the coast road towards Galway City, Catherine gazed at the turbulent sea-water, her heart heavy with the thought of the horrid massacre.

"The Blakes will come to appreciate our visit in due course," Bodkin said. "I did not have a mind to discuss the burials at this time."

Goodness, thought Catherine, to whom the point had not occurred. Would the Blakes object to the normal practice of burying Margery and little Oliver with her husband's family?

*　*　*　*　*

JOHN LOVED TO VISIT the walled city of Galway, a welcome respite from the dreariness of rural Carrowbeg. Even better was the presence of his beloved Catherine whose absence from the wake at Liscarrow had grieved him. He longed for an opportunity to explain why her father had arrested him. For the moment, he enjoyed the comfort of her body as they sat side by side in the chaise-and-four en route to Galway.

On arrival, their carriage drew up at Lynch's Castle, the medieval building that celebrated the supremacy of the Anglo-Norman tradition.

"So this is the house of poor Marcus Lynch," John said.

"May the Lord have mercy on his soul," Counsellor Bodkin intoned, clasping his hands together.

Having alighted from the carriage, they joined the mourners inside the prestigious building that bore the arms of Henry VII. John grasped Catherine's hand as they approached the corpse of Marcus Lynch on a marble-topped table in the drawing room.

"He looks at peace," Catherine whispered.

"I see no sign of throat damage," John said, surprised.

Having moved away from the corpse, Catherine asked, "Why was Mr Lynch in Liscarrow?"

"Because of a plague in Galway City: last winter was one of the coldest in living memory."

"I remember it well." Catherine rubbed her gloved hands together.

"The potatoes were rotten in the ground when the thaw set in last February." John was now in full flight, at ease with the undivided attention of his beloved. "A famine followed, succeeded by pestilence and evictions. Typhus fever broke out in Galway City—"

"My dear, I merely asked what brought Mr Lynch to Liscarrow."

John's face reddened. "Patience, my dear Catherine." John drew his breath. "The plague persisted into the summer, and the Galway Races were transferred to the healthier town of Tuam. Marcus received an invitation to stay at Liscarrow in order to attend the fun and games from there."

"Let us hope the plague has subsided by now." Catherine shuddered.

"Indeed it has since last Wednesday ... because, for the ten days previous, not one person had fallen ill." John smiled. "Now we can discard our posies of sweet-smelling herbs. Mama said the scent would protect us from the disease."

"Ring a Ring o'Roses ..." Catherine raised her eyebrows, having recited the opening line of the rhyme associated with the plague.

After paying their respects, Mrs Lynch drew the Bodkins aside into the parlour.

"My poor Marcus: how could this have happened? Why was he killed?"

John heaved a sigh of relief when his father took command.

"I am trying to understand that myself, Mrs Lynch. You live in Galway and I live in Dublin, both of us at a remove from events in the countryside."

"He was only in Liscarrow to attend the races."

"I was shocked when I heard the news," Bodkin said. "It appears that it may have been a family feud which caused the massacre."

"How could a family feud involve my poor husband?"

"I am not yet certain, but your husband lost his life because the scoundrels killed all those present, presumably to eliminate witnesses." Bodkin paused. "Please accept the heartfelt sympathy of my family."

John suspected that the feud arose from the disinheritance of Shawn Bodkin, the son of Oliver's first wife, Marie Lynch. He was about to explain that to Catherine when Mrs Lynch interjected in a trembling voice.

"The undertaker told me that my husband was repeatedly stabbed. His breast and belly were ripped open like a sheep in the slaughterhouse."

John wanted to retch. Lynch must have put up a struggle to prevent the slitting of his throat. No wonder Joyce had dissuaded John from entering that bedroom.

"You may know that my nephew, Shawn, and my brother, Dominick, have been arrested," Bodkin said. "If they are guilty, their hostility may have

12

arisen from the disinheritance of Shawn. I can only assume that the other fatalities arose from the need to get rid of evidence."

Mrs Lynch pursed her lips as tears streamed down her cheeks.

Bodkin continued, "Those charged will be brought to justice at the Assizes in Tuam within the next few weeks."

"It was good of you to come and to speak so openly. I shall attend the court hearing."

"We shall now leave you in peace."

John heaved a sigh of relief that his father had not mentioned the fact that his own son had also been a suspect.

* * * * *

CATHERINE UNDERSTOOD WHY MRS Lynch was so devastated by the barbaric murder of her husband: it was so pointless, an innocent man in the wrong place at the wrong time. It reminded her of the grief and bewilderment of John's parents on the death of their eldest son, Patrick, more than two years ago. She had been in the house that night when he passed away. Would the full story of that momentous event now emerge as a background to the current massacre?

Her thoughts were disturbed on the road home to Liscarrow when she heard a passer-by shouting, "The bloody Bodkins ... scoundrels ... murderers!"

"Who said that?" she cried.

"A man with a scar." John growled. "A trap approached us at speed out of—"

"What an ignorant fellow!" Catherine interjected while John opened his pocket telescope to peer at the trap vanishing in a cloud of dust. She was pleased that John still carried the instrument that had been her engagement present to him, even if it failed to identify the rogue.

"Ignore the vagabond!" Bodkin said as his cheeks coloured.

Catherine wondered if the man was a relative or sweetheart of one of the murdered servants. Was it possible they were about to visit his home or the home of his beloved?

On arrival at Liscarrow, the agent escorted them to the cabin of a grieving family. "I picked some late-flowering roses in case you might have need of them." Joyce said.

It was a pleasant afternoon with the western sun embellishing the yellow, brown and red colours of the autumnal leaves. That scene contrasted with an unsightly dungstead at the gable end of the peasant home. Catherine raised her handkerchief to lessen the noxious odour. She had never before been inside a servant's cabin, and found it very small with only one room, a straw bed by the rough wall, a centred fireplace beneath a hole in the roof and a small unglazed window to the east. *How could people survive in such deprived accommodation?* she wondered.

Joyce straightened his plate-buttoned jacket before saying, "There were two victims in this family, a footman and a maid, Thaddeus and Bridget McHugh."

A group of grieving neighbours had assembled outside the front door. More people were inside, waking the dead.

Approaching the parents of the deceased, the agent said, "This is Counsellor Bodkin, his wife, his son and Miss Catherine."

The heartbroken parents clung to one another. The man opened his mouth but the words got stuck in his throat.

Counsellor Bodkin said, "On behalf of my family, I wish to express my deepest sympathies on the cruel murder of your innocent son and daughter."

People stopped chattering, attracted by the authoritative voice of the respected counsellor.

"Your children have given great service to my late brother, Oliver, and his family. The authorities are determined to punish those who committed this heinous crime as soon as possible. I am pleased to see Friar Skerrett here today. This horrible tragedy must transcend any religious differences between us."

Catherine squeezed John's hand signalling how impressed she was with his father's response. The name of the priest stirred her memory because it was the maiden name of Anna, the widow of Patrick Bodkin. She had a vague memory of the priest attending Patrick's wake at Carrowbeg, suggesting a family relationship. John had told her that Anna was a distant cousin of his grandmother, known as the widow Skerrett.

After Bodkin's speech, the distraught parents seemed less uncomfortable in the presence of such exalted company.

"Allow me to recite a decade of the rosary," Friar Skerrett said, dusting his brown sackcloth. People dropped on one knee on to the earthen floor.

Catherine took care not to make a fuss of kneeling on her cream petticoat, as did Mary Bodkin beside her.

The *Our Father* was followed by ten *Hail Marys* and concluded with a *Glory be*. The prayer that impressed Catherine was the second part of the *Hail Mary*:

Holy Mary, mother of God,

Pray for us sinners,
Now, and at the hour of our death, Amen.

So now we are all sinners, Catherine thought grimly. Yet she experienced a feeling of spirituality occasioned by the repetition of the mantra and the soothing emotion of the common people. She wondered why her Protestant prayers never lifted her to the same extent.

After the worship, Friar Skerrett escorted the nervous parents towards the Bodkins.

The man of the house muttered, "Your presence here today means so …" His voice was checked by emotion.

"We are sorry for your troubles, too," his wife added.

"Thank you so much." Mary Bodkin hesitated before saying, "May we place a rose on each coffin?"

"Of course you may, and … while you're doing that, we'll get you a little drink."

Which is more than the Blakes offered, Catherine thought, as Mary placed red roses on the bodies of the son and daughter, both decked out in their Sunday best. They looked so peaceful and unmarked apart from the cravat and scarf shielding their respective throats.

The Bodkins bowed their heads when moving away from the rough coffins. It was a sacred moment marked by a silent tribute from those within the cabin and those outside.

Catherine sipped a glass of the peasant's fire-water for the first time in her life. It was just as well that neither her father nor her chaperone was present as the fiery poteen flowed down her gullet. *Goodness me! What an experience*. She leaned ever-so-slightly against John until the sensation eased.

A woman behind her began to keen. Other women in black shawls and red petticoats joined in the song of lament while kneeling around the coffins. Catherine felt the tears welling in her eyes.

After an extended interval, the Bodkins took their leave and set off towards the next cabin accompanied by the agent and priest. As they departed, Catherine saw a man with a scarred cheek stare intently at John with darkness in his eyes. John returned his gaze until the man moved away. Could he be the one who had verbally assaulted them on the road to Liscarrow?

Friar Skerrett broke the silence. "That went very well, Counsellor."

"Thank God." a relieved Bodkin exclaimed quietly.

"Your visit has been the talk of the estate," the agent said. "These people feel uplifted by contact with the Big House."

"Thank you for your help," Bodkin replied.

"I can take Miss Catherine home when the visits are over," Joyce offered.

"I shall ride with you," John responded after hugging his parents.

Catherine climbed into the agent's trap as John mounted his horse. Her journey home was uneventful until reaching Bermingham House where Lord Athenry was in quite a state, worried for her safety. Now was not the time to invite John to refreshments, given her father's mood. As she waved goodbye to her beloved, she knew they would meet again that evening at Saint Mary's Cathedral.

CHAPTER 3

JOHN BODKIN WAS STILL in a state of shock on the evening of the removal of the Bodkins to Tuam. Dressed in mourning black, he stood at the entrance porch before a large crowd that had gathered outside the cathedral. As he waited, John heard snatches of conversation. Who was guilty of the foul deed? Who had planned it? What was the motive? Could it have been blackguards from outside the area, fuelled with drink after the Galway Races?

After the tolling of the bell, Dean Bruce received the coffins at the door of the cathedral:

> *We receive the body of our brother, Oliver Bodkin,*
> *his wife, Margery and their son, Oliver...*

John walked behind the bearded priest as he escorted his grief-stricken parents to the top of the narrow nave. The Blakes followed, mourning their murdered daughter, Margery. The Bodkins sat opposite the Blakes, both on red upholstered chairs backed to the wall. John glanced at the tiny coffin of little Oliver lying between the coffins of his father and mother along the central axis of the nave. He shuddered at the memory of the bloodied axe that lay beside his seven-year-old cousin in his parent's bedroom. How could the murdering scoundrels have been so cruel?

As the sacristan removed the coffin lids, John was pleased to see Catherine arrive accompanied by Lord Athenry. A large contingent of professional people from the town and the landed gentry followed them. He directed his eyes at Catherine, who wore a black mourning gown with gold sleeve ruffles and white lambskin gloves. She carried three red roses, each one wrapped in silk. Her deportment reminded him of the time, two years ago, when they had mourned the death of his brother, Patrick.

Neither the psalms nor the prayers had changed in the meantime. Bruce raised his hands after the organist led the choir in the opening verses of the resurrectional psalm 119. Standing before the red-sandstone chancel arch, he prayed:

> *O Lord support us all the day long,*
> *till the shades lengthen and the evening comes...*

John prayed silently as Bruce walked from the altar and shook the hands of his parents and the Blakes as well as his own. Catherine followed with her father. When she raised her arms, John stood up and held her as the tears welled in his eyes. *Her tender embrace has filled my heart with the love I bear her.* He watched her placing a rose on each of the bodies of his relatives.

Afterwards, a procession of long-time friends expressed their sympathy to John amidst tears and loving embraces. The communal mourning soothed his soul. It continued through the evening and almost into the night against a background of flickering candles. From time to time, people stopped and stared in horror at the coffin of little Oliver and his heavily bandaged neck. They shook their heads in stupefaction at the sight, and that of his mother's advanced pregnancy.

As the crowd began to disperse, John became aware of an intense discussion among the Blakes, Dean Bruce and Lord Athenry. He saw Colonel Blake storming off from the south transept after much gesticulation. Standing by the High Cross of Tuam, Dean Bruce shrugged his shoulders while Athenry approached the Bodkins with Catherine.

"Please excuse me," Athenry said. "I need a few words with you."

John followed him with his father towards the quietness of the chancel.

"Colonel Blake would like to bury Margery in Oranmore." Athenry continued, "Dean Bruce said it was a most unusual request. The colonel replied that it was a most unusual situation."

John wondered what the fuss was about: nothing would restore their loved ones to life, no matter where they buried them.

Athenry furled his brow. "Blake insisted that his daughter could not lie with the Bodkins as members of the Bodkin family had murdered her. I said the court would soon decide on that matter."

Counsellor Bodkin responded, "We visited the Blakes this very morning. They did not raise the issue of separate burials."

"I understand, Counsellor."

"What does Dean Bruce think?" Bodkin asked

"He would prefer episcopal advice; however, Archbishop Synge's successor has not yet been appointed."

"Perhaps Blake should be told to leave well enough alone," John said.

"Indeed!" his father replied. "But what now?"

"Dean Bruce said he would pray for guidance. We must meet him before the funeral mass tomorrow." Athenry paused. "I shall now leave you in peace. Come along, Catherine."

John wanted to talk to Catherine but Athenry had in effect slammed the door in his face. After returning to the nave to meet the remaining sympathizers, he saw Anna, his brother's widow, approaching.

"Please accept my sympathies, John," she said, embracing him.

"Thank you, Anna. How is little Thomas?"

"He's thriving, thank God." Anna sighed. "This occasion reminds me of Patrick's death. I still cannot believe he died so young from natural causes." A tear trickled down her unadorned cheek as John proffered a handkerchief. "Please excuse me."

John wondered if Catherine had seen the exchange on her way out. Anna was not the only one reminded of the mysterious death of his elder brother two years ago.

As his sister-in-law departed, he became conscious of the falling night as the sacristan extinguished all but the coffin candles.

On the way home to Carrowbeg, the Bodkins travelled in a silence broken only by the creaking of carriage wheels. Clouds scudded across a moonlit sky on this balmy night. As his parents dozed off, John remained wide-awake still thinking about the exchange with Anna Bodkin. With these thoughts racing through his mind, the eerie screech of the barn owl reminded him of its reputation as an omen of evil.

Soon they were at Carrowbeg, and retired to bed after a quick nightcap. Even though he was physically tired, John slept poorly: haunted by images of the dead.

$$* \quad * \quad * \quad * \quad *$$

CATHERINE'S SLEEP HAD ALSO been unquiet, disturbed by the image of Anna Bodkin embracing her betrothed. She wondered if Anna had questioned the verdict of natural death pronounced by the coroner on her young husband. Catherine put these worries aside as she sat with her father at the breakfast table.

"Catherine, my dear …" She wondered why he spoke so loudly. "I want you to give Mr Bodkin a wide berth until things settle down."

"Papa! How can I ignore my fiancé?"

"Because of his possible involvement in this dreadful affair."

"You know he is innocent!" Catherine cried.

"I certainly hope so!" Athenry's voice then softened. "Now, my dear, we must make haste."

"Papa, you have destroyed my appetite." Catherine sipped her coffee but set aside her boiled egg and toast. "I shall be down in a moment." Annoyed and anxious, she ran upstairs to write a quick note to John. Then she hurried back so that her father would not leave without her.

Dressed in mourning black, the Berminghams were soon on the road to Tuam. Catherine underscored her annoyance by maintaining silence whenever Athenry tried to engage his favourite daughter in conversation.

However, she had been pleased with his invitation to accompany him to the funeral service. He was inclined to bring her along whenever faced with a challenging situation. Perhaps he believed that her presence softened the attitude of an aggrieved opponent. How would Colonel Blake respond to her presence, she wondered and, more importantly, how could she slip her note to John without her father noticing?

On arrival at the cathedral, Athenry and Catherine hurried to the vestry where Dean Bruce sat with the Bodkins and the Blakes. Catherine smiled warmly. She noticed that the dean fidgeted with his fingers. Was the poor man uncomfortable with the presence of women at contentious meetings?

"Ladies and gentlemen, we have a sensitive issue before us," Bruce said. "Colonel, would you like to say a few words?"

Dressed in military uniform, Blake fingered the scabbard of his sword, "We want to bury Margery in the Blake grave at Oranmore."

Counsellor Bodkin responded, "Oliver loved Margery with all his heart. He would not rest at peace without her."

Catherine saw her father nodding in approval while Blake glowered.

Bodkin continued, "In normal circumstances, I would bury Oliver, Margery and little Oliver in my father's grave in Belclare."

"Who else is buried there?" Bruce asked.

Catherine wondered why that mattered as Bodkin replied, "My parents are buried there with Oliver's first wife, Marie Lynch."

"That is unacceptable to us." Blake's sword rattled as he shifted his right foot.

Catherine held her breath. It was not the first time that her father had found himself amidst warring factions. *Who would try to break the impasse,* she wondered? She had always regarded Dean Bruce as a bit of a buffoon, with his booming voice and never-ending sermons, and expected little assistance from him.

On this occasion, he surprised her by saying, "I have prayed to the Almighty for guidance on this complex and sensitive issue. After careful reflection, I recommend that Margery be buried with her husband and son in a new grave in the grounds of the cathedral."

The colonel shook his head in disapproval as the dean resumed, "However, if you wish, I shall raise the matter with our new Archbishop, Josiah Hort, who will be inaugurated early next year."

"I strongly disagree with your recommendation," Colonel Blake said sternly. "I shall indeed raise the matter with the new archbishop. Come along, my dear." On his way out, Blake turned and said, "I must insist on carrying the coffin of my daughter with my own men."

Counsellor Bodkin nodded in agreement.

"Thank you, Dean Bruce," Athenry said.

While returning to the nave, Catherine stopped at the coffin of little Oliver as John followed her.

"You were very good to bring the roses last night," John whispered. "We must talk later."

Catherine said, "I saw you talking to Anna Bodkin."

"She was merely expressing her sympathy." John touched her arm gently. "We must take our seats."

Catherine slipped the note hidden in her white lambskin glove into the pocket of John's dark waistcoat. She joined her father sitting in the nave, hoping that he had not noticed her disregard of his instructions.

$$* \quad * \quad * \quad * \quad *$$

JOHN HAD NEVER SEEN such a large crowd in the cathedral. Every available seat was occupied. People stood at the rear and overflowed into the forecourt. Suddenly conscious of being under scrutiny from those nearby, he wondered what Uncle Dominick and Shawn were thinking in Galway Gaol. Did they hope for acquittal or clemency? Why had Shawn turned up at the scene of the crime in bloodstained clothes?

At that moment, the organist played a hymn that the choristers sang. Dean Bruce entered at noon, in a long black gown with white preaching bands at the neck. After the first reading of scripture, followed by a bout of muffled coughing, a deathly silence greeted his raised hands:

I am the resurrection and the life, saith the Lord ...

John was not sure if Dominick or Shawn would derive any solace from Bruce's vision of resurrection and a life hereafter. He was not looking forward to visiting Shawn tomorrow with his father. John glanced at Catherine for consolation but she had closed her eyes. It was time to read her note, now that people were beginning to doze off during the lengthy service.

Bermingham House,
Tuam,
County Galway.

21

Monday, 21st September 1741

My dearest John,

Papa says I must not see you for the moment. I am furious with him: but what can I do? Worry not, my dear heart, I love you all the more.

Catherine
Xxx

Zounds! What he feared most had come to pass. Damn! Athenry was determined to snatch away his dream partner in life. Now more than ever he needed to talk to her in private, the sooner the better.

While the readings of the service meant little to him, the solemnity of the psalms sung by the choir helped to calm his tortured soul. Dean Bruce briefly attracted his attention when he mounted the pulpit to deliver the homily:

My fellow Christians, we are gathered here today to witness

the ascension of Oliver Bodkin, his wife, Margery and their son, Oliver

to their heavenly reward. The tragedy that ...

As Bruce rambled on, John was impressed. It was just as well that neither Dominick nor Shawn could hear his chilling remarks about suffering in the afterlife. He gazed at Catherine, who was now alert. Mary Bodkin wailed inconsolably as did Mrs Blake. John attempted to console his mother. The commencement of the funeral procession soon interrupted his thoughts.

Dean Bruce led the procession from the altar through the south transept followed by the provost, the archdeacon and the coffins of the deceased. John felt the weight of Uncle Oliver's coffin on his shoulder shared by his father along with the agent and groom at Liscarrow. It reminded him of the time that he had shouldered Patrick's coffin to the family grave in Belclare.

The smaller coffin of little Oliver was carried by the groom and footman at Liscarrow, flanked on either side by Mrs Bodkin and Mrs Blake. Colonel Blake and three of his men carried Margery's coffin. A large crowd followed the procession into the open air under a darkened sky. An even larger crowd waited outside to view the tragic event that transcended the religious divide.

As John approached the graveside, the heavens opened. The rain pelted down on top of the coffin and on to his shoulders. He saw his father stumble and clutch his chest as he passed by a man with a scar on his right cheek. The man made to help his father but withdrew into the crowd once Bodkin had recovered. John tried to adjust his hat and raise his lapel with his free hand but the coffin on his shoulder hampered him. In any event, either action would have been of little use against the relentless rain.

Stopping by the graveside, Dean Bruce shielded his missal as best he could. He solemnly recited:

> *Forasmuch as it hath pleased Almighty God to take unto himself the*
> *soul of our dear Oliver Bodkin, his wife, Margery*
> *and their son, Oliver ...*
> *we therefore commit their bodies to the ground;*
> *earth to earth, ashes to ashes, dust to dust ...*

After a silent interval, the gravediggers lowered the coffin bearing Oliver Bodkin into the grave. John embraced his father who cried-out in anguish in an outpouring of grief that he had hitherto restrained. His mother dropped a red rose on to the coffin as the raindrops became indistinguishable from her tears.

The gravediggers lowered the second coffin so that Margery lay to the left of Oliver with both coffins facing east. After further prayers, John joined with the gravediggers in covering his relatives with a light covering of soil.

The third coffin was lowered so that little Oliver was overlaid equally on his parents' coffins and facing east as well. The keening of Catholic women on the outer ring of mourners lent an air of solemnity to the occasion. John joined the gravediggers again, this time with muck on his shoes. The thud of falling soil on to the coffin of little Oliver brought finality to the burials. John held his position by the grave as if transfixed by the enormity of the tragedy. After a discreet interval, Bruce and his entourage departed leaving the Bodkins and Blakes to meet their mourning relatives and friends.

Lord Athenry and Catherine were the first to join the Bodkins as the rain began to ease. A tearful Catherine embraced John and his parents, in turn, expressing her deepest sympathy.

He remained silent when his father addressed Athenry. "John and I shall visit Shawn Bodkin in Galway Gaol tomorrow, if you have no objection."

"I shall send a rider to Galway with a note to the Governor," Athenry responded.

As the Berminghams prepared to depart, John said, "We must wait to meet our mourners."

A long queue had assembled. An hour later, exhausted from efforts to recognize and converse with all their supportive friends and neighbours, Counsellor Bodkin suddenly collapsed but John caught him in his arms and held him until Mr Joyce arrived.

"Lord help us!" cried Mary Bodkin. "Call a doctor at once!"

In the meantime, John and the agent carried Bodkin into their carriage and laid him on the seat. When the doctor arrived, he examined Bodkin, checking his heartbeat, pulse and temperature.

"What is it, Doctor?" Mary Bodkin cried.

"Nothing to worry about, Mrs Bodkin," he said. "Counsellor Bodkin is suffering from exhaustion. He needs complete rest at home for at least two weeks."

Bodkin tried to raise himself from his prone position but could only mutter a response. "I must go to Galway tomorrow."

"You will do what the doctor says, and stay in bed," Mary spoke sternly.

"I can go to Galway on my own." John suggested.

"Good boy, John," Mary said. "Counsellor Bodkin can instruct you in the morning if he is feeling better."

John trembled at the thought of taking on the responsibility of the family at such a challenging time. In the first action of his new duty, he said, "Thank you, Doctor, for looking after my father."

"I could ask Doctor Ambrose Lynch to visit," the medical practitioner responded. "He has used waters from a deep chalybeate well in Galway to help his patients recover."

"Thank you, Doctor," John said. "That would be wonderful, would it not, Mama?"

When Mary nodded, John felt a glow of empowerment surging through his body; he was pleased to have an opportunity to prove his mettle under the scrutiny of the local community. At the same time, he was not looking forward to locking horns with cousin Shawn in Galway Gaol, given that their relationship was less than friendly and the situation fraught.

CHAPTER 4

AS HE AROSE FROM a restless night, John hated the thought of visiting his fractious cousin Shawn in gaol, never mind his intimidating Uncle Dominick.

At breakfast, his father said, "I should really visit the imprisoned scoundrels, but I know you will handle this task in my stead."

"We need to understand what happened," John retorted, having settled his nerves.

"Exactly!" Bodkin then glanced at his wife. "Would you like to travel with John, my dear?"

"I have no desire to see the murdering villains." Surveying the unkempt state of the breakfast room, she groaned. "I must have this pigsty set in order."

"How can you live in a place like this, John?" Bodkin asked.

"Uncle Dominick is in charge here. I have no say in the running of it. It is usually somewhat cleaner, but with all that has taken place …" His voice choked with emotion.

"You had no intimation of what Shawn and Dominick were planning?" Bodkin asked.

"None, whatever; you know what Uncle Dominick is like," John replied untruthfully and then quickly changed tack. "He hates everyone except Shawn and myself, and merely tolerates me."

"Does he hate me?" Bodkin asked.

"He feels that he was dealt a foul blow by grandfather's will. You got the ancestral home, Oliver got Liscarrow: he was left with nothing."

"That is why I put him in charge of Carrowbeg." Bodkin raised his hands as if exasperated.

"I suppose … you could have signed over some of the property to Dominick." John regretted the bluntness of his speech, but he was merely repeating what Blind Dominick never stopped saying.

"First I had to establish my legal practice which took years to achieve. Then I had to make proper provision for Patrick." Bodkin paused. "But if I had known he was so unhappy, perhaps I could have done more for him." A tear rolled down his unshaven face.

"Now, my dear, you must rest." Mary rose from her chair and adjusted her mob cap.

"I must take my leave." John reached for his riding crop.

"Take care on your journey, my darling," his mother responded.

John mounted his grey gelding and rode south from the village of Belclare. He enjoyed riding alone through the pleasant landscape: green pasture, dotted with fields of yellow corn against a background of wild heather on the mountains to the west. He stopped for a break at The Claregalway Inn as he approached the outskirts of Galway City. Tethering his horse, he joined the midday customers in the hope that he might be distracted from the family massacre.

His mood dipped when the proprietor approached, his expression grave. "Mr Bodkin, please accept my sympathies on your great loss."

"Thank you. Perhaps you could arrange a quiet table for me."

John was aware that every eye in the Inn had now focused on him, a member of the *Bloody Bodkin* family. The story was the talk of Galway, if not the whole country or even beyond its shores.

He ate bacon, cabbage and potatoes and washed it down with ale while the ostler supplied his horse with food and water. An hour later, he was back on the road to Galway when a heavy shower further dampened his spirits. It soon cleared away, however, and the sun and wind dried his clothes before he passed through the city gates and reached the Tholsel. This lofty edifice housed the town hall, a judicial chamber and the gaol, a basement apartment with a separate entrance.

Having displayed Lord Athenry's note, John asked the keeper to allow him to see his cousin, Shawn. He followed the warder along the dimly lit corridor, the noise of their shoes resounding on the stone floor. Against a background of clanging metal and the gaunt shadows of inmates, John thought he saw the silhouette of Blind Dominick but he was not sure.

John was surprised to see Shawn still wearing his bloodstained jacket and discoloured breeches. His hair was bedraggled, his face sullied and unshaven. Shawn managed a weak smile that could have passed for a grimace. The cell was small and dirty, with an earthen floor and bare walls; it contained merely a straw pallet and a chamber pot. A barred, unglazed window provided ventilation that had failed to disperse the pervasive smell.

"I did not expect any visitors," Shawn said.

"As head of the family, Papa asked me to visit you."

"Why did he not come himself?"

"He collapsed after the funeral," John replied, "He's not ill, but requires rest."

"Hmm!" Shawn directed his eyes at John. "How did you get out of gaol?" He asked slyly.

John had anticipated the taunt. "Lord Athenry concluded that I was innocent."

"Did he now?" Shawn snorted.

"You know that I'm not guilty," John retorted angrily.

"Or did he hope you could provide evidence for the prosecution."

The warder entered with wooden cups, and a pitcher of ale that John had procured. "You've got thirty minutes, Mr Bodkin," the warder said. "I'll be outside if you need me."

John heard the key turn, locking them in. He waited in trepidation to hear what Shawn had to say. John had often accompanied Counsellor Bodkin when interrogating one of his clients in gaol, providing him with experience in the art. The lawyer favoured a non-adversarial approach to encourage the person to confide in him.

"I'm not here to judge you ... only to listen," John said.

"I have nothing to say to you," Shawn hissed.

"You are in shock. We are all in shock." John walked around the earthen floor. He handed Shawn a cup of ale. Changing course, he said musingly, "I often wondered how you got on in Dublin."

"Did you indeed!" Shawn snorted. "You know that I failed in my studies."

"And your social life? Did you enjoy that?"

"Huh!" Shawn frowned.

John remained silent, as his father would have done, hoping that Shawn would speak.

"I was only seventeen when I came to the city, a naive country boy." Shawn wiped his nose with the sleeve of his jacket. "I got into bad company. Instead of going to lectures, I went to green rooms and socialized with demireps."

John wondered how Shawn had dealt with those women of doubtful reputation. "What happened next?"

"My father found out and was devastated." Shawn paused. "It reminded me of the days when I was an only child, and everything to my parents. I was distraught when my poor mother passed away. I was only seven."

John was relieved at the direction of the conversation. His cousin needed to cleanse his soul before he was hanged, if that were to be his fate.

Shawn wiped away a tear with a handkerchief proffered by his cousin.

"You must have missed her terribly."

"She taught me French, and spent many hours with me. Then suddenly she was gone." Shawn paused. "My father made some attempt to fill her place but could not; my life thereafter was empty. I had no brothers or sisters to play with and passed many hours alone."

John was pleasantly surprised that his cousin had opened his heart to him. It was almost as if Shawn was talking to Counsellor Bodkin rather than to himself.

"After some time, my father married Margery Blake, a sharp-featured woman who stood no nonsense. At first, I liked her bright and breezy presence. She organized my life and looked after my education. But when I behaved badly, she was angry and impatient." A tear trickled into Shawn's bristle. "A year later, her tummy had grown so big, I could not but notice it. When I stared at her bump, it made her cross. She scolded me and then began to beat me."

Shawn gulped down a cupful of ale before continuing. "One day, there was a great commotion in the house; women were running hither and thither with linen and hot water. My father ... oh, my God, what have I done?"

"Have another drink," John said, pretending not to notice the implied admission of guilt.

Shawn swallowed another draught. "My father was pacing around the house. I heard screams and thereafter ... silence. Then the unmistakeable cry of a baby pierced the air."

Shawn continued, "I now had a half-brother, little Oliver: someone I could play with. But my stepmother had difficulty nursing him and sent the infant to the wife of the shepherd, Shane Hogan. Mrs Hogan nursed the baby over the next three years."

John had to control his temper as he recalled the riding lessons he provided to little Oliver who now rested in his grave.

"Margery's moodiness became worse. As I grew into a youth, we clashed more frequently." Shawn gritted his teeth. "Her beatings became more severe. I grew to hate her."

"Love and hate are strong emotions." A knock was heard on the door as John drew his watch from his waistcoat. "Ods Bodkins! My thirty minutes is up. Let us talk again in due course. I shall bring you some food, fresh clothes and blankets."

"Thank you."

"I shall visit Dominick also. How is he?"

"As mad as ever, I doubt not. We're not permitted to be in each other's company."

John banged on the door to alert the warder who escorted him from the cell. He was relieved to leave, and slightly ashamed of his relief.

As he walked from the Tholsel towards the tethering point at The King's Head, John wondered if there was the slightest doubt of Shawn's guilt. The words of his father rang in his ears. *Any man is innocent until proven guilty*, he would have said. Encouraging Shawn to cleanse his soul meant he would be in a better condition to face his Maker, if it came to that.

A cold shiver ran up John's spine at the thought of a gallows ceremony. He had witnessed the hanging of the condemned in Dublin, surrounded by the inconsolable grief of their relatives; worse than that was the sound of onlookers baying for blood.

John wondered about Catherine. She had remained loyal to him even though her father had ordered her to suspend contact with him. Their wedding, planned for early October, would have to be postponed. Apart from that disappointment, he had a niggling fear that questions might arise during the trial relating to the death of his brother, Patrick.

$$* \quad * \quad * \quad * \quad *$$

HAVING RETURNED HOME, John noted the anxious look on his mother's face.

"What delayed you?" Mary asked. "Were you waylaid by a highwayman?"

"I spent some time with poor Shawn."

"Poor Shawn indeed!" Mary cried. "He has destroyed our family and deserves whatever fate awaits him."

"Home is where Shawn would rather be," John said.

"Indeed!" Bodkin paused. "And if Shawn is found guilty, you could become Lord of Liscarrow in due course."

This thought had not previously occurred to John, and it took him a little time to absorb it. Of course, the estate must have been entailed in such a way that it would automatically fall to him should Patrick die.

Mary looked at her husband. "Are you then convinced that Shawn and Dominick are doomed?"

"The law must take its course," Bodkin said. "The prosecution must prove their guilt."

"Proof will require evidence." As soon as the words tripped off his tongue, John regretted them; he feared being asked if he had suspected anything before the massacre.

"Well spoken, John," Mary said. "We shall make a lawyer of you yet."

John smiled weakly. When his father failed to pursue the issue of evidence, he relaxed and finished his mushroom soup. His appetite returning, he smacked his lips at the aroma of the roast chicken that permeated his nostrils when the footman served for the next course.

"I had forgotten to mention that Shawn had written to his father implicitly threatening his life," Bodkin said. "That letter, combined with his bloodstained clothes, was enough to warrant his arrest."

"Is that sufficient proof for the trial?" John wondered.

"That is precisely the point." Bodkin paused to sip some white Bordeaux. "The conspirators ensured a lack of primary evidence by leaving no witnesses. All remaining evidence is secondary."

"Do you have this letter?" John asked, realizing that his own evidence could be crucial if the letter was lost.

"No. I'm not sure if it still exists," Bodkin said. "Oliver informed Athenry as well as me at the time, but I know not whether he gave the letter to Athenry."

"What did the letter say?" John asked.

"I wrote down what he told me." His meal despatched, Bodkin walked towards the writing cabinet and opened the secret drawer. Rummaging through the papers, he found a copy of the letter and read it out:

Carrowbeg House,
Belclare,
Tuam, County Galway

.

Thursday, 15th September 1740.

My dear father,

I am greatly disappointed that you have chosen to disinherit your eldest son. I feel you acted under undue influence from my stepmother who unfairly despises me. In these circumstances, I respectfully request that you reconsider the matter and reinstate me as your rightful heir.

Should you fail to do so, I shall be forced to take appropriate action to remedy the situation.

Yours faithfully,
Shawn.

"But he did not explicitly threaten to kill him, and the letter is a year old." John laid down his knife and fork on his dinner plate and considered the words Shawn had used.

"That settles it," Mary said. "You must make haste with your study of the law."

John had commenced his legal training in London shortly after the unexpected death of his brother Patrick in 1739. He had transferred to the newly opened Law School in Trinity College Dublin in the following year.

"Indeed, I must," John agreed. "As soon as we recover from this terrible tragedy."

"Precisely," Mary said. "Remember that you now stand to inherit at least one if not two estates."

"Only if Shawn and Dominick are found guilty."

"Did Shawn indicate his guilt in any way?" Mary asked.

"Not directly; although he did say in an unguarded comment: *My God, what have I done?*"

"That sounds damning," Mary said. "Will either of you be called as a witness?"

"I expect so." John shrugged his shoulders.

"That is what I'm dreading." Bodkin frowned.

"You are far too sensitive, my dear." Mary touched her lips with a napkin.

Counsellor Bodkin drank the last of his wine. "Every family has the right to privacy. We can speak openly to one another, knowing that our words will go no farther." The Master of Carrowbeg tapped the table gently. "Tomorrow will be a time for rest and reflection. The day after, I would like John to talk to Dominick."

"But what about your legal practice, my dear?" Mary directed her eyes at her husband.

"My practice must wait until this unpleasant business has been brought to an end."

"That could take considerable time. We may find it necessary to remain here until the New Year."

"The trial of Shawn and Dominick begins on Wednesday, October 7th, two weeks hence."

"Good Lord!" John exclaimed. "The very day that my wedding to Catherine was to take place."

"What an unhappy coincidence!" Mary exclaimed.

"The vicar understood why I had to defer my wedding; but I regret the circumstance."

"It is indeed regrettable," Bodkin said. "After you have visited Dominick, your mother and I may return to Dublin if my health improves. I can then take measures to protect my practice."

Turning to John, Mary said, "Will you stay here or join us in Dublin?"

"I must talk to Catherine first." John now realized more deeply the impact that his cousins' trial might have on his relationship with the daughter of Lord Athenry. As he contemplated how to meet her, his parents brought the evening to a close by retiring upstairs.

Alone at last, John poked some life from the dying embers of the fire. He sipped his brandy thoughtfully, knowing that the next two weeks would be crucial to the rest of his life. What was Catherine thinking, at this very moment, he wondered? Would she honour her promise to marry him despite her father's injunction to keep her distance?

CHAPTER 5

"AAAH!" JOHN ROARED INTO the night, awakening as he did. He heard his parents' door opening, followed by the pitter-patter of footsteps into his room.

"What ails you, my dear boy?" Mary asked, almost tripping over her nightdress.

John sat up in the bed. "It was a nightmare, Mama. I'm sorry to have disturbed you." He blinked and rubbed his eyes. "I dreamt that Uncle Dominick was standing over me with a …"

"No more! I cannot bear to think on it," Mary said, holding her hands to her face. "This is a cursed place."

"Be easy, Mama, I shall see Dominick later today. Then I will suffer no more such dreams."

He felt the imprint of his mother's lips on his forehead. Rising up against the high pillows, he quivered at the real memory of his dream—Blind Dominick had stood, not by his bed, but his parents', a manic grin on his face. Brandishing a knife, he had glanced first at Counsellor Bodkin before moving the knife towards Mary Bodkin's throat.

Later that morning, Mary said, "John had a nightmare last night."

"That explains the roar I heard," Counsellor Bodkin replied, sipping his black coffee.

Cracking open her boiled egg, Mary asked her son, "How often do you have such nightmares?"

Without thinking, John replied, "I endured many such … after Patrick passed away."

He saw a tear trickling down his mother's cheek. "I told your father we should spend more time at Carrowbeg. You were too young to be left to yourself."

John nodded, and then changed course. "I must get some clothes, food and blankets to take along to Galway. Poor Shawn was shivering in his stained clothes."

"Well may he do so!" Mary cried angrily, "after the terrible thing he has done."

"I understand your anger," Bodkin replied. "My tolerance has its limit also, but the desire for revenge can be counterproductive."

The conversation was disturbed by a knock on the door. "Mr Joyce and Friar Skerrett to see Counsellor Bodkin," the housekeeper announced.

"Please show them in." Mary drank the last of her coffee.

"You are most welcome, gentlemen," Counsellor Bodkin said.

"I just called to see if I could help in any way," inquired Joyce.

"I'm glad you called." Counsellor Bodkin leaned back in his chair. "John goes to Galway today. We are to travel to Dublin tomorrow if Doctor Lynch pronounces me fit."

As the agent nodded, Friar Skerrett stepped forward.

"Please accept my sympathy on your terrible loss," said the priest.

"Thank you, Brother," Counsellor Bodkin replied.

"The six murdered servants have been buried. Their relatives appreciated your presence at their waking." The priest stroked his brown beard. "I fear they are now worried about their loss of income but are too proud to approach you directly about the matter."

Zounds! The massacre was bad enough, John thought; now his father had to deal with the demands of estate management also. It suddenly hit him that the burden could fall on his shoulders once his father returned to Dublin. Was this the kind of life that he wished to embrace, he wondered?

"We shall revisit the relatives upon our return from Dublin," his father responded to the friar. "I shall secure their future at Liscarrow."

"May God bless you; I shall leave you in peace now."

"I should have called on you before now," Counsellor Bodkin said. "I am yet a Catholic at heart, although we conformed to maintain our privileged position. Mayhap this is our punishment for so doing."

"Your family has suffered enough," Friar Skerrett replied. "Thank you for your response to the plight of those depending on you. It has warmed my heart."

* * * * *

JOHN WAS SOON ON the road again to Galway in a trap laden with blankets, clothes and food. He wondered how he would deal with the explosive character of his Uncle Dominick.

On arrival in the basement gaol of the Tholsel building, John said, "I have brought some provisions for Shawn and Dominick Bodkin."

"We'll take charge of those, Mr Bodkin."

"Counsellor Bodkin has authorized me to pay for the provision of separate chambers for the three accused."

"Just as well: each of them has been badly beaten by other prisoners in the holding area."

John held his breath as the warder escorted him to Dominick's cell. Wearing a worn eye patch on his pock-marked face, Dominick managed a twisted smile. He had lost the sight of one eye in an accident when he was a boy and had been known as Blind Dominick ever since.

"We shall do very well on our own," John said, feeling it time to live up to his new position in the family.

"I'll be outside if needed." The warder departed, leaving them a jug of ale and two wooden cups.

"What are you doing here?" Blind Dominick paced the floor.

"You are my uncle!" John cried.

"I am not your uncle." Dominick gritted his teeth. "I am your half-uncle. Your Uncle Oliver never ceased to remind me of my provenance. He also reminded me that I would inherit nothing."

"That is why Papa placed you in charge of Carrowbeg."

"But he did not sign it over to me." Dominick scowled.

"How could he?" John responded. "A father is duty-bound to will his inheritance to his eldest son."

"Not all of it."

John knew what was coming. He had heard this argument so many times.

"Father signed over a portion of the estate to Oliver and left me to fend for myself." Dominick clenched his fists.

"That is why Papa allowed you half the rent," John reminded him patiently.

"With what result? I do all the work and get half the credit and half the money. And when your father dies....." Dominick raised his hands threateningly, "I shall be turned out on the road with nowhere to go."

Dominick leaned back, the fingers of his left hand tapping against the wall. "So I ask again; what are you doing here?"

"I brought some food, clothes and blankets for you and Shawn."

"Keep your food and blankets," Dominick whispered. "Give me your knife and pistol."

"I left those outside with the warder."

"You're a good lad, John." Dominick's lips formed a smile which his eyes did not reflect. "Not beyond getting up to a bit of mischief."

John tried not to show his dismay at the maniacal laugh that accompanied that remark.

"Who will represent me at my trial?" Dominick asked, gulping down a cupful of ale.

"Whom would you like?"

"Counsellor Bodkin, mayhap."

"Father collapsed at the funeral and is still unwell. He will try for Mr Staunton to represent you; he's a good lawyer."

"You're lying." Dominick threw his wooden cup at the wall. "He does not want to represent us at all."

This time John exploded. "Of course he does not! How can he represent those who have murdered his brother, his pregnant sister-in-law and an innocent seven-year-old child ... not to mention poor Mr Lynch ... and six servants whose only crime was to be on the premises?" John spoke so loudly that the warder poked his head around the door.

"There's no problem here," John said reassuringly. Indeed, he had finally found his voice because of the tragedy. He regretted not having spoken-out before.

"So much for the presumption of innocence," Dominick replied.

"If you want to be defended effectively, you must tell me exactly what happened." John's confidence was beginning to grow.

"Why should I?"

"Nobody wants this poisoned chalice. If you relate the tale to me just as it happened, Papa will attempt to persuade Mr Staunton to defend you; otherwise you must take your chance."

John leaned back, relieved that the pressure was now on his uncle.

Dominick adjusted his eye patch and stared into his nephew's eyes. "And if I tell you nothing, what will happen then?"

"An inexperienced lawyer will be assigned to represent you. In that event, you can surely prepare your soul for eternity." John paused to let his words sink in.

Dominick grimaced before saying, "It was Shawn who pleaded with me to punish his father and his stepmother."

"Why?"

"You know why," Dominick said. "After Shawn failed in his studies, he returned home and began to socialize, having nothing else to do. His father refused to increase his allowance. Eventually, he left Liscarrow and asked me to take him in at Carrowbeg. He threatened to emigrate, but without money or contacts he had little chance of prospering abroad."

"You could have spoken to Uncle Oliver about him."

"Oliver was under Margery's thumb. Shawn received a solicitor's letter to the effect that his father had disinherited him. That was the final straw. He told me how his stepmother had made his life a misery for years. He had been willing to make another attempt at his studies in Trinity College but she scoffed at him, saying that all he wanted was his father's money."

Dominick paused as John passed him another cup of ale. He said in a low voice, "Shawn tried to poison Margery but without success. She suspected as much and persuaded Oliver to disinherit Shawn in favour of little Oliver."

"Shawn should have gone to my father in Dublin. He would have given him a second chance."

"Counsellor Bodkin was too absorbed in his legal work to look after his family in Galway." Dominick continued, "One night, flushed with drink, Shawn swore to recover his inheritance and be rid of his father, stepmother and little Oliver."

John was pleased at the manner in which he had encouraged Dominick to open his heart, but appalled at what he was hearing.

Dominick was now in full flow. "I asked Shawn how he might achieve that. He felt that poisoning was unsatisfactory; the action would have to be more direct. It soon dawned on me that the scheme was doomed to failure without help from someone at Liscarrow."

The details of the gruesome plan horrified John, reminding him that this had resulted in the death of ten people, one of them his adored cousin, little Oliver. It was, as if Dominick was relating the plot of a gothic novel, rather than a real-life event for all the emotion he displayed.

"I pointed out this problem to Shawn." Dominick drank some more ale. "He suggested the shepherd, Shane Hogan, as someone who might assist us."

"I do not comprehend. Why should he do so?"

"Margery sent her son for fostering to Mrs Hogan when he was a baby. After a time, her visits upset the feeding routine. Feeding Oliver and her own babe became too much for the shepherd's wife, and she wished to return baby Oliver to his mother. Hogan argued that his favoured position at Liscarrow would be at risk should she do so. His wife reluctantly agreed but a feeling of anger gradually festered into hatred when she lost her own child."

John topped up Dominick's cup with ale, anxious to hear the denouement and yet dreading it.

The fearsome man carried on, "I invited Hogan over for a few drinks, and he became a regular visitor. We told him he could become shepherd of Carrowbeg as well as Liscarrow if Shawn were to regain his rightful inheritance."

John noted to himself that Dominick had not hesitated to offer Hogan a position as herdsman without consulting Counsellor Bodkin: this, despite his complaint that he lacked authority at Carrowbeg.

"The guard dogs would recognize Hogan and would not bark to raise the alarm," Dominick said. "We explained that everyone present would need to be killed that night, so that no witnesses would be left."

John listened with incredulity and repugnance.

"Hogan was horrified. Shawn agreed to apologize to his father and stepmother and beg to be taken back into the family. When that did not answer, we put our plan in motion but Hogan was still reluctant to act. Shawn managed to find a tenant at Liscarrow who was at odds with Oliver; Hogan knew this man well and believed him to bear a genuine grievance against the Big House. It steadied Hogan's courage to have a colleague from Liscarrow, and we began to plan the finer details."

"Thank you, Uncle Dominick. I will try to ensure the best legal representation for your defence." John was trembling in shock to such an extent that Dominick had to knock on the door for the warder to let him out.

John needed time to work out the implications of Dominick's confession on his own situation. He must think clearly and tread carefully; this was dangerous ground.

CHAPTER 6

CATHERINE'S FATHER HAD INSISTED that she accompany him to Dublin at the beginning of the *Castle Season*. His mention of it brought her back to the occasion when John Bodkin had invited her to dance with him at a ball in Dublin Castle. His curly black hair, white-cuffed red jacket and tight white breeches had taken her breath away. What an elegant dancer, she had thought him, as he guided her through the intricate serpentine patterns of a minuet. They had initially met following a Sunday service in Tuam. Aged sixteen at the time, she was immediately attracted to the handsome young man with the flashing smile. When he gazed at her with his soft brown eyes, she knew herself lost.

The proximity of the family homes in Henrietta Street in the capital city facilitated their whirlwind romance. At Christmas, John asked her father for permission to propose to her; now seventeen, she had been thrilled to accept, although Athenry had insisted on deferring the official announcement for some time. Catherine believed her father to be concerned because John possessed no fortune and had limited prospects.

Now their romance was in jeopardy after the recent massacre of John's family. Her father's arrest of her fiancé on suspicion of murder had cast a further shadow on their liaison. She understood why John had felt compelled to cancel their October wedding and prayed that it would now take place early in the New Year.

The two-day journey to Dublin, with an overnight stay in Milltownpass, was exhausting but uneventful. On the morning after their arrival in Dublin, Catherine overheard the footman accept a letter from Counsellor Bodkin. Watching her father scan this letter at breakfast, she inquired tentatively if his correspondence contained anything of interest.

"I asked Counsellor Bodkin if I might call on him this morning on a private matter." Athenry walked to the chafing dishes for an extra helping of bacon and eggs. "I would like you to accompany me."

"Gladly, Papa. I shall be ready on the instant." Catherine rushed upstairs to complete her grooming and apply a dash of jasmine and orange blossom scent. She knew John would be at home because he had sent her a note to that effect. She wondered briefly at her father's volte-face, but decided not to look a gift horse in the mouth.

At precisely one minute before eleven of the clock, Catherine stepped on to the pavement wearing a hooped cream dress with a yellow petticoat flashing. She admired the elegance of her tall, blue-eyed father who wore a cutaway red jacket over a decorative cream waistcoat, dark breeches and white stockings. They walked from their red-bricked house at 11 Henrietta

Street to the adjoining Bodkin residence at Number 12. She was surprised to see that the shutters were still drawn on a third floor window. Knocking on the tripartite door, they were soon escorted by the footman to the drawing room of the tall house.

"My dear Mrs Bodkin, Counsellor, and Mr Bodkin, please forgive my intrusion in your hour of devastation."

"No intrusion: we are delighted to see you," Counsellor Bodkin said. "I feared I might be unable to journey to Dublin, but Doctor Lynch has fortified me with his magic water."

Catherine curtsied to the family. John motioned her into the chair he had being sitting on and stood behind her.

"I am so glad to see you on the road to recovery," Athenry said. "I have never seen such carnage as that morning in September when I was summoned to Liscarrow. No wonder it has taken its toll on your health."

Catherine wondered what was in his mind. Her father was not a man who engaged in social visits without a motive.

After the footman had served coffee and freshly baked buns, Athenry glanced at Counsellor Bodkin, "How will you cope with your practice under the circumstances?"

"After this visit, I fear it will be necessary to absent myself until after the trial in early October, perhaps even into the New Year. I can only hope my practice will survive this interruption."

Sipping his coffee, Athenry replied, "As you know, I am acquainted with some of your clients in Parliament. I would be happy to have a word with them if you so wish it."

"That would be of great assistance, thank you. John will need to talk to them as well; there are some matters that will require negotiation if I am to retain my clientele. Then I may return to Galway to complete my recuperation before the trial."

"Capital!" Athenry hesitated for a moment. "May I ask a favour? Lady Browne was to chaperone Catherine during our visit to Dublin, but at the last minute, she became unwell and was unable to travel. This presents me with a small dilemma."

"I hope your poor sister is soon recovered," Mary Bodkin said. "I should be very happy to chaperone Catherine while you are on business."

"I am indebted to you, Mrs Bodkin. It should only be necessary this afternoon when I have a meeting with Justice Rose." Athenry now turned his head to Counsellor Bodkin. "I suspect that my consultation with him may have implications for you. May I call on you tomorrow morning to discuss the matter?"

"Of course," Bodkin said, raising an eyebrow.

Athenry rose and embraced Catherine. "Behave yourself, young lady," he smiled.

She walked with him to the door where a coach from their stable mews was waiting to take him to the House of Parliament.

After her father departed, Catherine directed her eyes at John's mother. "Your home is beautiful, Mrs Bodkin."

"John will be delighted to show you around, I'm sure." Mary Bodkin smiled. "I shall accompany you."

"My pleasure, Miss Catherine; please follow me." John bowed ever so slightly. He wore a dark jacket with cream breeches over white stockings.

Catherine followed him as they climbed an ornate staircase of cantilevered stone to the third floor where John slept.

"Which room was Patrick's?" Catherine asked.

"The room next to mine," John said. "It remains locked. I have not entered it since he died."

"Nor have I," said Mary Bodkin.

Although Patrick had behaved badly to her, Catherine still felt a morbid curiosity to see the chamber that had been his. Now she understood why the window of that room had remained shuttered.

"Perhaps we could visit his room together. What think you?" John said.

"If your mother consents," Catherine replied, pleased that John could read her mind as well as ever.

"I should consult with Counsellor Bodkin first," replied Mary.

"Very well, Mama," John said. "Upstairs is the attic where Patrick and I used to play as young children." He looked at Catherine as if anxious to accommodate her lively mind. "Now, you might like to spend some time in the library; our collection of books is thought to be quite fine."

Opening the door for her, he touched her arm lightly; a frisson coursed through her body. She hoped anew that their wedding would not be long delayed.

"After lunch, we shall sit in the garden and enjoy the sun. Would you like that?"

Catherine nodded and they entered the library together in perfect amity.

* * * * *

ON THE FOLLOWING MORNING, Catherine sat in the library while her father spoke with Counsellor Bodkin in an adjoining chamber. Searching for a suitable book to read, her eyes were drawn to a portrait of a young woman that hung between two bookcases. She could just discern the name of the artist, Elisabetta Sirani. It appeared to be a self-portrait: the woman held a palette with a thumb-hole in her left hand and a paintbrush in her right hand. She wore a purple gown tipped with white lace at the décolletage, and her dark brown hair fell to her shoulders in a mass of curls. Catherine had never heard of a distinguished female painter. She wondered if her Aunt Bridget, a self-proclaimed art expert, might know of her.

Fascinating as the portrait was, it did not prevent her from overhearing the discussion in the next room. She had left the adjoining door slightly ajar after the footman had brought coffee to both rooms.

Catherine was not surprised when her father came straight to the point. "Mr Justice Rose is anxious about representation for the defence at the forthcoming trial in Tuam."

The decorative teacup rattled in its saucer as Counsellor Bodkin presumably sought to control his surprise. "Is there a problem?"

"He's having difficulty obtaining a defence lawyer with the necessary experience to ensure a fair trial."

"Nobody wants to defend the indefensible," Bodkin said, "but these people are betraying the ethics of their noble profession; shame on them!" The delft rattled again.

"There's no shortage of lawyer counsel who would be delighted to seize this opportunity, but such an appointment could lead to the charge of an unfair trial, as you know. The prospect of a subsequent appeal to the Chief Secretary...." Athenry's voice tailed off in apparent despair.

Catherine knew that her father had been anxious for her to accompany him to Dublin in the hope that she would locate the missing letter that could ensure a guilty verdict. He had put her in charge of filing his papers in an orderly manner. She loved this work because of the sensitive nature of some of the documents. Sworn to secrecy by her father, she had resisted the temptation to share any of this information even with John. The threatening letter written by Shawn Bodkin to his father should form a key item of evidence for the prosecution in the forthcoming trial: but, it was missing. Catherine had searched her father's papers at Bermingham House without success; now she needed to go through his papers at 11 Henrietta Street and in his office in the Irish Parliament.

Her thoughts were drawn away from Elisabetta Sirani when her father said, "Justice Rose suggested that you should lead the defence. You would not have to cross-examine: all that could be done by lawyers under your supervision."

Bodkin exploded, "You are asking me to defend my half-brother, Dominick, who has allegedly murdered my brother, Oliver."

The tone of her father's response revealed his embarrassment. "I know, and I deplore the need to do so, but what alternative is there?"

"I shall tell you, Lord Athenry."

Catherine had never heard the lawyer speak so forcefully. The massacre of his family must have impacted appreciably on the head of the Bodkin family.

"Both Shawn and Dominick asked John if I would represent them." Bodkin paused. "John told them that I would approach Mr Staunton instead on their behalf. I would request him to act for the defence as a personal favour, but only if they were prepared to tell my colleague the full truth of what had happened."

Catherine was fascinated by how cleverly Bodkin had concealed the fact that John now knew most of the story of that dreadful night. John had told her about his meetings with Shawn and Dominick Bodkin in Galway Gaol, although he had respected their confidence. Had Counsellor Bodkin admitted to such knowledge, her father would have advised the prosecuting counsel accordingly.

"Splendid! Staunton is an excellent counsellor," Athenry responded.

At that point, Catherine retired to the comfort of the parlour where she found Mary in conversation with John. "I did not hear you return last night," Mary said. "The hour must have been late."

John scowled. "I went to The Brazen Head, but everyone there questioned me about the massacre. I went from one tavern to another trying to escape the interrogation. I fear I indulged overmuch in strong liquor." He glanced at Catherine. "I even challenged someone to a duel but the innkeeper intervened and had me taken home."

"You poor boy," Mary said. "We are all suffering from this dreadful business."

At that point, they were joined by Bodkin and Athenry.

"We shall return to Galway tomorrow." Bodkin looked at John. "I shall need your assistance again."

"What do you wish me to do?"

"To visit the shepherd, Shane Hogan, in Galway Gaol," Bodkin said. "I also need to know who else visited Dominick and Shawn at Carrowbeg, apart from Hogan."

"I…I cannot be sure," stammered John.

"The time for discretion is over," Mary informed him. "You must tell your father what you know."

Catherine quivered to see her betrothed under pressure. She herself knew the visitor to be the man with the scarred face: the agrarian agitator who was a legend among the local community.

"I believe it was Roger Kelly, the infamous Whiteboy and brother of Mrs Hogan," John said.

"I must have speech with him also," Counsellor Bodkin replied.

"Should I speak to Mrs Hogan, do you think?" Mary asked.

"Let me consider that," Bodkin said, running his fingers through his greying hair.

Catherine began to appreciate that talking to those accused of the massacre helped the Bodkins to grieve; they needed to understand the motivation that had driven members of their own family to commit such a horrendous crime. She wished to accompany John to Galway Gaol, but knew that this was not the time to ask. In any event, her father would forbid it unless she could show a compelling reason; could she find one? Now that he knew about the possible involvement of Roger Kelly in the conspiracy, he might cooperate in the expectation of finding relevant information. With that thought in her mind, she departed with her father to search for the missing letter.

* * * * *

JOHN BODKIN HAD BECOME increasingly agitated at the persistent interrogation that had resulted from his residence at Carrowbeg at the time leading up to the massacre. The trial was to commence in less than a week. He was concerned that it seemed almost certain he would be called as a prosecution witness. Interrogating Shane Hogan would help to focus his mind on the evidence he could provide to the court.

As he prepared to leave, the servants were covering the furniture at 12 Henrietta Street. The house would remain closed until the New Year. Their silver plate and jewellery were packed and ready to go with them.

His mother had assembled the servants in the dining room that overlooked the Georgian elegance of Henrietta Street. "Counsellor Bodkin would like to say a few words," she told them.

"I want to thank you for your support over the past few days. My family and the servants in Galway have been through a horrendous experience," Bodkin said as a tear trickled down his cheek.

"We are now trying to resolve matters there and bring the culprits to justice. To do this, it is necessary to reside in Galway for the time being. With God's blessing, we shall return in the New Year." Bodkin paused while the servants listened quietly.

"Thank you again for your support. Let us all pray for a happy and prosperous New Year." He crossed himself with a blessing, as his late mother would have done, and the servants followed suit.

Mounting the city coach, John wondered when indeed they would return. He was silent as the horses trotted over the cobblestones towards the centre of Dublin. As they crossed the bridge at Sackville Street, Trinity College came into view. John handed his telescope to Catherine, the better to see the university.

"That is where Shawn started the great journey of life, before falling at the first hurdle," John said. He was now following in Shawn's footsteps in the new School of Law established there last year, having abandoned a transitory liberal arts education.

Now that Patrick was dead and Shawn discredited, it made sense for him to pursue the law and inherit his father's lucrative practice.

As the coach journeyed westward along the River Liffey, Dublin Castle came into view. John pointed to the impregnable fortress to the south, the seat of British rule in Ireland. "I wonder if the Chief Secretary has heard about our problem in Liscarrow."

"I hope he never will," Counsellor Bodkin said.

Soon they were on the stagecoach heading west. After an overnight stop in Milltownpass, John was mortified to hear the Bodkin massacre being discussed by two lady passengers unknown to them.

Just after crossing the River Shannon, he heard a voice cry, "Halt! Stop the horses."

The coach ground to a halt and a hooded highwayman wrenched open the door.

"Everybody out," he cried. "Hand over your money and jewellery and nobody will get hurt."

Experience had prepared John for this eventuality. As he alighted from the coach, closely following his father, he drew his compact flintlock pistol from his waistband under his coat. Catherine had given him the decorative gun as a Christmas present. That morning, he had rammed the single-barrelled weapon with black powder and lead shot, and primed it with gunpowder. Now he released the safety lock and shot the second highwayman, who was currently searching the coach.

The ladies screamed on hearing the gunshot. Blood spouted from the man's thigh through his dark breeches. His accomplice took fright and sped off into a nearby copse, making his escape before the arrival of six yeoman soldiers. John maintained guard over the injured highwayman, who was clutching his leg in pain but anxious to mount his horse and make his escape.

"Do not move, or I shall stove in your head," John said holding the butt of the pistol over the man's head.

"Your name, sir?" the sergeant asked.

"John Bodkin."

The name Bodkin riveted the attention of the soldiers and the two unknown passengers. John understood their curiosity. "This is my father, Counsellor-at-law Bodkin of Galway and Dublin, my mother and my betrothed, Miss Catherine Bermingham."

"Thank you, sir. We shall take this rascal into custody and hunt down his partner: safe travel for the remainder of your journey."

The elderly woman who had led the earlier conversation said, "I must apologize for unknowingly intruding on your grief. Please accept my sympathy on your great loss."

The younger lady nodded, apparently relieved that the danger was over. "You are very brave, Mr Bodkin. You saved us from those evil men."

John blushed to find himself the hero of the moment. As he displayed his bossed and engraved pistol, he wondered if his father had recognized the voice of the escaped highwayman.

"Who was he?" John asked as he replaced the pistol in his waistband.

"It sounded like the man with the scar who verbally abused us on our way back from Galway."

The ladies stared at Counsellor Bodkin, raising their eyebrows and opening their lips ever so slightly.

"Roger Kelly?" Catherine asked.

"The Whiteboy himself!" The older lady trembled with excitement.

"We shall soon find out," Counsellor Bodkin said.

"Indeed we shall," John responded, looking forward now to his imminent meeting with Shane Hogan, the brother-in-law of Roger Kelly.

CHAPTER 7

JOHN BODKIN WAS DEEP in thought at breakfast in Carrowbeg. He was relieved that his father had made satisfactory arrangements to protect his practice, and that Athenry had assisted him in doing so. Even better was Athenry's surprise decision to allow Catherine to visit his home in Dublin for the afternoon.

Thus encouraged, and having regained his appetite, John helped himself to a bowl of porridge from the sideboard. As he ate the morning repast, he looked through the window at the garden that Dominick had allowed to run wild. "'Tis a blustery day out there. An early start would be best."

After his parents nodded, John rode to Galway. As he cantered on his way, an oncoming coach suddenly slipped off the road after its wheel dipped into a pothole. John wondered if another hold-up was being attempted and prepared to be of assistance. He reined in his horse and fingered his concealed pistol as a group of farm workers from the neighbouring fields neared the carriage.

"Not a bloody Bodkin again!" one of them shouted.

"Watch your tongue," John warned, brandishing his weapon.

"No need for that," laughed the leader of the group. "Pay no heed to that hothead."

When John had satisfied himself that the coach slippage was truly an accident, he checked to see if anyone was hurt. Apart from the shock, and some bruising to the coachman, they all reported as fit to resume. The men from the fields helped to pull the scratched but otherwise undamaged coach back on to the road.

John thought he recognized the voice of the man who had spoken to him. He had been unable to confirm whether the man bore a scarred cheek, being limited to a left view of his face. He thought of the previous day's highway robbery, and how, he seemed destined to renew acquaintance with Roger Kelly one way or another.

As he approached the city, John stopped and sniffed the posy of sweet-smelling herbs. His mother had placed them in his pouch as a protection from any lingering plague infection. He saw a group of ragged and haggard people at the city gates. The famine had taken its toll. Hunger was driving these unfortunates to seek entrance to the city now that the disease had past. One of the women cried, "My children is starving, sir. My husband is dead and my poor brother's throat was slit at Liscarrow."

Before John could respond, the sentinel cleared the way and allowed him through. John paled. He had no problem shooting highwaymen but it was hard to ignore starving people, especially one who claimed that her brother was a victim of the Bodkin massacre.

He shouted, "Whoa!" and slipped down from his horse. John walked back to the city gates and called the woman aside. "I am John Bodkin of Carrowbeg. Please accept my sympathy on the death of your brother."

"Thank you, sir," the dishevelled woman replied. "My brother, James Fallon, worked as a servant for poor Mister Oliver ..."

Tears welled in John's eyes as the woman broke down. Her little boy and girl cried and held on to their mother's petticoat. John pressed a florin into her hand. "That should tide you over until after the trial. Counsellor Bodkin will arrange assistance for the relatives of the victims."

"May God bless you, sir," she said. The woman dried her tears, blessed herself and consoled her little ones.

"I shall ask the sentinel to arrange a ride for you without charge on the next available coach back to Tuam." John explained the situation to the guard who agreed to make the necessary arrangements. For the first time in his life, John felt that he had done something good for the wretched of the land. He left the money for the fare and returned to his horse with a spring in his step. However, his mood darkened on realizing that the agent must have failed to look after at least one of the relatives of the victims. John was furious that the poor woman, one of the bereaved at Liscarrow, had been reduced to begging at the city gates.

The cruel reality of the situation returned when John saw a professional acquaintance waving in sympathy, as he rode down Shop Street, and shaking his head in apparent despair.

He tethered his horse at The King's Head and walked to the domed Tholsel building, not far removed from Lynch's Castle, the home of Marcus Lynch—murdered at Liscarrow.

* * * * *

"GOOD MORNING, MR BODKIN," said the warder. "Is it yourself again?"

John responded with a weak smile. "I would like to see Mr Hogan, please."

The warder nodded. John followed him through a dark corridor to a tiny cell where Hogan lay on a straw mat, unshaven and unkempt. Bruise marks on his face confirmed the wisdom of separating the three accused from those in the larger holding chamber. Hogan was a well-built man, middle-aged, with a slight stammer. He averted his eyes from his visitor.

"What brings you h…here, Mr Bodkin?" Hogan stood up slowly.

"Counsellor Bodkin has been asked to act as your defence attorney but that is not possible."

Hogan listened with apparent surprise on his weather-beaten face.

"Justice Rose had been unable to find you a defence counsellor experienced enough to ensure a fair trial."

"So they think me guilty," stammered Hogan.

"You are entitled to a presumption of innocence. You may enter a plea of *Not guilty* at your forthcoming trial in Tuam, if you wish it so."

"Has a date been set?" Hogan said, leaning forward.

"The court convenes next Wednesday."

"How could your father serve as defence counsellor when his own brother, his sister-in-law and …" Hogan broke down.

John proffered a handkerchief.

"Papa refused to act as defence counsel for that reason."

Hogan nodded sadly. "Who then will represent me?"

"Papa has asked Mr Staunton to do so. He will need to know the full story of what happened."

"Will your father be called as a witness?"

"I don't think so."

Hogan wiped his sweaty brow with the white handkerchief. "Has the prosecution any witnesses?"

"I know not."

John shuddered as Hogan directed his eyes at him. "Will you be called?"

"I expect so, as I lived with Shawn and Dominick before the massacre."

John prayed that Hogan would cease the interrogation but the shepherd fixed his eyes upon him. "What do you know?"

John felt like replying that Hogan should mind his own business; but his father had trained him well. "I know that you visited Carrowbeg with Roger Kelly on a number of occasions. We expect that Kelly will be called as a witness."

Hogan clenched his fists.

"I understand he's a tenant at Liscarrow," John said. "How well do you know him?"

"He's my brother-in-law."

"Was he disaffected with Uncle Oliver?"

"That is a long story not worth the telling."

"Why did he accompany you to Carrowbeg?"

"I asked him," Hogan replied in an apparent tone of truculence.

John sighed. It was going to be a long morning.

"Why did you invite him to accompany you there?"

"I was asked to do a job of work and needed the support of someone I trusted." Beads of sweat broke through on Hogan's forehead.

"What did Mr Kelly think?"

"He took against it. He tagged along reluctantly but he backed out at the last minute."

"Will he tell the truth under oath?"

"If he does, he'll regret it," Hogan shouted and kicked his chamber pot.

The warder put his head through the opened door.

John smiled. "Everything is fine, thank you."

The warder directed his truncheon at Hogan and then departed.

John tried to replicate his father's course of conduct. "Let us consider this carefully." He felt strange using the somewhat pompous expression. "What does Kelly know?" John paused and then answered the rhetorical question. "He knows that you, Shawn and Dominick Bodkin were planning a mission. He withdrew at the last minute, and therefore does not know if you carried out that mission."

Hogan grunted. "What of it?"

"The prosecution will look for more direct evidence." John allowed Hogan time to ponder his words. "They may ask you to turn evidence in return for clemency."

Hogan's eyes narrowed. "I would be marked out a…as an informer." His stammer had returned.

"You would be alive, Mr Hogan. Your wife would have a husband. Your children would have a father."

John wondered what Hogan was thinking, as the enormity of the decision was borne in on him. Even if he was granted clemency, the court would probably sentence him to transportation to America; at least, though, he would be alive.

John continued, "You should be aware that Mr Staunton will also represent both Shawn and Dominick Bodkin. Do you think that Dominick would turn evidence?"

"Your uncle terrifies me…more than anyone I ever met." Hogan drew in a deep breath. "He would not turn evidence, and he would surely kill me if I did."

"He would not be able to harm you if your evidence proved him guilty because he would be hanged immediately." John pointed out.

Hogan wrung his calloused hands. His position was vulnerable: he was the only accused person to be married with children.

"Do you think that Shawn would turn evidence?" John forced the shepherd to consider all the options.

"If he could hold on to his inheritance, he might."

"Papa would understand your reluctance to turn evidence." John paused. "You need time to consider the matter."

John knocked on the door to gain egress. As the warder responded, John continued, "With your permission, I shall return in the afternoon to continue my discussion with Mr Hogan."

The warder nodded as Hogan lay down on his straw pallet.

John stepped out on to High Street on his way to The King's Head. He breathed a sigh of relief. Although at an early stage in his legal training, he felt that he had handled the consultation with assurance. It was time for luncheon.

$$* \quad * \quad * \quad * \quad *$$

ENTERING THE KING'S HEAD, John was surprised to find Lord Athenry chatting to friends in the hallway with Catherine in attendance. He thought she looked sublime in a lightly-hooped dark dress with a cream petticoat, her auburn hair a cloud of curls on her shoulders.

Athenry raised his hand in greeting. "Mr Bodkin, I am delighted to see you. You must join us for lunch."

John almost fainted with surprise. "I could not think of intruding, Lord Athenry," he replied.

"Nonsense, man!"

Catherine intervened. "Papa will only take *yes* for an answer."

"I am just come from Galway Gaol," John said. "I have now visited each of the three accused."

"You must be exhausted from all the travelling," Catherine responded.

"Nothing that good food cannot cure." John smiled.

Enjoying a repast of lobster and vegetables, John was aware of people turning their heads towards their table from time to time and whispering behind their napkins. The notoriety of the *Bloody Bodkins* was now well-established.

White wine having been poured, Catherine looked at her father and whispered, "We must invite the Bodkins to dinner."

"Excellent notion, my dear!" Athenry replied and then glanced at John. "When the trial is over and Counsellor Bodkin has recovered, I hope you and your family will join us for dinner one evening."

"Papa would be delighted," John said. "The trip to Dublin set him back a bit but his constitution is good." He was relieved that Athenry had issued the invitation even if his favourite daughter had manipulated him.

Over coffee, John remarked, "I saw Hogan this morning. He needed time to consider his position, and I must now renew my session with him before returning to Carrowbeg. Thank you so much for your hospitality. Please excuse me."

"I shall walk with you to the door, Mr Bodkin," Catherine said. Before Athenry could respond, she had smartly followed John to the exit.

In the open air, amidst the clamour of the busy town, John touched Catherine's arm. He whispered, "I need to talk to you before the trial."

"Not now, my dear; perhaps after luncheon in The Bagworth Inn, or after service on Sunday."

"I'm worried about what may come out when I testify."

"Just tell them the truth," Catherine flicked back a wisp of her hair that had strayed over her eye.

"I wish it were that simple," John sighed forlornly.

"It is that simple. Do not fret overmuch."

"I must leave now before your father has a seizure."

Catherine drew her fan across her cheek as a symbol of her love for him, and returned to her father.

Back at the Tholsel, the warder escorted John along the prison corridor. The moaning of Blind Dominick that he heard suggested that even the toughest could be broken in captivity. In Hogan's cell, he produced a bun he had wrapped in a napkin that the shepherd ate rapidly.

"Have you thought over what I said, Mr Hogan?"

"I don't know about turning evidence." Hogan walked around the earthen floor. "What questions would they ask me?"

"They would ask for your name, age, marital status, occupation and how long you have worked at Liscarrow." Bodkin blew his nose. "They would then inquire about your relationship with the Bodkins there."

Hogan stammered in response, "My r...relationship with Oliver Bodkin, could not have been better. I had a good plot of land and a senior position as shepherd. It all started to go wrong when his first wife, Marie Lynch, a lovely woman, passed away. He married again and two years later Margery Blake gave birth to little Oliver. She asked Mrs Hogan to nurse the infant after she had difficulty feeding the baby."

John was pleased that Hogan had opened his budget without being asked a direct question.

Hogan resumed, "Little Oliver became our foster child. We loved him dearly, but Mrs Margery had my wife tormented, criticizing everything she did. When our only baby boy died from pneumonia, she didn't even pay her respects, let alone give us time to mourn. I had a quiet word with Master Oliver. That was a mistake. After that, we had dog's abuse from Mrs Bodkin."

John passed Hogan a naggin of ale that the sweating shepherd quickly gulped down.

"I will save the rest of the story for Mr Staunton. I want to talk to Roger Kelly as well."

John figured Hogan must have realized that he should not incriminate himself further.

"Thank you, Mr Hogan. You need time to reflect."

Departing from the Tholsel, John relieved his tension by shouting, "Onward to Liscarrow," as he mounted his grey gelding. The startled reaction of pedestrians and the squawking of seagulls amused him as he turned for home.

CHAPTER 8

JOHN UNDERSTOOD WHY SHANE Hogan was so nervous about turning evidence even though it might moderate his sentence. It made him think of what might happen if someone were to inform Lord Athenry of the true nature of Patrick's death. The snide remarks of Shawn and Dominick Bodkin about his behaviour had unnerved him; either, they were shooting in the dark or they knew more than they should about the matter. Why had they brought it up now, after more than two years? Presumably, they thought he knew more of their conspiratorial discussions than they liked, and sought to dissuade him from revealing such evidence in court.

After breakfast on the following morning, John told his parents, "I met Lord Athenry and Miss Catherine yesterday in Galway."

"How is Lord Athenry?" Mary looked up from her letters.

"He insisted on my joining them for lunch in The King's Head." John leafed through a copy of *Pue's Occurrences* on the off-chance that it might carry a report on the forthcoming trial. "I was taking a break from questioning Hogan. After luncheon, Catherine prompted her father to invite us to dinner in Bermingham House."

"I thought Athenry had forbidden Miss Catherine to see you for the time being," Mary said.

"Catherine knows how to charm him," John smiled. "However, he did defer the invitation until the trial is over."

"Indeed!" Mary blinked her brown eyes. "How did you fare with the shepherd?"

Their conversation was suspended while the housemaid tidied the fireplace and added fresh wood to the fire. When they were alone again, John replied, "I suggested that he turn evidence in return for clemency."

"Clemency, after the terrible crime he committed!" Mary cried.

"Mama, he is the only accused with a wife and family; in any event, clemency would result in transportation or hard labour rather than execution. He would not escape punishment."

"What do you think he will do?" Mary asked, eyebrows raised.

Counsellor Bodkin interjected, "He would be reluctant to be labelled an informer. It is the worst thing one Irishman can call another."

"It might be useful to talk to Roger Kelly." John recalled the intervention of the man with the scar when his colleague had verbally abused him on the road to Galway.

"I cannot call at his home. Neither can I invite him here; tongues would wag," Bodkin said. "We could meet in Athenry's office in Tuam, where we could speak in confidence. I shall draft a note seeking permission from Athenry to use his premises, and another inviting Kelly to meet me there."

John joined his father in the library to perform this chore while Mary departed to discuss the daily routine with their housekeeper.

Brandishing a quill at his writing desk, Counsellor Bodkin said, "The note to Athenry is routine." He looked into the middle distance as if seeking inspiration before drafting the letter to Kelly, then passed it to John, asking, "How does that read?"

To Mr Roger Kelly
Liscarrow,
Belclare, County Galway

Friday, 2ⁿᵈ October 1741

Dear Mr Kelly,
I would be most grateful if you could meet me in Lord Athenry's office in Tuam tomorrow at eleven of the clock to discuss the situation of Shane Hogan.

Thanking you in anticipation,

Yours faithfully,
Counsellor Bodkin
Carrowbeg House.

John appreciated being consulted on this sensitive matter; after all, it was not every day that a member of the landed gentry invited an agrarian rebel to a meeting, unless it were to ambush him.

"Capital," he said, having scanned the note. "But will Athenry agree?"

"There's only one way to find out. I shall ask the footman to deliver the letter to Lord Athenry immediately."

Once permission from Athenry was granted, the letter to Kelly was delivered. The Whiteboy also replied in the affirmative, although the footman reported that Hogan's brother-in-law appeared nervous.

At the appointed time on Saturday morning, a knock sounded on the door of Athenry's office. "Thank you for coming, Mr Kelly," Counsellor Bodkin said. "Please take a seat."

John poured three small whiskies. "With the trial approaching next week, a tot will help to keep us calm."

The glass of whiskey wobbled in Kelly's hand.

"John has spoken to your brother-in-law in Galway Gaol," Counsellor Bodkin said. "We know that you were involved in the conspiracy at Liscarrow, but wisely withdrew at the last minute. The question now is: can you do anything to help your brother-in-law to avoid conviction or, if convicted, to avoid hanging?"

"What's that to you?" Kelly asked.

"I'm concerned about the welfare of my tenant, Mrs Hogan, and her children," Bodkin said.

John thought that a more persuasive, and more truthful, answer would have been that they wished to ensure the conviction of Shawn and Dominick Bodkin by securing direct evidence.

"How can I help?" Kelly asked.

"If you can explain how you and he became involved in the plot, then maybe I can provide guidance." Bodkin leaned forward.

"Anything I say must remain between us." Kelly narrowed his eyes. "Can I trust you?"

Placing his right hand on his heart, Bodkin said. "I swear by Almighty God that any information you give me shall remain strictly confidential unless you direct me otherwise."

Kelly sipped his whiskey with a steadier hand. "All we want is a fair deal for the tenants. Rotten potatoes have led to famine and evictions. We want to protect people from the whim of a landlord."

John could see the steely determination in the grey-green eyes of the rebel.

Kelly clasped his hands. "I was threatened with eviction when I could not pay the rent because my potatoes were rotten. I asked Hogan if he could help. He said that Mrs Margery was driving his wife demented; my sister, Mrs Hogan, held her responsible for the death of her only son. We both had a grievance against the Big House." Kelly continued, "Hogan said he was approached by Shawn Bodkin, who wanted to recover his inheritance. We paid a call to Carrowbeg."

John topped up the glasses of whiskey.

"Hogan and I thought the plan was madness, and said so. Blind Dominick went berserk," Kelly recounted. "He threatened he would murder both of us if we refused. Hogan was frightened enough to reluctantly agree. I did not; I patted the side of my jacket where my pistol lay and Dominick backed off."

Kelly stood up. "Later on, I asked Hogan to cry off. I promised him protection but he was afeared. He begged me to take part along with him.

When I refused again, Dominick drew his sword to kill me. I drew my pistol on him and he yielded."

John recalled the roaring and the shouting that he had heard that night before retiring to bed.

"Once I put my gun away and headed for the door, Dominick seized me from behind throwing his arm around my neck. Shawn aimed his pistol at Hogan and ordered him to sit down. Hogan was too frightened to intervene on my behalf. They gagged me and bound my wrists and ankles. I struggled to free myself but failed."

John's face lit up. "That was the noise I heard the following morning when I was summoned to Liscarrow."

"We need time to reflect on what you have said," Counsellor Bodkin added. "Can we meet again here at three of the clock?"

Kelly nodded.

"It would be better if we went our separate ways at this point," John said. "We are to lunch with the Berminghams."

Kelly gulped the last of his whiskey and departed alone.

The dialogue between two informed and intelligent men on opposite sides of the barricades had intrigued John. Even more interesting would have been the interaction between Blind Dominick and Kelly, two men capable of inspiring fear in their enemies. No wonder he had heard voices raised that night.

And, then it hit him. Now he knew why Kelly had not forewarned the servants of the impending massacre. He could not have done so because he was under house arrest. Had the Whiteboy been allowed to walk free that night, as a tenant and a man of the people, he would have warned the servants personally or close members of their families, also tenants. The forewarned servants, particularly the butler and the housekeeper would have alerted Master Oliver of the impending attack. The invaders would have been shot, or intercepted, by Lord Athenry's yeoman soldiers, had they been mobilized in time.

* * * * *

CATHERINE WAS PLEASED THAT the Bodkins had invited Lord Athenry and herself to luncheon in The Thomas Bagworth Inn. Much to her surprise, her father had accepted; mayhap, she thought, he and Counsellor Bodkin were scheming together in anticipation of the trial. She sat at her dressing table buffing and polishing her nails with a chamois cloth, wondering if John would notice the effort she had made to impress him. She hoped so, although she was more anxious to hear the outcome of the meeting with Hogan. The trial was due to commence next Wednesday, the very day that she and John were to be united in matrimony. And then, she wondered, what in heaven's name would she do with her elaborate wedding cake?

Determined not to dwell on this disappointment, she focused on the trial instead. She was determined to attend, and had ensured that her Aunt Bridget was also eager to do so and would accompany her. The lure of the trial of the decade had led to Lady Browne's remarkable recovery from the vapours.

When they arrived at the inn, John was admiring hunting portraits in the hallway, while Counsellor Bodkin chatted with some local dignitaries on their way to the Galway Races.

"Thank you so much for the invitation," said Lord Athenry.

"Papa and I are delighted you could join us at such short notice," John responded. "We have reserved a private room. This way, if you please."

Catherine was impressed with this new and more assertive John. As they walked through the bar, a hush descended upon the customers; the notoriety earned from the recent massacre was inescapable.

They were served a meal of soup and roast pork with onions, accompanied by a Bordeaux white. Conversation, at first confined to social topics, finally turned to the subject occupying all of their minds.

"Are you ready for the trial, Counsellor?" Athenry tapped his lips with a napkin while the footman served dessert and coffee.

"Not quite yet, but good progress has been made."

"Was that Roger Kelly I saw earlier leaving my rooms?"

"Father had a few words with him this morning," John said.

"I heard he withdrew from the conspiracy," Catherine remarked.

"My dear," Athenry cautioned, as if shocked, "that information is strictly confidential."

Catherine wondered why her father had not arrested Kelly on a charge of conspiracy to murder and withholding information.

"It may well be confidential," John remarked, "but the whole affair is the talk of the town."

"Hmmm," Athenry murmured. "Interesting fellow; that man Kelly."

Catherine was aware of Kelly's membership of the Whiteboys; their name derived from the white smocks the members wore in their nightly raids. Their activities on behalf of the dispossessed impressed her, although her father was said to be a prime target. She knew also that he would not hesitate to have Kelly hanged, given the opportunity.

Athenry resumed, "We may expect an invasion of journalists and scandalmongers from Dublin, Galway and London for the trial next week. It is deplorable, but this case has caught the public interest and we are going to be in the news for all the wrong reasons."

"May I attend, Papa?" Catherine inquired.

"Not for the Grand Jury in the morning," Athenry said. "That will be closed to the public."

"I wish to attend the trial," Catherine persisted. "May I do so?"

"You would do better to concentrate on your painting, my dear," Athenry replied sternly.

"Aunt Bridget said she would chaperone me there. She is feeling much improved." Catherine smiled with that easy charm with which she had captivated John. "I could sketch the accused and then paint them at home."

Athenry sighed.

"I shall certainly attend the trial," John said.

"Indeed you must, young man," Athenry riposted. "I presume you have received your court order to attend as a witness."

As John nodded, Catherine interjected, "Aunt Bridget said it could become very heated. She expects that it will be attended by people of all classes."

"Quite so," Athenry replied.

"I would be quite safe in her company."

"I shall consider the matter," Athenry responded, rising. "Thank you so much for a delightful lunch. We shall meet at the trial. Come, Catherine."

"John and I must return to meet Mr. Kelly. Thank you for facilitating us in this matter," Counsellor Bodkin said.

Catherine trembled with excitement. How she would have loved to attend the meeting with the Whiteboy! She could not wait to speak to John in private as soon as possible; perhaps, the trial would provide an opportunity to do so.

∗ ∗ ∗ ∗ ∗

THE INTERACTION WITH A rebel had fascinated John as well, an experience new to him although their paths had crossed before.

Looking Kelly in the eyes, Counsellor Bodkin said, "You were a wise man to withdraw from the conspiracy. What can we do now—?"

"May I ask a question?" John interjected.

After Counsellor Bodkin nodded, John carried on, "Why did you not inform the servants of the impending massacre?"

"That's a smart lad you have there, Counsellor." Kelly paused. "After I was bound and gagged, I was locked into a room at the far end of the house."

"But you were gone when I returned." John said.

"My sister Julia set me free when it was all over. I still have nightmares thinking of all the misery I could have prevented had I escaped earlier."

"Unfortunately, what's done is done and cannot be undone." Counsellor Bodkin furled his brow. "Now what can we do to help Hogan?"

John now understood that his father was inviting Kelly to become an informer without actually putting it into words.

The man with the scarred cheek remained impassive. "I know what you have in mind," Kelly said. "If Hogan turned evidence, he might escape execution. Did you ask him?"

"I did," John said.

"How did he answer?"

"I formed the impression that he would not do so." John ran his fingers through his black curls. "I reminded him that he was the only man among the accused with a wife and children to think about. He is torn."

"Could I see him?" Kelly asked, "without harassment?"

Bodkin let out a breath he had not known he was holding. "You are his brother-in-law; armed with a letter from me, may be sufficient to gain you entry. I have drafted a note in the expectation that you might want to visit him."

Passing the note to Kelly, one of the few literate tenants at Liscarrow, Bodkin said, "If you are happy with this letter, I shall sign it, and seal it; then tomorrow you can bring it to Galway Gaol and show it to the keeper."

Kelly scanned the contents:

The Keeper,
Galway Gaol,
The Tholsel,
Galway City

Saturday, 3ʳᵈ October 1741

Sir,

Following consultation with Lord Athenry, I wish to request permission to allow the bearer of this note, namely, Roger Kelly of

Liscarrow, to visit his brother-in-law, Shane Hogan, tomorrow at noon, and later in the afternoon at three of the clock should that be necessary.

This visit is in relation to the trial of the accused in Tuam next Wednesday under Justice Rose.

I can assure you that Mr Kelly will present himself in an exemplary manner in keeping with the behaviour expected of a visitor.

Yours faithfully,

Counsellor Bodkin,

Carrowbeg,
Belclare,
Tuam, County Galway.

"That seems in order." Kelly said. "Perhaps it should be marked *Urgent* on the outside?"

Bodkin nodded. "The easier to pass the sentinel at the city gates." He passed the letter to John after adding the requested amendment.

John lit a candle from the wood fire. He softened the vermilion wax with the candle flame and allowed it to drip on to the fold of the letter before embossing it with the Athenry seal. The smell of the molten wax permeated the room, lending a formal air to the proceedings.

Counsellor Bodkin continued, "Hogan may still refuse to turn evidence."

"You are assuming that I will ask him to do so," Kelly said and then, raising his eyebrows, "And if he does refuse?"

The counsellor regarded Kelly steadily. "It is the only course left to us, I believe."

"I know what you're asking, Counsellor." Kelly returned the eye contact. "I will not inform. I would be signing my own death warrant."

"I understand, but …" Bodkin stood up with his back to the crackling fire. "I fail to see how your friends could object to evidence that might lighten the load on a misfortunate man of the people."

"You have a clever tongue, Counsellor, but among my people that is not how matters work." Kelly smiled grimly. "Are we done here?"

"Not quite. There is another option." Bodkin paused. "Your sister."

"Zounds!" Kelly found his voice. "You want my sister to be an informer."

"I just want you and Hogan to think about the possibility. Mrs Bodkin and I considered visiting Mrs Hogan but decided against it. The grieving tenantry would not have understood."

For the first time, John saw an apparent glimmer of uncertainty on Kelly's face. His father had presented the rebel with a dilemma.

"I understand how difficult this is for you," Bodkin said.

John understood that Hogan's life now resided in Kelly's hands. Did the Whiteboy know what to do for the best?

"I shall be at home at eleven of the clock on Monday morning if you should wish to discuss the matter further," Bodkin said.

Kelly gave the counsellor a look that could only come from a person operating outside the prevailing system: resentment of the rich man, who did not have to do manual work for a living, mixed with admiration for an intelligence like his own, and accompanied by cynicism, about the possibility of a beneficial outcome.

John donned his cocked hat as the meeting of the titans ended. Both men left with an apparent grudging respect for the other. It was time to move on.

CHAPTER 9

ROGER KELLY WAS THOUGHTFUL as he sat by the small fire in his cabin on the Bodkin estate at Liscarrow. Never before had he engaged in conversation with a member of the landed gentry. Up to now, he had dedicated himself to protecting the poorest of the poor from the worst excesses of the rich. If that meant straying beyond the limits of the law, it was a gamble that he and his Whiteboy friends were prepared to take.

He had been surprised when invited by Counsellor Bodkin to discuss *a matter of mutual interest.* In normal circumstances, he would have burnt the letter and laid low for a while; however, the massacre of servants at Liscarrow and the involvement of his brother-in-law persuaded him to attend that meeting. He wondered if John Bodkin had recognized him at their chance meetings on the road to Galway, or on the occasion when he had held up the stagecoach.

These thoughts swirled through his mind when riding from the meeting to inform his sister of developments. On his arrival, he told her, "Counsellor Bodkin said I should visit Shane. He gave me a letter to allow me in."

"Why so?" inquired the distraught woman.

Kelly chose his words carefully. He knew how vulnerable his sister was. "Bodkin made a suggestion to him earlier."

"Tell me, Roger."

Kelly drew a deep breath. "Not a word to anyone."

"I promise." Mrs Hogan sat down by the turf fire.

"He asked Shane to turn evidence in the hope of a milder sentence." Kelly warmed his outstretched palms at the fire.

"He wants him to inform?" When Kelly nodded, she resumed, "What do you think about that?"

"It will be up to him to decide. I'll see him tomorrow. Would you like me to carry a message?"

"Tell him we love him. Tell him we pray for him." A tear trickled down her weather-beaten face. "Tell him to come home to us; we miss him so much."

Roger Kelly departed from the Hogan cabin with those words ringing in his ears. A cold chill accelerated through his body. His sister was instructing her husband to turn evidence. If the Whiteboys knew that he was supporting an informer, they would surely kill him.

Early on Sunday morning, Kelly rode to Galway Gaol. The sentinel at the city gates looked hard at him before letting him through. Without Counsellor Bodkin's note and the Athenry seal, the man at the gate would probably have refused entry or ordered his arrest. Kelly had to control his anger when he saw the forlorn women and children begging entrance to the city. That was an issue for another day.

Tethering his horse at The King's Head, he presented the counsellor's sealed note to the warder at the basement of the Tholsel. The officer slammed the door in his face while he conferred with the keeper. After an interminable wait, the warder escorted him to Hogan's cell. On his way there, he could hear the muffled moaning of prisoners. Kelly wondered if he would eventually end up there, like his brother-in-law. He stepped into a tiny, stinking chamber.

"What are you doing here?" Hogan stammered. The shepherd had lost weight and looked as white as a sheet.

"Counsellor Bodkin asked me to see you."

"He wants me to inform." Hogan clenched his fists at the prospect.

"He's trying to save your neck." Kelly presumed that Bodkin's real motive was to ensure the hanging of Dominick and Shawn Bodkin rather than to save Hogan, but that was of no account if the result suited them both.

"What does Margaret think?"

"She sent her love and is praying for you," Kelly paused. "Her message was *Tell him to come home to us.*"

"She wants me to inform?" Hogan quaked. "What do you think I should do?"

"That's for you to decide."

Hogan lowered his voice. "I would be branded an informer. The shame would be handed down to my children."

"Not when you're informing against the gentry."

"I would be informing against Shawn and Dominick Bodkin," Hogan said.

"Yes! On behalf of six innocent servants who lost their lives."

Hogan buried his head in his arms and cried. "My God, what have I done?" he spluttered. "I have nightmares every night. When I refused to kill little Oliver, Blind Dominick threatened to kill me ..."

Kelly tapped Hogan on the arm, pointing to the barred unglazed window, and whispered, "Keep your voice down!"

Hogan leaned closer to Kelly and whispered, "I smeared him with blood and told him not to move, hoping they would think him dead; but Dominick knew. He handed me an axe with one hand and held a pistol to my head with the other. My poor little boy screamed, *Papa, do not kill me! Please, Papa.* I took a mighty swipe but aimed away from the boy."

Kelly realized that Hogan was far too emotional just now to be reasoned with. "Try not to think about it for a while. I'll return this afternoon when you are calmer."

As Kelly departed from the gaol, the sights and sounds therein made him grateful for his freedom. He shuddered at the thought of incarceration.

The gusty autumnal wind helped to dispel the wretchedness of the gaol from his mind as he walked south towards the River Corrib. What a pleasant change to walk beside the turbulent waters and watch the swans gliding to calmer regions.

After a while, he repaired to The King's Head for a tankard of ale and lost himself in thought. How could he save the life of his brother-in-law? How could he protect the welfare of his sister and her children? When he left, he purchased some poteen from a backstreet *shebeen*, an unlicensed public house, and concealed it in the inside pocket of his jacket. Normally he would have used the proceeds of highway robberies to ease the plight of the poorest of the poor. On this occasion, he made an exception for his misfortunate brother-in-law. Luck was on his side: the warder refrained from searching him on this occasion. The note from Counsellor Bodkin had worked wonders, gaining him free passage if not respect.

"I have a surprise for you," he whispered to Hogan in his cell. "A naggin of poteen."

Hogan smiled for possibly the first time since the massacre. He took a mighty slug of the fire-water. "You took a chance, smuggling that in."

"If they found it, they would've kept it themselves. A knife would have been another matter."

"No talk of knives!" Hogan wrung his hands like a penitent. "I cannot do it, Roger; even to save my life."

"That's a fine handkerchief you have," said Kelly, turning the subject.

"It belongs to John Bodkin; I forgot to return it."

Kelly shifted his feet on the earthen floor. "If you won't do it, I can." The rebel paused. "I mean stand as a witness."

Hogan's eyes widened in astonishment. "I never thought I'd see the day when a Whiteboy turned informer. Have you lost your senses?"

"Maybe so. It's you and my sister I'm thinking of."

Hogan stood up. "Your evidence wouldn't be enough to save me. All you know is the plan you heard before you withdrew."

"You have told me all I need to know."

"That was confidential, Roger."

"I would not lie under oath if I can save you."

"The Whiteboys will hunt you down and kill you."

"That is what I told Bodkin," Kelly admitted. "But they must catch me first. Being single has its merits."

"You have no money to escape with."

"Enough to get by."

Kelly understood why Hogan was not overjoyed at his offer, generous though it was. The prospect of clemency was slim. Even if it were granted, Hogan would be banished from his country. Transportation was better than execution, but could it ever banish the image of little Oliver begging for his life?

"I will speak to Bodkin later today," Kelly said.

"I'll talk to him the day after in Tuam." Hogan drained the final drops of liquor from the naggin. "May God bless you, Roger Kelly."

* * * * *

As KELLY RODE BACK to Carrowbeg, he thought about his offer to stand as a witness. It was uncharted territory, because the massacre was the result of a feud within the landed gentry. Hogan was a reluctant accomplice. The servants had been slain to eliminate witnesses. Should he talk to the Whiteboys about Hogan's dilemma? Probably not, he decided: they would only see it as an opportunity to strike back at their oppressors.

Kelly reached Carrowbeg as the sun began to dip in the sky. The peace of the verdant estate was in stark contrast to the conflicting emotions jostling within him. Salutation by a footman and formal announcement was a new experience for a Whiteboy.

"You are welcome, Mr Kelly," John said. "Papa is in the library."

Kelly nodded. Sitting in a room laden with learned books was another novel experience for him.

Counsellor Bodkin looked up from his writing desk, surrounded by documents and legal journals.

"I spoke to Hogan," Kelly said without any preliminaries. "He refused to do it, even with poteen to give him false courage."

Bodkin paused as if absorbing the information. "Thank you for trying. Will you join me in a brandy?"

Kelly nodded. "I'm willing to bear witness in his stead."

"That is a brave decision, Mr Kelly." Bodkin acknowledged. "I must make it clear that I cannot guarantee your safety; nor can I guarantee that your evidence will be sufficient to gain clemency for your brother-in-law."

"Hogan said that to me as well."

Bodkin tapped the table with his fingers. "I will not be allowed to talk to Hogan on Tuesday because Mr Staunton might object. Instead, I shall seek permission for Mrs Hogan to visit him after he is transferred from Galway to Tuam."

"To give her a final chance to change his mind?"

"Exactly," Bodkin replied. "Should he remain obstinate, then you can act as a witness."

"I'll speak to her. If she cannot persuade Shane, then I will act as a witness."

"Thank you, Mr Kelly."

Leaving the opulence of Bodkin's estate at Carrowbeg, Kelly rode the long mile to Liscarrow facing into red-tinted clouds just after sunset. A few local people waved to him as he passed by. Soon he reined in his horse at Hogan's cabin. What a contrast that was to Carrowbeg House, even though it was a palace compared to his own single-room shanty.

Margaret Hogan sat in her chair by the turf fire, clutching her rosary beads, a string of fifty-five beads including five sets of ten smaller beads, used for keeping count in the recital of prayers. Her children were asleep. "Will you join me in the rosary for poor Shane?"

Roger knelt by the chair normally occupied by the shepherd. The second half of the *Our Father* struck a chord with him for the first time.

> *Give us this day our daily bread,*
> *and forgive us our trespasses,*
> *as we forgive those who trespass against us;*
> *and lead us not into temptation,*
> *but deliver us from evil.*

Kelly knew that the requirement of *daily bread* was a constant struggle for tenant families now that famine had struck. Those evicted and the homeless suffered most, left defenceless on the side of the road. How could the Lord expect him to *forgive those who trespass against us* when people were faced with such inequality and exploitation? That is why he had succumbed to *temptation* and joined the Whiteboys.

Kelly wanted to deliver the countryside of the *evil* of poverty, although the authorities did not see it that way. Now he was sworn to stand witness in support of a murderer. *What a strange world we live in*, he thought, as the *Hail Mary* refrain rolled mechanically from his tongue.

"How is he?" Margaret asked when the prayer was finished.

"I cheered him with a little poteen. He smiled for the first time in weeks. He'll be transferred to the Bridewell in Tuam on Tuesday morning. Counsellor Bodkin said you can visit him there."

"What has he decided to do?"

Kelly sighed in despair. "I told him what you said, but he cannot bring himself to speak. You can talk to him yourself on Tuesday."

"Well, the old fool!" she cried, thumping the hearth with the poker. A little cry came from the bedroom as her youngest child woke up. "Never mind; she'll go back to sleep."

"I've offered to stand as a witness instead."

"God bless you, Roger."

She stood up and hugged him tightly. Kelly felt the heat of her body against his chest.

"My evidence is mostly what I heard from Shane, that's the problem," Kelly said. "Shane's own evidence would be stronger."

"I know, Roger. I'll talk to him."

"I can arrange for the children to be looked after, if needs be."

"Please pray for me. I don't know if I can win this battle."

* * * * *

EARLY ON THE MORNING of Monday, 5th October 1741, Counsellor Bodkin was deep in thought in his estate at Carrowbeg. He was anxious to ensure that Hogan would turn evidence, or that Mrs Hogan or Kelly would act as witnesses; that would bolster the case for the prosecution and ensure that Dominick and Shawn Bodkin would swing from the gibbet.

"Are you ready for the trial, my dear?" Mary asked as John sat down to the breakfast table.

"I have never before experienced such disorder of the nerves," Bodkin replied, absent-mindedly tapping a boiled egg. "The thought of my own flesh and blood in the dock fills me with gloom."

"Think of the ten people they murdered, two of them, your own flesh and blood," Mary responded but placed her hand gently on his. "What is happening today?"

"Justice Rose, Prime Sergeant Stannard and the Honourable St George Caulfeild will arrive in Tuam this morning amidst great fanfare. Lawyer counsel, clerks and journalists on horseback will accompany their coach. Lord Athenry, Mr Staunton and some local dignitaries will join them on horseback a few miles outside the town."

"I would have joined them myself were it not for our misfortune," John remarked. "Have you met them all previously?"

"I know them well," Counsellor Bodkin said. "Athenry asked me to join them later for tea."

"You forgot to eat your egg, my dear," Mary reminded her husband.

"I have no appetite today." Retiring to the library, he considered the situation. For once in his life, he felt powerless: not in command of the situation, and depending on the vagaries of court procedures, and the state of mind of Hogan or Kelly. He was grateful that John had offered to drive him into Tuam that afternoon.

Traversing the four miles to Tuam later that day, John asked a question to which he thought he knew the answer. "Why are you so anxious for Hogan to turn evidence?"

Bodkin hesitated, but his fury and grief at the murder of his beloved brother and nephew could no longer be contained. "Because I want to ensure that Dominick and Shawn swing from the gibbet. It is all I can think of ever since that day." Tears welled in his eyes.

"I understand, Papa. It's a heavy cross to bear." John shook the reins and urged the horse forward.

By the time they reached Lord Athenry's office, Bodkin had composed himself. He found Justice Rose and Chief Sergeant Stannard deep in conversation. The Honourable St George Caulfeild and Mr Staunton soon joined them in their respective capacities as prosecuting and defending counsels.

"Counsellor, please accept my sympathy on the terrible tragedy visited on your family." Justice Rose stood and extended the hand of sympathy.

"Thank you, sir."

Justice Rose continued, "I understand why you felt unable to act as defence counsel. Thank you persuading your esteemed colleague, Mr Staunton, to act in your stead."

"I understand the prisoners will be transferred from Galway to the Bridewell tomorrow morning," Bodkin said.

"Sheriff Shaw will escort the three accused from The Tholsel to Tuam under armed escort early in the morning," Rose responded.

"My brother Dominick and my nephew Shawn would like me to visit them to discuss some family issues arising from the trial." Bodkin could feel beads of perspiration forming on his forehead. "I do not feel myself capable of such a visit, but my son John has offered to perform the duty. I hope that is acceptable to you."

"Provided the discussions are unrelated to the trial itself," Rose said. "I would not wish to compromise the positions of the prosecution or defence." He glanced at Caulfeild and Staunton, who nodded in agreement.

"I would also like to request permission for Mrs Hogan to visit her husband in the Bridewell tomorrow. She is a respectable tenant of mine. With several small children, she was not in a position to visit her husband in Galway Gaol."

"I shall be happy to facilitate those visits," Athenry said.

Bodkin relaxed, being pleased with the ready acquiescence to his requests. He wanted very much to know if Shawn Bodkin's threatening letter to his slain father had been unearthed, but did not feel in a position to inquire.

Caulfeild relieved his curiosity when he said, "May I ask if Lord Athenry has found the missing letter?"

Athenry blushed. "Not yet, but the search continues, Mr Caulfeild."

Apparently displeased, Caulfeild said, "That letter is a vital piece of evidence."

Bodkin took his leave, a little easier in his mind. Athenry followed him out.

"I can provide you with a copy of the letter from memory, if you so wish," Bodkin offered.

"I hope that will not be necessary, but thank you." Athenry frowned. "Catherine is searching my files at Bermingham House after my staff failed to locate it. If anyone can find it, she will. What would I do without her?"

Bodkin wondered if Athenry's final remark was meant indirectly for John. Was Athenry about to dash his son's hopes of marriage to his daughter? He put that thought aside to focus on the here and now. "I shall instruct John to bring a copy to the trial, just in case."

"Thank you, Counsellor. I must check that all is in order at the Bridewell and the Courthouse."

Bodkin returned to The Thomas Bagworth Inn where John was waiting outside in their trap to bring him home to Carrowbeg.

CHAPTER 10

JOHN BODKIN HAD SLEPT poorly. He dreaded the thought of standing up in court for examination by the leading prosecutor in the land. However, he decided to reveal all that he had overheard discussed by the conspirators on the night of the heinous massacre. To put his mind at rest, he needed to discuss the matter with someone, but Catherine was the only person with whom he could speak freely.

Counsellor Bodkin's distress was obvious as they sat down to breakfast. "I feel such hatred towards my brother and my nephew," he said. "You will have to face them alone; I cannot bring myself to do it."

John understood that his father was still inconsolable after the callous murder of his brother, Oliver, and nephew, little Oliver: the fact that those accused were also family members made the situation even worse.

"Very well, Papa. I will make haste; the sooner I leave, the sooner this unpleasant business will be over." John finished his meal rapidly and rode the four miles east to Tuam.

While he was tethering his grey gelding outside the Bridewell, a voice shouted from a group of agitated countrymen, "Let the murderers roast in hell."

John ignored the taunt, knowing that the yeoman soldiers would ensure him safe entrance. He approached the keeper of the gaol. "Justice Rose has given me permission to visit Shawn and Dominick Bodkin."

"Is the counsellor with you?" asked the keeper in an unfriendly tone.

"No. He is not in the best of health today."

"Very well: I shall allow you access, Mr Bodkin." The keeper rose slowly from his desk. "Lord Athenry has ordered that the accused be held in separate chambers, so you will be obliged to see them one at a time."

John nodded perfunctorily at the public servant, who seemed reluctant to deal with one so young.

Entering Shawn's cell, John was not surprised to find his cousin in a sorry state—unkempt, pale and shivering.

"Not you again?" Shawn hissed.

John gritted his teeth. "Dominick said you wished Counsellor Bodkin to defend you. That was not possible, so my father persuaded Mr Staunton to act for you instead."

"What defence has he prepared?" Shawn asked.

"He will discuss that with you later today." John blew his nose in the hope that he might relieve himself a little from the smell. "I am not allowed to mention anything related to the trial."

"Then why are you here?" Shawn raised himself from his straw pallet.

"As things stand, you now own Liscarrow."

"For all the good it will do me." Shawn grunted. "If I am found innocent, I won't need a will; if guilty..."

"Have you made a will?" John interjected, meeting Shawn's eyes.

"You think me guilty, then?" Shawn said in a truculent tone.

"Father believes that anyone in your position would want to make a will," John replied, ignoring the question.

"And if I do not?" Shawn punched the palm of his hand with his fist.

"If you are found guilty, the estate of Liscarrow will pass to my father."

"I am aware of it." Shawn glared at John. "I suppose there is little point in willing it to Dominick?"

"That is for you to decide," John responded coolly.

"I could leave it to Patrick's son, little Thomas." Shawn roared with a mirthless laugh, "I shall not will it to you, at any rate. It would be a pointless act."

"What do you mean?" John cried.

"That you shall discover soon enough." Shawn bared his yellowed teeth in what passed for a smile.

"I shall take my departure now," John said, losing patience. "Whatever the outcome, we'll visit again after the trial."

John saw the tears welling in Shawn's eyes as he departed. Although he had never liked his first cousin, he pitied him; the predicament he was in, and its almost inevitable conclusion, was something he would not wish on any man.

John walked in silence to the nearby cell of Dominick Bodkin. The visit here proceeded along similar lines. Towards its conclusion, Blind Dominick stared into his eyes and muttered, "You would do better to look to yourself." John shivered at the menace in his voice.

He then recalled what Shawn had said. What were Shawn and Dominick attempting to achieve? Deep down, he already knew: they wished to intimidate him and ensure he would not testify against them, using Patrick's mysterious death as a lever. Now he needed a brandy. As he sat with a glass in The Thomas Bagworth Inn, the image of Patrick's corpse entered his mind. He banished it with an effort of will, and focused his mind instead on the coming ordeal of the witness stand. How could he remain in command of himself when unsure of how much they knew?

* * * * *

AFTER LUNCHEON THAT DAY, John saw Mrs Hogan passing by. She looked disconsolate, with tears in her eyes.

He walked towards her. "How are you, Mrs Hogan?"

"Not the best," she whispered. "I begged him to turn evidence, but he would not."

"What did he say?"

"He told me that when he arrived at the Bridewell, some people shouted *murderer* to his face."

"Probably relatives or friends of the slain servants."

"He shuddered in the telling of it." Her voice trembled. "Shane said he would be found guilty, without a doubt."

"But his sentence might be commuted if he bore witness."

Mrs Hogan shook her head. "He said he could not allow an informer's shame to pass on to our children."

But what about passing on a murderer's shame, John thought, but could not bring himself to say it. Instead, he asked, "Might he yet change his mind, do you think?"

"If he does, he will let us know by nodding his head. That much he promised me."

"We must trust he may yet see his way." John paused. "I regret that I cannot offer you transport home, as I rode here."

"No matter, thank you. I want to visit the church and say a prayer before I go home." Mrs Hogan wrapped her shawl around her and walked slowly towards Bishop Street.

On his way home, John shook the reins and urged his horse forward. He travelled the four miles west in a silence broken only by the sound of clattering hooves and the wind whistling in the trees.

Back at Carrowbeg, John still worried about the taunting remarks from his accused relatives in the Bridewell. In a moment of foolishness, he considered riding the six miles to Bermingham House to talk to Catherine but thought the better of it. He missed her so much; she knew how to calm his troubled soul.

John was not surprised to see Roger Kelly arrive at the house that afternoon. He escorted him into the library to see his father.

"I spoke to Mrs Hogan after lunch today. She was unhappy with her husband's decision," John said.

"If she could not change his mind, I doubt that anyone can." Kelly looked at Counsellor Bodkin.

"I cannot tell you what to do," Bodkin said, "but I can tell you what will happen now. The Grand Jury will indict Hogan with murder, and the prosecution will call John as a witness."

John shrank under Kelly's regard. He remained silent, unsure of what to say, and was relieved when his father resumed, "I expect John will testify that you and Hogan visited Carrowbeg on a number of occasions before the massacre."

When John nodded, Bodkin continued, "After John has finished in the witness box, you will be called to testify under oath."

"What will they ask me?"

"You will be asked to provide evidence of the conspiracy."

"And how will that help Hogan?"

John said, "By demonstrating how reluctant Hogan was to participate in the heinous crime."

"Reluctant or not, he was there," Counsellor Bodkin said, "but he bears less guilt than the others because he was threatened into it."

Kelly said, "Shane insists that he did not kill little Oliver."

"You could tell the court that Hogan killed no one," John said.

"But I have no evidence of that," replied Kelly.

"You were part of the plot. You could emphasise Hogan's assertion of innocence of murder by way of a character reference," John said. His own testimony would also be in Hogan's favour to some degree.

"Mr Staunton could then make an impassioned plea for clemency." Bodkin steepled his fingers. "But I cannot guarantee its success when public abhorrence of this crime is so great."

John was glad that his father was being honest about the possibility of a commutation in Shane Hogan's sentence, allowing Kelly to make a balanced decision.

"I'll see you in court tomorrow, God willing," Kelly said. He rose to depart. "And if I'm not there, you'll know I've changed my mind."

* * * * *

JOHN AWOKE IN AN odd humour on the morning of Wednesday, 7th October 1741. Much to his surprise, he had slept well. During the night, he had fantasized about Catherine, and had kissed and hugged her to distraction. How he longed to be with her! He looked forward to doing so after testifying at the trial.

But how would he testify? He had the advantage of having persuaded Athenry during interrogation that he had nothing to do with the massacre. John hoped he would be able to handle the prosecutor with poise and confidence. Why should he not? His approach reflected an emerging maturity that would help him with the examination no matter how cunning the prosecutor.

Arriving in Tuam from Carrowbeg, John was alarmed by unruly scenes outside the courthouse. A large crowd had gathered, as the prisoners arrived from the Bridewell, heads bowed low. Someone shouted, *Hang the bastards!* The crowd surged forward but the yeoman cordon stood firm, though not without difficulty. Without their presence, the accused men would have been ripped apart, limb from limb.

As the clock chimed nine in the tiered courthouse, the clerk of the court announced, "All rise." Justice Rose entered—the elderly icon of the Irish legal system.

John was reminded that the eyes of Ireland and further afield would rest on this court. Their family affairs were no longer a private matter; one night of horrific violence had seen to that.

"The first duty of this court will be to swear in a Grand Jury," Rose said. "Lord Athenry has compiled a list of respected gentlemen from the Tuam district."

Having sworn in the Grand Jury, Rose carried on, "Gentlemen, it is your duty to determine if true bills can be found against the accused for the murder of ten people at Liscarrow on Saturday, 19th September 1741."

John knew that *true bills* meant that the evidence was sufficient to serve an indictment on the accused.

Rose cleared his throat. "The prosecution will present their case. You must decide if I should order the indictment of one or more of the accused. I now call on the Solicitor General, the Honourable St George Caulfeild, to present the case for the Crown. The counsel for the defence, Mr Staunton, may observe the proceedings in the interests of his clients."

Justice Rose turned to Caulfeild. The Member of Parliament for Tulsk rose imperiously, lightly dusting his gown. "My lord, I shall start with Shawn Bodkin, originally of Liscarrow and currently of Carrowbeg, who is accused of conspiracy to murder his father, Oliver Bodkin of Liscarrow, his stepmother, Margery, and his half-brother, Oliver, along with Marcus Lynch Esquire of Galway and six servants, namely, Henry Burke, Mrs Agnes Burke, James Fallon, Bridget MacHugh, Thaddeus MacHugh and Michael O'Brien." Caulfield paused to adjust his papers.

"The massacre was discovered by an out-servant at Liscarrow on the morning after the horrific event. The distraught man immediately raised the alarm. When Lord Athenry arrived at the scene of the tragedy, he found the accused, Shawn Bodkin, standing outside the house, pale and shaking in bloodstained clothes. Athenry had previously been given a letter by the late Oliver Bodkin, written by his son, Shawn, threatening him and demanding that his inheritance be reinstated. With this motive established, the young man was arrested on suspicion of murder." Caulfeild paused to adjust his wig while gazing at the members of the Grand Jury.

"Lord Athenry soon found that Dominick Bodkin of Carrowbeg, known as Blind Dominick, a younger half-brother of the murdered Oliver, and Shane Hogan, a shepherd at Liscarrow, had both fled; they were nowhere to be found in the community. He ordered their arrest. The army discovered them on their way to Dublin and detained them before sunset."

Caulfeild walked towards the Gentlemen of the Grand Jury. "I understand that, shortly before he was disinherited, Shawn Bodkin left home to live with Dominick Bodkin at Carrowbeg. I also understand that a shepherd, Shane Hogan, visited Carrowbeg on a number of occasions shortly before the massacre. He participated in what appears to have been conspiratorial conversations with Dominick and Shawn Bodkin, some of which were overheard by Counsellor Bodkin's son, John, who was also temporarily dwelling on the premises."

Caulfeild glanced at John, who felt a flutter of nervousness in his belly. The Honourable Member continued, "Lord Athenry also briefly arrested John Bodkin due to his residency at Carrowbeg during the crucial period, and a blood stain acquired from contact with his cousin, but released him when persuaded of his innocence and his unblemished character. The same does not apply to Dominick Bodkin, who resented his unfavourable treatment in his late father's will, and fled the scene of the crime in a manner suggestive of guilt."

"The case of the shepherd, Shane Hogan, is more complex. The conspiracy was crucially dependent on one member being well-known to the guard dogs and trusted by them. The two dogs were found knifed to death by the out-servants on the fatal morning. Only Hogan of the three accused conspirators could have accomplished such a deed without raising the alarm."

"Having carefully considered all these relevant matters, I have concluded that each of the three accused should be indicted and brought to trial."

"Thank you, Mr Caulfeild. I shall now call a recess to allow the Grand Jury to deliberate on the case presented by the Crown."

"All rise," cried the clerk of the court as Justice Rose departed to the keeper's office. Receiving an invitation to refreshments, John Bodkin joined him there, accompanied by Athenry, Caulfeild, and Staunton.

"I understand there was quite a commotion outside the courthouse this morning," Rose said.

"It would have turned ugly were it not for the presence of the soldiers," Athenry responded.

"It was quite understandable, given the grief of the relatives of the slain servants," John Bodkin was sufficiently emboldened to add, despite being a young man among distinguished elders. The silence that followed his remark, punctuated only by the sound of delicate cups clinking on saucers, suggested that he might have done better to hold his fire. To his relief, the clerk of the court soon intervened to say that the Grand Jury had concluded their deliberations

Court reconvened, Justice Rose said, "I understand you have reached a decision."

"Yes, my lord," the foreman of the jury replied. "We have found true bills against each of the three accused."

Justice Rose responded, "The indictments will now be finalized for the commencement of the trial at ten of the clock this morning."

"My lord," Caulfeild interjected, "if you are agreeable, once I have examined John Bodkin and Roger Kelly, I would like to continue with Hogan, then Dominick Bodkin and finally Shawn Bodkin."

Judge Rose directed his eyes at Staunton who raised no objection. "Very well, Mr Caulfeild."

CHAPTER 11

WHEN JOHN BODKIN RETURNED to the courtroom, he found it empty apart from his mother who was conversing animatedly with Catherine and Lady Browne. When he caught the eye of his betrothed, she drew her fan across her cheek as an expression of her love for him. He smiled in return.

Lord Athenry joined them. "Good morning, ladies, Mr Bodkin. Is the charming Anna Bodkin joining us this morning?"

John wondered why Athenry had inquired about Patrick's widow. He was not a man inclined to casual conversation.

"Anna is at home, looking after little Thomas," Mary said. "He is somewhat feverish at the moment."

"Poor child," Lady Browne said.

"I'm sure he will recover very soon," Mary responded. "Anna may join us later today."

Athenry then changed tack. "Do excuse me, please. We have a mass of people outside hoping to gain entrance. The army is on high alert."

"Have you seen Roger Kelly?" John asked.

"Not the Whiteboy!" Lady Browne paled.

"He's present already," replied the departing Athenry. "My men are watching him."

"I should hope so, indeed." Lady Browne sniffed.

Shortly afterwards, the doors were thrown open to the public. John sat by Catherine at the end of a long bench. The army controlled the rush for seats by organizing people into a queue and restricting entrance to small groups at a time. When the disturbance distracted the attention of Lady Browne and his mother, John took the opportunity to move closer to Catherine. He could feel the comfort of her body and enjoyed the rare pleasure of physical contact. How long more did he have to wait before they could enjoy intimacy?

When Mrs Lynch and the Blakes of Oranmore sat on the same bench, John made a little more space by drawing Catherine even closer to him. Behind them, people crushed together on the benches until standing room only remained. Shortly afterwards, the gowned attorneys took their seats in the front row accompanied by clerks, clergy and journalists.

John could feel the breath of the grieving servants behind him as they pushed into the third row. When the clerk of the court cried, "All rise," the thought of his impending testimony made him quiver again—his skin, goose-pimpled with the emotion of the occasion.

Justice Rose opened the proceedings. "Ladies and Gentlemen, we are here today to adjudicate on the appalling murders at Liscarrow. Allow me to extend my deepest sympathy, and that of my colleagues, to the relatives and friends of the bereaved. Earlier this morning, the Grand Jury handed down an indictment against the three accused. I now call on the prosecution to proceed."

"Thank you, my lord." The Solicitor-General, St George Caulfeild, commenced for the Crown, "Gentlemen of the jury, I shall present evidence that the accused, namely, Shawn Bodkin, Dominick Bodkin and Shane Hogan, are jointly and severally guilty of the aforesaid murder of ten people."

Caulfeild paused, to the rapt attention of the packed courtroom. "My lord, I wish to call my first witness, John Bodkin."

John glanced at Catherine who bit her lip as he walked to the witness box. Nervously he swore to tell the truth, the whole truth and nothing but the truth.

Caulfeild said, "John Bodkin, I understand that you were living in the adjoining property of Carrowbeg, one mile distant from Liscarrow, in the period before and during the September murders."

"Carrowbeg is owned by my father, Counsellor Bodkin. We live in Dublin but I usually stay in Carrowbeg during the summer and early autumn."

"With whom do you share accommodation at these times, Mr Bodkin?"

"With my Uncle Dominick and my cousin, Shawn." Out of the corner of his eye, he could see Catherine looking at him intently.

"In the period immediately preceding the murders, did you observe any visitors to the house?"

John directed his eyes at the dock where the three accused sat impassively. "I saw Shane Hogan and Roger Kelly of Liscarrow visit the house on a number of occasions, including the night of the murders."

"Do you know what they talked about, and to whom?" Caulfeild said.

"They spoke to Dominick and Shawn Bodkin. I absented myself on these occasions. Sometimes they spoke loudly and heatedly, and I could then hear a little of what was said; words or phrases rather than sentences."

"What words did they use?" Caulfeild raised his eyebrows.

John grew heated under the examination as all eyes focused on him. He replied, "I heard words like *inheritance, Margery, Oliver,* and so on."

"Did you hear any of the words, *murder, kill,* or *knife,* Mr Bodkin?" Caulfeild continued.

"I heard those words."

"Was there anything unusual about the gathering on the night of the murders?"

"I heard shouting and banging, and then silence for a while until the conspirators left."

"Thank you, Mr Bodkin."

John returned to sit beside Catherine in the second row. He was surprised that he had not been questioned about his visitations to the three accused in the Tholsel in Galway and in the Bridewell in Tuam. Perhaps Caulfeild had decided to make haste to the three accused with an option of returning to him if necessary.

"I now call on Roger Kelly." Caulfeild boomed. "Is he present?" A collective gasp of astonishment emanated from those present as the man with the scarred face rose at the back of the courtroom. Leaving behind his weeping sister, he came to the stand, and was sworn-in.

"Roger Kelly, I understand that you are the brother-in-law of the accused, Shane Hogan, the shepherd of Liscarrow."

"I am."

"Why did you leave the meeting at Liscarrow on the night of the murder?"

"I tried to leave because of a disagreement."

"Can you outline the nature of this disagreement?"

"We had been trying to frighten Oliver Bodkin and his wife at Liscarrow ..."

"What was the motive for this, Mr Kelly?"

"To recover Shawn's inheritance. His father had cut him out of his will and he was angry."

"How did you become involved?"

"The guard dogs had to be controlled at night to get close enough to make the Bodkins afeared. Shane Hogan was the man for that. He was nervous and asked me to join him. I did so because Oliver Bodkin had threatened me with eviction when my crop failed and I could not pay the rent."

"Go on, Mr Kelly."

"The Bodkins were not easy to frighten. Hogan and I wanted no more of it. Dominick and Shawn threatened us; Hogan stayed and I motioned to leave."

"Can you confirm that it was the intention of the accused to murder all the occupants of Liscarrow House on the night in question, Mr Kelly?"

"I cannot do that because I was bound and gagged and dispatched to another room at the far end of the house. I could no longer hear what was being said."

"Are you certain of that, Mr Kelly?" Caulfeild walked to the witness stand and fixed his eyes on the Whiteboy. "May I remind you that you are under oath?"

"I'm certain."

Caulfeild paused but Kelly remained impassive. "Thank you, Mr Kelly. You are excused for the moment."

John was surprised that Kelly had failed to complete his testimony; this meant that no one had provided direct evidence of intent on the part of Dominick and Shawn Bodkin. He glanced at Catherine, who shrugged her shoulders.

Justice Rose intervened, "I suggest we take a short break at this point."

* * * * *

JOHN LISTENED TO THE busy whispering as people stretched their legs in the courtroom. Others conversed in conspiratorial tones. The two names that he heard repeatedly were Roger Kelly and Blind Dominick. The man with the eye patch had been motioning aggressively towards the Whiteboy, who was now nowhere to be seen. Cocking an ear to the conversation of the journalists, he found they were equally fascinated with Kelly and Dominick. They were busy comparing notes and beginning to write copy.

"You did well in the witness box," Catherine said.

"Thank you." John then looked at his mother. "After Hogan testifies, perhaps Lady Browne and Miss Catherine might join us for luncheon."

"But of course!" Mary Bodkin replied.

Lady Browne smiled. "Thank you. I suspect that Catherine will have no objection." She then looked at John. "I thought you sounded like the Counsellor when you were giving your evidence. Have you considered a career in the law?"

"Indeed I have! Especially since Patrick passed away." John saw Catherine rolling her eyes. He cursed himself for not thinking first before opening his big mouth. Tears formed in his mother's eyes.

"Poor Patrick. I never understood how it could have happened," Mary said. "We were all devastated, and now this ..." Tears dribbled down her rouged cheeks.

John proffered a handkerchief to his grief-stricken mother.

"Forgive me; I did not intend to remind you of your loss," Lady Browne said.

"It is good to speak openly and shed tears." Mary dabbed her eyes. "Now, what were we saying?"

"We were discussing my future career." John smiled, happy that the conversation had moved on from the subject of Patrick. "I am making good progress in the new Law School at Trinity and helping Papa with his practice."

"Splendid!" Lady Browne said.

The clerk of the court called for order.

Justice Rose said, "Please call your next witness, Mr Caulfeild."

"Thank you, my lord. I would like to call Shane Hogan."

John watched Hogan walk slowly towards the stand under the gaze of his tearful wife. Here was the man without whom the atrocity against his family could not have taken place. John knew he should hate Hogan, and yet, pity stirred in him for the broken man he had become. He wondered if Kelly's evidence had been helpful to Hogan; would Hogan now testify against his partners in crime.

"Mr Hogan, you are the shepherd at Liscarrow. Is that correct?"

"Yes."

Caulfeild continued, "Why did you remain in the conspiracy when your brother-in-law abandoned it?"

"Roger Kelly is a single man. I have a family. Blind Dominick had threatened my wife and children."

"What happened after Roger Kelly was bound and gagged and removed from the room on the night of 19th September?"

"Dominick said that I should be revenged on Margery Bodkin and must stand my ground."

"What was your grievance against her?"

"She had insisted that my wife nurse her son, Oliver, as well as our own son. It was too much for my wife; she fell ill with exhaustion, and begged Mrs Bodkin to take Oliver back. Margery refused. Our little boy fell ill and ..." Hogan wrung his calloused hands.

"Take your time, Mr Hogan." Caulfeild proffered an initialled handkerchief to the shepherd.

Wiping his tears, Hogan resumed, "Our only son died while little Oliver thrived. We are still distraught at our loss, although we always loved little Oliver as our foster son."

"Did you hate Margery Bodkin?"

"I did, but I have learned to live with it."

"Did you conspire to murder Margery Bodkin?" Caulfeild walked across the courtroom.

"No."

"What transpired next on the night in question?"

"I said I would ask Kelly to come back when he had cooled down."

"Please continue, Mr Hogan," Caulfield paced the floor before a silent audience.

"They agreed. Kelly was ungagged but refused to rejoin us."

"Is it your contention that Dominick and Shawn Bodkin carried out the murders on their own?"

"No. The guard dogs would have eaten them alive."

"So who then committed the massacre at Liscarrow on the night of the 19th September?"

"I don't know." Hogan's face reddened.

"I think you do know, Mr Hogan." Caulfeild threw his notes on to the podium. "You approached the guard dogs, who knew you well, cut their throats with a razor and then proceeded unimpeded into the house with your companions."

"I did not." Hogan cried, trembling under the unrelenting gaze of the Solicitor General.

"Thank you, Mr Hogan. You may step down for the moment."

"This court is now in recess until after luncheon." Justice Rose tapped his gavel and departed.

∗   ∗   ∗   ∗   ∗

THE EXCITEMENT OF THE court proceedings had enthralled Catherine. Her discreet sketching of the witnesses had greatly impressed Aunt Bridget. She was proud that John had given a good account of himself in the witness box. Poor Hogan, she sighed: what a tragic figure he had presented while testifying. She wondered how the fearsome Dominick would appear in the witness box. With these thoughts whirling in her mind, she was glad to break for lunch, an opportunity denied to those in unreserved seats.

She walked with John towards the nearby Thomas Bagworth Inn followed by Lady Browne and Mary Bodkin at a discreet distance.

"You performed very well in the witness box," Catherine said. "Aunt Bridget admired your self-possession in such a crowded courtroom."

"I'm thankful it is over. I was afeared that I might inadvertently mention some matter for Caulfeild to pounce on."

"You told the truth—what wrong could he have found in that?" Catherine inquired, puzzled.

"I did not lie, but I knew more than Caulfeild drew from me," John said.

"But you were not in any way involved? I know you were not."

"Of course not, my darling," John replied. "I learned my lesson the night Patrick died."

Catherine froze. Her shoulders stiffened; it seemed that every time she tried to banish the thought of Patrick's death from her mind, someone mentioned it and it returned to haunt her once more. She had often considered discussing the matter with Dean Bruce; but she could not be sure if her secret would be safe with the old windbag. Opening her mind to her father or her aunt was another option, but she feared they would not understand.

"Forgive me: I should not have mentioned Patrick's death," John apologized.

"You must keep a guard on your tongue." Catherine chided him gently.

"What are you two discussing?" Lady Browne had caught up with the young couple at the entrance to the inn. Without waiting for an answer, she continued, "If there is time enough after we have eaten, perhaps we could take a short stroll by the River Nanny."

"Capital!" John agreed as the proprietor escorted them to a private room.

Over freshly baked bread, partridge and lemonade, Lady Browne said, "What did you think of that scoundrel Kelly giving evidence in the case?"

Catherine banished Patrick to the back of her mind and sought to allay John's discomfiture, noting how he shifted in his seat.

"I mentioned him in my evidence because he visited Liscarrow a few times before the murders," John said. "Nobody knew if he would appear to take the stand."

"They say he's a Whiteboy," Catherine replied.

"Indeed!" Lady Browne snorted. "Not only that, he has threatened your father."

"Why, Aunt Bridget?"

"Because he had to evict some of our tenants who would not pay their rent."

"Maybe they could not do so," Catherine replied. "It is likely they had no money because of the failure of the potato crop."

"My dear young lady, you are becoming excessively opinionated," Lady Browne chided. "Your father can explain the matter to you when he returns home this evening."

John turned the subject. "I would appreciate a stroll along the River Nanny. Shall we set off?"

"Well said, young man," Lady Browne remarked. "Mrs Bodkin and I shall follow in your wake."

Leaving the inn, John and Catherine walked north on Shop Street before turning west along the river that powered the town mill. Catherine looked over her shoulder to find that the chaperones had stopped to admire the swans. Rounding a bend, she moved closer to her fiancé. They were effectively alone for the first time since the massacre.

"I love you, Catherine," John said. "I have missed you so much."

Catherine felt a frisson of excitement surging through her body as his arms encircled her. She snuggled close to him and felt his heart pounding. When his fingers lifted her chin, she kissed him. Lips open, she felt his tongue swirling round in her mouth. *If only we were married*, she thought.

They walked arm in arm by the surging water. "Let us marry as soon as the trial is over," John decided, "I can wait no longer."

"I'm ready, John. I love you so much."

"We shall honeymoon in Paris and settle in Dublin, away from this horrid mess."

"That is my dream."

Suddenly a voice called, "Catherine!" She looked around to see Lady Browne beckoning the young lovers to return.

Catherine rushed back, flushed with excitement over John's expression of love and reiteration of his desire to marry. She was very aware that this was the day, their wedding should have taken place. But now the trial was about to recommence and she was eager to see Dominick on the witness stand.

CHAPTER 12

AFTER THEIR WALK BY the River Nanny, John sat beside Catherine in the courtroom alongside Lady Browne and his mother. In normal circumstances, Aunt Bridget would have sat between them as chaperone but the excitement of the occasion resulted in a more informal seating arrangement.

The warmth of Catherine's body reminded John of their kiss at the riverside and awoke in him a renewed longing for physical contact. He thought joyfully of their decision to marry as soon as possible. Once the trial was over, they could move on after a period of mourning. A new chapter in their lives beckoned, or so he hoped.

Meanwhile, an air of excitement pervaded the courtroom preceding the examination of the fearsome Blind Dominick.

The clerk of the court called for order. Adjusting his wig, Justice Rose said, "Mr Caulfeild, please call your next witness."

"I call Dominick Bodkin of Carrowbeg," Caulfeild responded.

Blind Dominick stood in the dock. With his eye patch complemented by a pockmarked face, he presented the appearance of someone to be reckoned with.

John dropped his eyes from his uncle's baleful glare. He felt Catherine nudging closer helping to calm him.

A hush descended in the courtroom as Caulfeild commenced examination for the Crown, "Dominick Bodkin, you are charged with conspiracy to murder, and with the murder of ten people in Liscarrow House on the night of the 19th September 1741. How do you plead?"

Dominick remained silent at first. Just as his defence counsel, Mr Staunton, motioned to rise, the accused cried, "Not guilty!"

"Murderer!" cried numerous voices from the crowd. Justice Rose called for order.

Caulfeild resumed, "Mr Bodkin, can you explain to the court why you are called Blind Dominick?"

"Objection, my lord," Staunton interjected. "What is the relevance of this question?"

Justice Rose looked at Caulfeild, who responded, "The question is designed to establish motive, my lord."

"I shall allow it for the moment. Please answer the question, Mr Bodkin."

Dominick grasped the bar of the dock until his knuckles turned white. "As a young boy, I played with my older brother, the late Oliver Bodkin. We played all sorts of games including swordfights. When we fenced, we used blackthorn sticks with sharpened tips. Father warned us never to point the weapon at the face. One day, as Oliver lunged forward, he slipped and his stick pierced my eye. I screamed in pain until Mrs Bodkin came. She rushed me to the surgeon in Tuam but it was too late. My eye was lost. I was nicknamed Blind Dominick and known by that name ever since."

John whispered to Catherine, "Dominick never stopped reminding us of that."

Caulfeild asked. "It was an accident, was it not, Mr Bodkin?"

"Maybe it was, but my life was ruined. I had to wear a hideous eye patch. People were repelled by my appearance."

"Did you hate your half-brother, Oliver?"

"No."

"Tell the court about your childhood illness."

Blind Dominick continued, "Shortly after I lost my eye, I picked up the smallpox. The doctor cured me, but I was left pockmarked for life. The older boys at school bullied me. They called me *Pock face*, *Black eye* and other such names."

"Did not your older brothers protect you?" Caulfeild asked.

"Counsellor John tried to, but not Oliver."

"What happened when your father died?"

"We buried him." Blind Dominick flashed his maniacal grin, looking at John who remained impassive, refusing to respond to the black humour.

The lawyer pursed his lips. "I should have asked *How did he distribute his estate?*"

Dominick replied, "I got nothing under my father's will. Carrowbeg was left to Counsellor John, and Liscarrow was left to Oliver."

"Why were you excluded from the will?"

"I had no idea; but after Mrs Bodkin died, Oliver said I was illegitimate, and that was why I was left out of the will."

John had heard that rumour. His father had confirmed Dominick's illegitimacy although the identity of the mother was unknown to him.

"The poor man had such a burden to bear," Catherine whispered.

"What is your position at Carrowbeg?" Caulfield asked.

"Counsellor John asked me to look after Carrowbeg while he concentrated on his legal career in Dublin. He also asked me to take care of his two sons, Patrick and John, over the summer months. The young lads brought joy to my heart until poor Patrick died, more than two years ago."

"Did you consider marrying?" Caulfeild asked.

"I wanted to marry." Dominick paused as a tear rolled from his remaining eye. "No woman ever gave me a second look. My scarred face and lack of a fortune did not help. I was the butt of jokes at dances and at the hunt, but having grown strong, I defended myself with fist and sword."

"Dominick Bodkin, you have had to bear a difficult station in life, the loss of your eye, your affliction with smallpox, the insult of illegitimacy, exclusion from your father's will and your failure to attract a wife. These afflictions would be sufficient to destroy most men, but you managed to successfully run an estate and establish good relations with your nephews."

Caulfeild persisted, "Now please tell the court why your nephew, Shawn Bodkin, came to see you."

John anticipated that Caulfeild was about to twist the knife.

Blind Dominick smiled grimly. "My nephew was a young lad of eighteen who had gone astray. His mother died when he was only seven. He missed her terribly. Two years later, Oliver Bodkin married Margery Blake. She treated Shawn badly."

Colonel Blake, Margery's father, coughed loudly.

Dominick carried on, "After failing his studies in Dublin, Shawn was refused an increase in his allowance. Oliver eventually disinherited him and transferred Shawn's inheritance to his new son, little Oliver, at Margery's insistence."

"My late daughter did nothing of the kind!" Colonel Blake interjected.

"Colonel Blake, I understand your distress but you must allow the court to follow its own procedures. I must ask that your comment be stricken from the record and that the jury must ignore it," Justice Rose responded. "Please continue, Mr Bodkin."

"Shawn asked if he could stay at Carrowbeg because the atmosphere at Liscarrow was poisonous. I reluctantly agreed. He said he had written to his father requesting re-instatement as his rightful heir."

Caulfeild walked towards Dominick. "Were you aware of a conspiracy to murder Oliver Bodkin?" The prosecutor raised his voice, "I shall take this opportunity to remind you that you are under oath."

"No."

"Liar!" shouted a voice from the rear.

"On the morning after the massacre at Liscarrow, Lord Athenry ordered your arrest on suspicion of murder. You were nowhere to be found. Why did you run away, Dominick Bodkin?"

"I did not run away! Hogan and I went to look at some sheep in Roscommon."

"Nonsense!" A woman screamed. Blind Dominick remained impassive.

"I do not believe you, Dominick Bodkin. My lord, permit me to tell the court what I believe to be the truth of the matter."

"Objection, my lord!" cried Staunton. "Mr Caulfeild is about to embark on speculation for which he has no evidence."

"I shall allow it, if it helps to unearth the truth," Justice Rose countered. "Tread carefully, however, Mr Caulfeild."

"Thank you, my lord. The events of the 19th of September were as follows: a number of men approached Liscarrow House under cover of darkness; one of these men, Shane Hogan, ensured that the dogs would not hinder them by slitting their throats—"

"Objection, my lord! Staunton interjected. "There is no evidence whatever to show that Shane Hogan killed the guard dogs."

"I apologize, my lord. I withdraw Hogan's name." Caulfeild looked at Justice Rose, who nodded permission to continue.

"These men entered the servants' quarters and slit the throats of the three men and one woman present."

"Murderers!" cried several voices from the crowd while the mothers of the slain servants moaned in grief.

John would have been fascinated by the cut-and-thrust between the two barristers had the situation not involved his own family and servants known to him. He glanced at the jury to gauge their reaction but they remained impassive.

After restoration of order, Caulfeild continued, "The conspirators then entered the main dwelling and murdered the butler and the housekeeper. Marcus Lynch, a visitor from Galway for the races at Tuam, was killed next. Finally, Oliver and Margery Bodkin had their throats slit in their bedroom, and—most horrifying of all—their small son, Oliver, was decapitated with an axe."

Pandemonium broke loose in the court. Tears welled in John's eyes at the memory of the savage murder of his lovable cousin. He saw similar grief all around him: on the faces of his mother, the widow of Marcus Lynch, the parents of Margery Bodkin and the parents of the slain servants.

The Solicitor General walked slowly towards the witness stand and looked Blind Dominick straight in his remaining eye. "Dominick Bodkin, all the evidence suggests that you were a participant in this massacre. What do you say to this?"

Silence descended on the courtroom as the fearsome man stood erect. "No, I was not."

"Thank you, Mr Bodkin."

Just before Dominick moved to resume his seat in the dock, a rotten egg hit him on his pockmarked cheek. It burst on impact and soiled his fine clothes, but he retained his composure as the warder tried to clean him up.

"The accused must be treated with respect. I shall not countenance mob rule in this court. We shall adjourn and resume in twenty minutes." Justice Rose departed.

* * * * *

THE BACKGROUND INFORMATION DRAWN from Blind Dominick had fascinated John. He now had a better understanding of the motivation of the man; yet he felt there was more to the story than had been unveiled.

"How will Shawn Bodkin testify?" Catherine asked.

John shook his head. "At this point, I know not."

An eerie silence descended upon the courtroom: Caulfeild's description of the massacre had rekindled memories of the gruesome crime. Even the journalists looked askance as they recalled the decapitation of little Oliver and the murder of a pregnant woman.

When Justice Rose returned to the bench, he announced, "Ladies and gentlemen, please show forbearance for the appearance of the last accused, Mr Shawn Bodkin."

Caulfeild fixed his eyes on the accused. "Shawn Bodkin, you are charged with conspiracy to murder and with the murder of ten people on the night of 19th September 1741. How do you plead?"

The colour drained from the young man's cheeks before he said, in a barely audible voice, "Not guilty."

Angry catcalls and the wail of weeping women assailed John's ears.

Caulfield resumed, "Dominick Bodkin has said in evidence that you were closely attached to your late mother, Marie, a cousin of the slain Marcus Lynch."

Mrs Lynch cried out at the mention of her late husband.

"Marie Lynch was the first wife of your father, Oliver Bodkin," Caulfeild said. "She passed away when you were only seven, ironically the age at which your half-brother, little Oliver, was murdered."

Shawn grimaced as Caulfield said, "How well did you know, Marcus Lynch?" Caulfield asked.

"He was a frequent visitor while my mother lived."

"Did you like him?"

Shawn answered in the affirmative. Caulfield continued, "Were you previously aware that Marcus Lynch was visiting Liscarrow on the night of 19th September 1741?"

"No."

Caulfeild changed tack. "How did you get on with your new mother, Margery Bodkin, otherwise Blake?"

"Not very well," Shawn replied.

"Why?"

"My Uncle Dominick has already explained this."

"Did you hate your mother, Margery Bodkin?" Caulfeild approached the dock.

"Objection, my lord—Margery Bodkin was his stepmother," Staunton said.

"Sustained," Justice Rose responded.

"Did you hate your stepmother, Mr Bodkin?"

"No."

"Did you try to poison her?" Caulfeild paced the floorboards.

"No, I did not!" Beads of perspiration broke out on Shawn's forehead.

"Did you write a letter to your late father requesting the reinstatement of your inheritance?" Caulfeild asked.

"I did."

"To what result?"

"My late father refused my request."

"Lord Athenry has testified to the Grand Jury that you threatened your father should he refuse. Although your letter cannot be produced in court, Counsellor Bodkin has corroborated this description of the contents of your letter to me."

"I just said I would take further action." Shawn wiped his sweaty forehead.

"And that's what you did on the night of the 19th of September," Caulfeild raised his voice, "when you and others brutally murdered your father, stepmother, half-brother, Marcus Lynch and six servants."

"I did not!" Shawn's denial was drowned out by the shouting and wailing that followed.

"Why did you go to Liscarrow on the morning after the massacre?"

"Julia Kelly told me that Mr Joyce had summoned my cousin John there as a matter of urgency."

"Why were your clothes bloodstained when Lord Athenry arrested you at Liscarrow?"

"From slaughtering animals on the previous day."

"You had no opportunity to change your clothes after your work on the farm?" Caulfeild glanced at the gentlemen of the jury. "I have no further questions, my lord."

"Thank you, Mr Caulfeild," Justice Rose said.

"We shall now recess for ten minutes. Then, we shall hear the recommendations of the prosecution and defence."

"Hang them now!" someone shouted.

The labyrinthine procedures of the court were frustrating to the crowd, to whom the culpability of the accused seemed so obvious as scarcely to need a trial.

The judge called again for order. "It is vital that the verdict of this court is seen to follow due process and therefore cannot be overturned by an appeal to the Chief Secretary. Following the closing remarks, the jury will deliberate on the proceedings of this court. I shall then announce their verdict and my findings arising therefrom."

* * * * *

CATHERINE WAS RELIEVED THAT neither Dominick nor Shawn Bodkin had referred to the circumstances of Patrick's death. If only she were a Catholic, a priest could hear what she knew in the privacy of the confessional. Her thoughts were interrupted by Aunt Bridget's voice.

"That was extraordinary!" Lady Browne exclaimed, looking at John, "to think that you were resident in the same house as the conspirators on the night of the massacre."

Mary Bodkin's brow wrinkled as she looked anxiously at her son.

"I knew something was wrong when Hogan and Kelly came to visit that night," John said. "They refused to talk in my presence, so I went to bed early. I could hear loud voices, and then footsteps as a door banged. That must have been Roger Kelly's dispatch to another room. I heard the clanging of bottles, as if they were drinking—then more footsteps and then silence …"

"Were Shawn's clothes stained on the night before?" Lady Browne asked.

"Not that I was aware off," John replied.

"You should have said that on the stand, young man." Lady Browne frowned.

"He would have, if he had been asked, Aunt Bridget," Catherine said.

"Hmm, of course," Lady Browne said.

Catherine smiled reassuringly at John. Her volatile aunt was occasionally big enough to withdraw an unfair accusation but never to apologize. How strange it was that Caulfeild had failed to ask him that question.

"I'm worried about the mood of the mob," Mary Bodkin whispered.

"So is Papa," Catherine said. "That is why the yeoman soldiers are on high alert."

"Well said, my dear," Lady Browne responded. "Lord Athenry will assure our safe journey home once this unpleasant business is over."

Catherine wondered if she should confide in Aunt Bridget. She knew little about her apart from her interest in art and that she was a childless widow. As an older sister, she was inclined to act imperially towards Lord Athenry—much to Catherine's amusement and to the amusement of those who lived and worked in Bermingham House. She could not talk to her father because the knowledge would shatter him. First, Catherine decided, she would talk to John before making a move.

CHAPTER 13

WAITING FOR THE COURT to resume, John tried to summarize the respective cases for the prosecution and the defence in his mind. The only documentary evidence that had existed against Shawn was the threatening letter he had sent to his father, and even that had gone astray. It had defied Catherine's best efforts to find it; its contents existed only as remembered testimony. Apart from that, the letter could easily be interpreted as implying legal action rather than violence. As such, Staunton should be able to launch a strong defence on behalf of the three accused. Whether it succeeded might depend on the emotional impact of the crime and the thirst for revenge among the bereaved.

As Justice Rose returned, the clerk of the court cried again, "All rise."

Having resumed his seat, the judge said, "Gentlemen of the jury, you have heard the case for the prosecution against each of the accused, Shawn Bodkin, Dominick Bodkin and Shane Hogan. I now call on the Solicitor General, The Honourable St George Caulfeild, to present his closing statement."

Caulfeild rose imperiously while adjusting his wig. "Gentlemen of the jury, we have before us three defendants accused of executing the worst massacre in the history of this county. Each of the accused has pleaded innocent to the charges and yet the evidence of their complicity is overwhelming. We know from the testimony of John Bodkin that the defendants secretly conspired. We know from Roger Kelly that the conspiracy was directed against Oliver Bodkin, his wife Margery and their son and heir, little Oliver. It appears that when the conspirators were unable to intimidate the Bodkins covertly, they decided to murder everyone in the house. This was an insane attempt to escape indictment by eliminating witnesses."

Caulfeild paused and looked around the silent courtroom. He walked slowly towards the jury and fixed his eyes upon them. "We know that Shane Hogan was the most likely person at Liscarrow to have silenced the guard dogs by slitting their throats. We know that Hogan, along with Dominick Bodkin, absconded the following morning thus implicitly acknowledging their guilt. Their unlikely story of inspecting sheep in Roscommon carries no weight. We know that Shawn Bodkin visited the scene of the crime in bloodstained clothes on the following morning. His apparent paroxysm of grief fooled neither Lord Athenry nor the Grand Jury, who indicted him and his two co-conspirators. Each of the defendants had motivation and opportunity to commit these premeditated murders. I could go on, but the case against the defendants is so overwhelming that to do so would be unnecessary. My recommendation to the jury is clear—Shawn Bodkin, Dominick Bodkin and Shane Hogan are jointly and severally guilty of the murder of the ten residents of Liscarrow on the night of the 19th September 1741. Gentlemen of the jury, you must return a verdict of *Guilty* to all the charges. I rest my case, my lord."

"Thank you, Mr Caulfeild," Justice Rose said. "I call on Mr Staunton to conclude for the defence."

"Thank you, my lord," Staunton said. "I share the feelings of horror felt by all law-abiding citizens at the massacre that occurred at Liscarrow on the night of the 19th of September. However, the Solicitor General has sought to persuade you that the accused have perpetrated these heinous crimes with evidence that is wholly circumstantial in nature. The fact of the matter is that nobody has come forward who has witnessed any one of the ten murders. Nobody has come forward who can testify that any one of the accused has admitted culpability for the planning or execution of these crimes. Thus, Mr Caulfeild has failed to prove beyond a reasonable doubt the guilt of any one or all of the three accused."

Staunton walked slowly towards the jury. "Gentlemen of the jury, in the absence of credible evidence of guilt you have no option other than to return a verdict of *Not guilty*. Thank you, my lord."

"Nonsense!" cried a voice from the crowd accompanied by loud whispering.

"Order in court, please," Justice Rose banged his gavel and waited for the rumpus to dissipate. "I thank the Solicitor General and Mr Staunton who have presented their briefs with their customary competence."

Justice Rose paused. "Gentlemen of the jury, it is now your duty to adjudicate on the innocence or guilt of each of the accused. You must consider if any one or all of them is guilty of conspiring to murder the occupants of Liscarrow on the night of 19th September 1741. Secondly, you must consider if any or all of them is guilty of murdering one or more of the victims in that house on that night, namely, Oliver Bodkin, Margery Bodkin, Oliver Bodkin Jr, Marcus Lynch, John Burke, Mrs Mary Burke, James Fallon, Bridget MacHugh, Thaddeus MacHugh and Michael O'Brien. You must be satisfied beyond a reasonable doubt that one or more of the accused is guilty of one or both of the charges laid against them."

As the jury prepared to deliberate on the evidence, Justice Rose said, "This court is now in recess until a verdict is reached."

"All rise," the clerk of the court said, standing up. "The town crier will announce the time of resumption of the court when a verdict has been agreed."

* * * * *

"AUNT BRIDGET, I'M IN need of air, if I am not to faint," Catherine said, in the hope of talking to John alone for even a few moments.

"Very understandable, my dear—the heat and odours in the court are overpowering." Lady Browne vigorously waved her fan.

John said, "I shall look to her."

"And so shall I," Lady Browne retorted.

Catherine walked briskly towards the exit, escorted by John. Glancing over her shoulder, she saw Aunt Bridget trying to extricate her hooped dress that had caught between the front bench and the protruding end of Colonel Blake's scabbard.

"Let us perambulate until Aunt Bridget disentangles herself." Catherine suggested.

"As you wish—is aught troubling you, my love?"

"Firstly, tell me …" Catherine lifted her petticoat over a foot-scraper on the flagstones, "… how you think the jury will answer."

"They will find them all guilty—I'm sure of it," John said.

"And then?"

"Justice Rose will sentence them to hang."

"When?" Catherine looked towards the dipping sun.

"Tomorrow, I would imagine." John raised his eyebrows. "Not enough time for the hangings this evening."

"Nor enough time for us to get married," Catherine said ironically. "Were it not for the massacre, we would have married today." She feared that her father's reservations about John's suitability as a husband might yet prove an obstacle to their marriage. Her father had used Patrick's death to delay the wedding to allow time for mourning. A similar delay would now result from the Bodkin massacre. John's mature performance as his father's deputy following the Counsellor's collapse at the Bodkin burials was the only bright spot in their present landscape.

"I am at the end of my patience," John responded. "As soon as one delay is overcome, another emerges to dash our hopes."

Lady Browne rushed towards them. "There you are," she puffed, pink in the face from exertion.

"We took a short stroll, enjoying the fresh air and waiting for you to join us," Catherine said.

"I have never seen such a crush here." Lady Browne sighed.

Catherine could sense a rise in tension now that judgement was imminent. She listened to those who came out of the courthouse regaling their friends with details of the testimony of the three accused. Animated discussion ensued, with tempers rising and calls for revenge if any delay occurred in executing the accused.

Fearing that such anger could result in violence, Catherine said, "Shall we walk to St Mary's and enjoy a little solitude?"

"We could say a prayer at the Bodkin grave." John suggested.

"What a lovely idea." Lady Browne added.

They walked up High Street in silence towards the cathedral. Silence prevailed in the churchyard, broken only by the crunching of gravel under their boots. Catherine recognized the grave that bore for the moment a simple wooden cross, inscribed with the word *Bodkin*.

John knelt down on the grass beside the freshly filled grave and prayed. "May the Lord have mercy on the souls of Oliver Bodkin, Margery and little Oliver."

Catherine and Lady Browne held their hands together and bowed.

After an interlude of silence disturbed only by another group of mourners passing by, John said, "Papa has ordered a Celtic cross to commemorate our lost family."

"Very suitable," Lady Browne said.

As they lingered in the spiritual atmosphere, Catherine whispered, "Aunt Bridget …"

Lady Browne peered from under her green taffeta hat. "What is it now, young lady?"

"When all this is over, John and I would like to arrange a new date for our wedding."

"I shall speak to your father," Lady Browne replied. "Sometime in the New Year would answer, I imagine. The Bodkins will need time to mourn. In the meantime, you can work on your art."

Catherine rushed towards her aunt, almost knocking her over as she hugged her.

"Do restrain yourself, my dear." Lady Browne then paused. "What is that noise I hear?"

Cocking his ear to the wind, John said, "I believe it is the Town Crier."

"I can faintly hear him," Catherine added.

"For goodness' sake, what is he saying?" Lady Browne asked anxiously.

"Court is about to resume," Catherine replied. "Here ye, hear ye—court is about to resume."

They hurried back to take their seats in the courtroom, coinciding with the entry of Justice Rose.

* * * * *

WHEN THE CLERK OF THE court had subdued the chattering crowd, silence descended on the courtroom. "Gentlemen of the jury have you reached a verdict?" asked the judge.

"Yes, my lord," replied the foreman.

"Please announce the verdict."

Clearing his throat, the middle-aged man spoke solemnly. "On the count of conspiracy to murder, we find Shawn Bodkin guilty, Dominick Bodkin guilty, and Shane Hogan guilty."

The foreman glanced at Justice Rose, who nodded for him to continue. "On the count of murder, we find Shawn Bodkin guilty, Dominick Bodkin guilty, and Shane Hogan not guilty."

The foreman paused as a gasp of astonishment greeted Hogan's acquittal on the charge of murder. "In the case of Shane Hogan, we humbly request that clemency be considered as the court may deem appropriate."

John was relieved that Shawn and Dominick Bodkin would now swing from the gibbet. The work he had done with his father and Roger Kelly to secure a guilty verdict against the disgraced members of his family should have impressed Lord Athenry. The partial acquittal of Hogan allied with a plea for clemency would ease the pain on the Hogan family: but would it save Hogan from the ultimate sanction? Looking around the courtroom, he saw a glimmer of hope in Mrs Hogan's tearful eyes.

Justice Rose inquired of the jury. "Are you of one mind in your verdicts and your request for clemency in the case of Mr Hogan?"

"The verdicts and our request for clemency were unanimous, my lord."

"Thank you, gentlemen of the jury. The court is grateful for your service and for the service of all those who have helped this court to perform its grave duty." Justice Rose raised his hands to steeple his fingers. "It is now my solemn duty to pass judgement. May the good Lord guide me in this onerous task."

Disturbed only by a few bouts of coughing, Rose continued, "The murders committed on the night of 19th September 1741 at Liscarrow constitute one of the most horrific events in living memory; ten innocent people done to death, including a pregnant woman and a young boy. It is necessary to act with firmness and severity in order to prevent further crimes of such a gruesome nature."

John was very conscious of the black cap sitting on the bench beside Justice Rose.

"The jury has pleaded for clemency in the case of Shane Hogan, presumably because of a *reluctance to act*. However, as this contemptible conspiracy could not have succeeded without his involvement, however reluctant, I cannot therefore afford him such clemency."

Hogan paled in the dock. Mrs Hogan sobbed quietly at the back of the courtroom. Roger Kelly made a quick exit as Lord Athenry signalled to his sentinel. John suspected that the signal was an order to arrest Kelly.

Justice Rose slowly donned his black cap. At sight of it, an eerie silence descended on the courtroom. "I hereby sentence Shawn Bodkin, Dominick Bodkin and Shane Hogan to be hanged tomorrow morning at Liscarrow." Looking at the accused in the dock, he said, "May the Lord have mercy on your souls".

"All rise," cried the clerk of the court. "This court is now in recess." Justice Rose tapped his gavel and departed.

As the courtroom emptied, the Blakes and Mrs Lynch joined the Bodkins and the Berminghams. "Thank the Lord this trial is over," John said. "We may now attempt to move on."

"I need to see them hang first." Colonel Blake rattled his sword.

"I, too," Mrs Lynch cried, "although I have always avoided hangings in the past."

"We shall meet then tomorrow at Liscarrow." John concluded.

CHAPTER 14

AFTER THE ANNOUNCEMENT OF the verdicts, John lingered in the courtroom with his mother while they waited for people to disperse. He found it hard to believe that his cousin and uncle would hang tomorrow. Quietly he whispered to Catherine, "I feel I should visit Shawn and Uncle Dominick in case they have any last requests."

"How can you face those horrible men?" Catherine knitted her brow.

"It is my family duty."

"I hope you do not find the experience too gruelling." Catherine hid her eyes behind her open fan. "I shall have a quiet evening at home, unless Aunt Bridget sees fit to stir the pot with father tonight."

John said cautiously, "After quitting the Bridewell, I should pay a call upon Patrick's widow, Anna. She is visiting in Tuam with little Thomas."

"Poor child. Thank goodness he is too young to understand the horror."

Lady Browne approached the couple, saying, "Catherine, my dear, we should go now."

John escorted the ladies to the Bermingham coach and waved them away. He made his way towards the Bridewell; as he approached, he saw Mrs Hogan departing. He wondered how much she had known of the heinous conspiracy. It was unlikely that Hogan would have burdened his wife with such an appalling course of action.

"Please forgive him, Mr Bodkin," she said, tears streaming down her cheeks. "He would speak with you, if you will."

John hesitated but reluctantly agreed.

"He's with Friar Skerrett now," she said. "Shane has been put in chains."

John entered the Bridewell, the characteristic odour now familiar to his nose, and told the warder, "I would like to visit the three condemned men."

The warder escorted John to the office of the keeper, who shook his head sadly. "A bad business, Mr Bodkin. We shall escort you to the prisoners one at a time."

Entering Hogan's cell, John gazed at the broken man. "I met your wife on my way in."

Hogan wept. "I failed her, and I failed your family. How could I have become involved in such a business?"

"Why did you wish to see me?"

"Please help my wife and children, Mr Bodkin. They are innocent victims of my sins." Hogan wiped his tears with the tattered sleeve of his coat. "Mayhap they could stay on in our cabin, at least for a while?"

"That depends: did Mrs Hogan know about the conspiracy?" John furled his brow.

"I never told her a...aught," Hogan stammered.

"Very well. I will try to smooth her passage because of your children, whether they remain at Liscarrow or go elsewhere."

"Thank you. You're a decent man. Please forgive me for my sins."

"Tomorrow you shall meet your Maker. May the Lord have mercy on your soul!"

John left with mixed emotion. How could he feel sorry for a man who had conspired to murder his uncle, his pregnant aunt and his little cousin? His real sympathy lay with the innocent children of the Hogans who would have to bear the shame of their father's disgrace.

Next he entered Shawn's cell, wary of this last confrontation with his troublesome cousin.

"Staunton was useless," Shawn hissed angrily.

"He did the best anyone could in the circumstances."

"It was set up to afford me no chance. Once you and Kelly opened your big gobs, it was a foregone conclusion."

John remained silent, knowing nothing he said could improve Shawn's outlook.

"What are you doing here, anyway?"

"Have you any last requests?"

"Give me your pistol. Help me escape from this hellhole."

John opened his coat jacket and raised it above his waistband, turning full circle, to show that he carried no weapon.

"I'm glad I killed my stepmother." Shawn grimaced. "She was an evil bitch who manipulated my father against me. Because he was so spineless, I'm glad I killed him too."

"You had no justification for killing your father," John cried. "He gave you every opportunity to make progress in your life."

"I had no interest in the law. He tried to force me to follow in the Counsellor's footsteps."

"He was merely trying to assist you towards a career."

Shawn said with an evil gleam in his eye, "You always have an answer, cousin John—but what of your own secret?"

John tried not to betray himself. "What is it you speak of?"

"You shall find out soon enough ... unless ... you get me out of here." Shawn smirked. "Now get out and leave me in peace!" he shouted.

The warder unlocked the cell door and John emerged, still unsure as to how much Shawn knew about the death of Patrick. Even if he knew all, what could he do with his knowledge on the brink of the scaffold? His confused thoughts added to his trepidation on visiting Blind Dominick again.

A sense of tedious familiarity came over him when his uncle barked, "What are you doing here?"

"You are my uncle, after all ..."

"Why are you here?" Dominick persisted.

"To say goodbye and to deal with any requests you might have."

"After they hang me, you can cut me up and throw me to the dogs." Dominick stretched out his hands and lurched forward.

John held his ground, knowing that Dominick would not strangle him. He was silent long enough to allow his uncle to compose himself.

"I have no wife, no children, no property—nothing, except my regrets."

"I hope you may meet your Maker with a mind at peace."

"And if there is no Maker? What then?" Dominick raised his hands.

John remained silent.

"I have a little money hidden away," he said. "You will find it beneath the floorboards under my bed in Carrowbeg. I shall not bequeath it to Counsellor John because he did not find me a good lawyer." He leaned back against the wall as his mood mellowed. "You shall not inherit it either, unless you can get me out of this hellhole."

John shook his head; Dominick must surely realize that rescue was impossible, even if John had wished to help him. What did his uncle mean by his veiled threats? Peace of mind would not be attainable again until the hangings were over.

Dominick drew a deep breath. "I shall bequeath it to my grand-nephew, little Thomas, although he will have little need of it once he inherits the estates—which will be soon enough. Perhaps you could arrange that for me."

"I shall draft a note for you to sign. The keeper and the warder will witness your signature."

John departed, fearful of the morrow. Dominick's threat was now clear: his own life was in danger. Otherwise, why say that Thomas would inherit the estates *soon enough*?

* * * * *

WHEN CATHERINE ARRIVED AT Bermingham House, one thought was uppermost in her mind: this should have been her wedding day. If the massacre had not taken place, she would now be in her boudoir preparing for a night of intimacy with John. Of course, it was a small matter compared to the loss of lives, and she knew she should put it from her mind; but how could she forget her wedding when her gown hung yet unworn in her wardrobe? It felt almost as if she had been jilted at the altar.

That evening at dinner, Catherine said, "Papa, I feel so ashamed; my mind keeps returning to my postponed wedding. Instead, I should mourn the poor people whose murders were the cause of its postponement."

"That is only natural, my dear; but life goes on," Athenry said. "When the hangings are over, we may begin to recover from this dreadful act of violence."

"What shall I do with my wedding cake?" Catherine had gazed many times at the fabulous creation in the pantry. "Will it keep until John and I marry?"

Athenry frowned but made no comment.

"Have you any thoughts on the matter?" Lady Browne asked. "It is possible to preserve the cake."

"In what manner?" Catherine wondered.

"By removing the icing," Lady Browne said, "inserting a knitting needle into the case and pouring brandy or another spirit into the holes."

"I have another idea." Catherine found it difficult to concentrate on the main dish of venison awaiting her attention. "I would like to auction it off and donate the proceeds to the relatives of the deceased servants." She spoke with trepidation, fearing that her suggestion would meet with scorn.

Following an interval of silence, Lady Browne said, "What think you, Francis?"

Athenry cleared his throat and spoke, "That cake was a costly one, my dear."

"I know it, Papa," Catherine acknowledged. An image of the *chinoiserie* cake flashed through her mind. Her friends had come from near and far to admire it. Based on Chinese motifs, the sage-coloured tiers were complemented by stencilled white blossoms. The elegant tier separator featured edible pink peonies and two blue and white birds.

"I would not expect another of its kind when our marriage takes place."

"As to that," Athenry snorted, "are you certain you still wish to marry John Bodkin, my dear?"

"Papa! Of course! How can you ask such a question?"

Catherine knew her father well enough to let his comment lie. She attacked her venison, feeling easier in her mind. Her expensive wedding gown was the next subject that required discussion.

"It would be better to have some more items for the auction," Catherine said tentatively.

"Have you considered your portraits?" Lady Browne suggested.

"Goodness me, no, Aunt Bridget. They're not good enough."

"They are just as good as those of Miss Sirani," Lady Browne said with a sparkle in her eye. "Apart from that, you could have my wedding gown; I only wore it the once."

"Bless you, Aunt Bridget!" Catherine said. "Papa?" She wrinkled her brow inquiringly.

Athenry smiled. "You may have my late father's blunderbuss." He placed his napkin on the table. "You will find it hanging in my display case."

"Would you like to act as auctioneer?" Catherine glanced at her father.

"Good heavens, no!" Athenry said.

"What about John?" Lady Browne suggested.

"That would be suitable; he is well able to speak in public," Athenry said.

Catherine was pleased with the response. She nerved herself to ask if she might also donate her own wedding gown; fidgeting with her napkin, she felt a fluttering of sensations in her chest.

"Speak up, young lady. What ails you?" Lady Browne tapped the table with her fingers.

"I would also like to donate my wedding gown." There, she had said it. Her friends had greatly admired the elegant creation, and so had she; but for whatever reason, she felt that she should wear the gown, only on this very day, the day of her planned wedding. Superstition, perhaps, but the feeling was very strong.

Tears in her eyes, Catherine excused herself and hurried to her bedroom. She called for her maid, and asked her to help her don her wedding gown. If she could not wear it again, she must try it on now. She stood in front of her mirror as the full-length gown was draped over her shoulders. Her maid laced her bodice at the back until it perfectly fitted her bosom while exposing a discreet décolletage. The feel of the gorgeous pink taffeta on her arms was so sensuous. When the dress was on, she held out her arms to enjoy the elegance of the pearl-laced, double-sleeved flounces in silk and ivory lace. She walked about the room to get the feel of the pannier-style drapes of her skirt that swished around her legs.

After admiring herself in the mirror one more time, she sat down by the window overlooking the entrance avenue. It was almost as if she were waiting for John to arrive and whisk her away. A strange feeling came over her, as she sat there, watching the rosy redness of the horizon fade to a dull pink. *How she could ever feel as ready to marry as she now felt?* Closing her eyes, she thought about John and their uncertain future.

* * * * *

AFTER VISITING THE CONDEMNED, John retired to The Thomas Bagworth Inn for a brandy. He was prey to conflicting emotions and craved temporary solitude. If the massacre had not occurred, he would now be a married man, preparing for a night of intimacy with his beloved Catherine. Then he would have whisked her away to Paris for a glorious honeymoon, far away from the mundane reality of family life. After gulping down one brandy, he was tempted to call it a night and dream about the wedding that had not taken place, but duty called.

He felt obliged to visit Anna, the widow of his late brother, Patrick. After Patrick's demise, she had returned to her parents' home in Galway with baby Thomas. Recently, however—because of her desire to attend the trial—Anna had temporarily moved into the Skerrett townhouse in Tuam. As John approached the terraced two-storey house in Vicar Street, a well-dressed young man was leaving the premises. The man nodded politely as the housekeeper escorted John into the drawing room. Anna's father dozed by the fire.

Anna embraced her brother-in-law. "How are you bearing up, John?" she asked.

"I'm coping. We all are, but it is my father who has been hit the hardest."

"I was distraught when I heard about the massacre," Anna said. "It reminded me of poor Patrick's death; sudden and unexpected. I miss him so much." She sat down by the fire of wood. "Little Thomas is too young now to understand, but I shall tell him about his father before he begins his studies."

John smiled as the faint cry of a child filled the air through the open door.

"That is he now: please excuse me while I have a word with the nursemaid."

John warmed his hands by the fire. He still felt uneasy about Patrick's death, and was tempted at that moment to open his heart to Anna but wisely refrained. He should have spoken to someone years ago to shed some of the burden, but had kept deferring the move in the hope that his discomfort would fade, which it never had. Catherine advised him to talk to Dean Bruce or another worthy man of the cloth, but that option had remained unexplored.

As he waited for Anna to reappear, John wondered if his sister-in-law was seeing the well-dressed young man. He rose on hearing steps on the staircase and a cooing sound.

"Now, Thomas, this handsome young man is your Uncle John."

John was happy to hold his only nephew, now three, who responded with a sneeze. He smiled and reminded Thomas that:

The Bodkins sneeze like the grim Chinese.
They come from the Phoenicians.

Both John and Anna laughed at the silliness.

"Thomas seems like a fine lad. It is so good to see him. He is now the only Bodkin member of a younger generation until I start a family myself."

"How is Catherine?" Anna asked.

John wondered why Anna's cheeks had slightly reddened. "Very well. She's at home in Bermingham House."

"Such a pity you had to cancel the wedding, but of course you had no choice. Have you set a new date?"

"Sometime early next year, I trust."

"You're taking your time." Anna raised her eyebrows.

"We must allow a period for mourning," John replied with as much diplomacy as he could muster. Her comment reminded him of the way that Patrick used to rile him about his lack of ambition.

"I hear that the Berminghams are a fertile family. Little Thomas will soon be joined by many more Bodkins, I suspect!"

"As things stand, Thomas is now the heir apparent to Liscarrow."

"My, oh my!" Anna said as Thomas began to yawn. "He must be exhausted at the prospect." She hoisted the young boy on to her shoulder and disappeared upstairs with him.

Anna's perky mood put John in mind of the handsome young man who had left the house as he entered. When she returned, he said, "I must apologize for disturbing your visitor."

"Not at all. He's a friend of the Skerrett family. He visits occasionally when my father is here. It is pleasant to have company."

"I should not delay my return any longer. Once things have settled down, I would like to see you and Thomas again."

"Thank you, John. I would welcome that."

CHAPTER 15

SILENCE PREVAILED AT BREAKFAST on the morning of Thursday, 8th October 1741, the day John and Catherine should have left on their honeymoon. Instead of enjoying the excitement of Paris with Catherine, he would travel to the hanging tree at Liscarrow with his heartbroken father.

"I have attended hangings before but never one of my own relatives," John said. The porridge he had taken from the chafing dishes repelled him, and he left most of it.

"I cannot bear to think on it," Mary replied.

Counsellor Bodkin blew his nose. "This is an ill day for all of us."

"You must wrap up well." Mary Bodkin advised. "It is raining heavily and looks to continue so."

John was concerned about his father since his collapse at the funeral of his slain family. His doctors had advised rest and a cessation of his legal work until his health improved. Despite the inclement weather and the advice of his wife, Counsellor Bodkin insisted on attending the hangings. John was glad of his company: it demonstrated the unity of the surviving Bodkins in the face of adversity.

Soon they were on the one-mile journey from Carrowbeg to Liscarrow, close to the village of Belclare. In spite of the bad weather, the road was jammed with people heading for the site of execution.

Raising his voice, Counsellor Bodkin said, "A triple hanging is a rare occurrence, and not one to be missed by the people."

"Especially when such a heinous crime has been committed," John replied, clenching his fists. "Justice must be seen to be done."

As the carriage came to the end of the narrow road, known as a boreen, the density of the traffic blocked their entrance to the main road. "I shall walk on to determine the situation," John said.

Covering the remaining quarter of a mile on foot, he found Lord Athenry directing the local yeomen. The soldiers were attempting to accommodate the huge crowd gathering alongside the hanging tree that flanked the fields of Liscarrow. The gold-and-black painted woodwork of the Bodkin carriage contrasted sharply with the mud-spattered donkeys and carts of the common people.

"Where is your carriage?" Athenry asked, parading on his black mare.

"About a quarter of a mile back: our groom is waiting for the road to clear," John replied. Rain dripped from his tricorn hat on to his nose and shoulders. Adjusting his hat only made matters worse.

"Go back: stay in your carriage," Athenry said. "My men shall find you a favourable position in sufficient time."

Meanwhile, a flurry of activity in the crowd alerted John to the arrival of the condemned from the Bridewell in Tuam. Each man sat in separate horse-drawn carts. The crowd jeered and shouted *murderers*. Unprotected from the rain, the prisoners were soaked to the skin after the four-mile journey to the gallows. The continuing arrival of people, mostly on foot, delayed their passage. The muscles in John's belly tightened. He would not have minded if the prisoners were torn limb from limb to atone for their grievous crimes.

Eventually the Bodkin carriage reached the gallows.

Athenry peered in. "The business shall soon be under way, Counsellor."

"John insisted we bring the carriage, but it has been difficult to get through the crowds."

"You deserve a little comfort after the horrendous ordeal you have been through."

John noticed a bedraggled Mrs Hogan struggling through the crowd and approached her.

"God bless you, Mr Bodkin," she said. "'Tis a terrible morning, surely; and a terrible day for us all."

"I am sorry for your distress," John said.

"Shane gave me one of your handkerchiefs. He asked me to wash it and return it to you." She rummaged in her leather bag and produced an ironed handkerchief with the initials *J B* clearly visible.

John accepted the embroidered fabric with a lump in his throat, conscious of the eyes of the people on them. "Thank you, Mrs Hogan." He turned away and rejoined his father.

After a period of silence, John gazed through the window of the carriage. "The hangman has attached three nooses to the oak tree. The army has lit a fire of wood nearby."

"They will have impregnated the wood with lamp-oil to make it more flammable in this rain," Counsellor Bodkin said.

A loud roar erupted from the crowd as the prisoners approached the hanging tree. Some people tried to break through the cordon that extended to a narrow path along which the condemned men approached. The yeoman soldiers tried to secure order, but could not prevent the hurling of mud-balls, stones and clumps of grass at the murderers. John would have liked to fling such missiles himself, his anger fed by the bloodlust of the crowd. What a contrast it made to the Roman emperors who threw sweets and perfumes at their condemned prisoners.

Finally, the shackled felons arrived at the gallows accompanied by Lord Athenry, a friar and a vicar. The presence of Friar Skerrett and the sight of Mrs Hogan whispering a rosary on well-worn beads reminded John of the Catholic past of the Bodkins.

Shane Hogan was the first to have the noose tied around his neck as he and his co-conspirators were unshackled. Friar Skerrett approached the shepherd. He raised his voice as the crowd fell silent. "Shane Hogan of Liscarrow, will you confirm your guilt as you prepare to depart from this mortal life?"

Hogan responded emotionally. "I am guilty," he cried. "Lord, forgive me. I have such sorrow for the relatives of the dead. I beg their forgiveness." He shuffled his feet and looked first towards his wife. "I beg the forgiveness of my dearest wife and children." He paused and then directed his eyes towards the Bodkin carriage. "I also promise to look after little Oliver in heaven should the good Lord admit me."

"Shame on you, you murderer," a voice roared from the crowd as Hogan broke down in inconsolable sobbing.

The graphic details of the murders flooded through John's mind as the hangman placed a black hood over Hogan's head.

"May the Lord have mercy on your soul!" Friar Skerrett blessed himself with the sign of the cross, an action repeated by many in the vast crowd.

In the silence, disturbed only by the pitter-patter of rain, the hangman drew the cart away, jerking the prisoner's neck and leaving Hogan hanging in mid-air. Mrs Hogan opened her eyes to witness the last dying kicks of her husband.

Please close your eyes, Mrs Hogan, John thought as worse was to follow. Athenry's men took Hogan down within minutes, and laid him on the cart, even though his feet still twitched. After restraining him with cord, they emasculated and disembowelled him. When the army threw his bowels into the fire, the people roared their approval. The army then quartered and decapitated him. Mrs Hogan collapsed in a heap at the sight of her husband's mutilated body. Her grief did nothing to temper John's anger at the shepherd who had brutally murdered his family.

"Hogan has received his just deserts," John said, pumping his foot on the carriage floor.

* * * * *

NOW IT WAS TIME for John to witness the execution of his own relatives. *How had these terrible events ever come to pass*, he wondered? Had Counsellor Bodkin neglected his extended family in Galway while expanding his legal practice in Dublin? John felt helpless and forlorn; his characteristic optimism could not withstand these events.

The hangman approached his Uncle Dominick; this image would stay with him always. Unable to tear his eyes away, he watched the hangman place the noose around Dominick's neck to the accompaniment of hurled missiles and loud insults. His condemned uncle was one of the most feared men in Galway and few, if any, had sympathy for him.

Suddenly, Shawn Bodkin broke away from his guard. He rushed at Blind Dominick and grabbed the condemned man by the neck, shouting, "You have destroyed my life!" The soldiers seized Shawn and pulled him away.

As the commotion settled down, Dean Bruce approached: "Dominick Bodkin of Carrowbeg, as you prepare to depart from this mortal life, will you confirm your guilt please?"

Dominick glared at the hostile crowd before responding, "I greatly regret the deaths of the people I murdered at Liscarrow. They were innocent victims of our family feud."

"You devil!" roared a voice from the crowd. "May you rot in hell!"

The hangman then dispatched Dominick Bodkin to eternity to the approving roar of the crowd.

"Dear God," cried John, overwhelmed by renewed grief for his murdered family. The power of prayer that he had hitherto ignored came home to him now as Mrs Hogan told her rosary beads.

The crowd began to chatter as the rain cleared, perhaps reminiscing about Blind Dominick, a legend within the Galway community. John's uncle had been a violent man, as those who crossed him soon found out. Now that he was gone, many blessed themselves in feigned sympathy; but those whose relatives he had murdered did not pretend to any emotion except satisfaction that their loved ones had been avenged.

Once Blind Dominick had been gibbeted, and exposed to public contempt, the hangman placed the noose around the neck of Shawn Bodkin. As Dean Bruce approached, Shawn spoke loudly, "I wish to make a statement before I depart this earthly world."

John paled. Shawn's last threat in the Bridewell came back to haunt him.

A Story of the Bodkin Murders

Shawn pulled a tattered page from his jacket and read from it. He raised his voice so that he could be heard from a distance despite the whinnying of horses:

> *Two years before the murder of my father, another*
> *murder was committed by my cousin, John Bodkin, of*
> *Carrowbeg,*

John flushed red. "Absolute nonsense!" he cried. "That is completely untrue, Father."

Counsellor Bodkin paled. Silence reigned. Every face was turned towards the speaker on the gallows. Shawn continued,

> *It was that crime which led me to commit the murder for*
> *which*
> *I am now about to die. John Bodkin murdered his elder*
> *brother, Patrick,*
> *in order to gain his inheritance.*

John rushed to the hanging tree and strongly denied the allegation, much to the astonishment of the multitude.

Shawn's strong voice boomed across the landscape,

> *On the night of that occurrence, John and I slept in the*
> *same room.*
> *In the middle of the night, he rose from his bed*
> *and entered Patrick's room, carrying with him a pillow.*

"Absolute rubbish," John shouted, moving away from the scene of execution. He listened to Shawn's concluding remarks,

> *It was John who reported Patrick's death on the following morning,*
> *having smothered him with his pillow.*
> *The failure to detect that murder inspired me to devise a plan*
> *to recover my inheritance in the hope*
> *that I also would evade detection.*

John heard gasps from the crowd. He cursed Shawn for having made that sensational statement. It would destroy his reputation; no one would believe in his innocence, although he had not murdered Patrick. Before he could be interrogated, he un-tethered a grey gelding and raised himself on to the saddle urging the horse forward. He rode up the hill away from the scene of execution. Once he came to a secluded clearing, he stopped at a vantage point from which he could still see the hangman through his pocket telescope.

* * * * *

THROUGH THE EYEPIECE, HE saw Athenry approach the Bodkin carriage on his black mare. His father slowly alighted. Counsellor Bodkin held his arms up and would have collapsed to the ground were it not for the quick-witted groom who caught him in time. *Thank God, he is alive and well,* John thought, as his father regained his feet. After a period of animated discussion, Athenry departed, gazing around the horizon as if searching for his prospective son-in-law.

John shifted his attention back to the gallows. Shawn was speaking to Dean Bruce. How ironic it was that both he and Catherine had considered discussing their dilemma with that man of the cloth. Had they done so, Shawn's sensational statement would not have surprised the priest. Damn Shawn! He was attempting to destroy another member of his family even as he died. Shawn's vindictiveness had plunged the Bodkins into yet another family scandal that could reach out to taint the Berminghams as well.

He watched the dying kicks of his cousin on the gallows. What a waste of a young life, driven by insecurity and jealousy that had apparently driven him to madness. Any hope that John entertained of disproving Shawn's statement disappeared when he saw the journalists from *Pue's Occurrences* and *The Gentlemen's Magazine* eagerly making notes as they conversed with the locals.

He could not bear to think of his poor father and mother who would be shocked to the core. How could he ever explain what had happened on that dreadful night two years ago which resulted in Patrick's death? His parents would not understand. Neither would Lord Athenry. He must reach Catherine before the story reached her or reached Lady Browne.

The rain had stopped. As John prepared to ride to Bermingham House, he saw a puff of smoke curling upwards from the direction of Liscarrow. The redness of a flame soon burst upon the grey sky. People began to walk northward toward the source. As they rounded the final bend of the boreen, Liscarrow House was seen to be afire. The agent and servants made frantic efforts to control the blaze, but their efforts were in vain. Athenry sent half of his soldiers to quell the inferno but it was too late. The fire was visible for miles around, attracting even more spectators. The dark clouds lifted and soon the sun shone with a rare autumnal intensity. It struck the watchers as a signal from heaven that recompense had been paid, and a stern reminder that murder would not be tolerated.

John remained transfixed as the memories of his boyhood returned. Would the nightmare ever end? He focused his telescope on the Blakes and Mrs Lynch, and on the relatives of the murdered servants muttering among themselves. They no doubt felt that justice had been done: the scene of the horrific crime had been destroyed, even purified, by fire. He wondered who had set the place alight—most likely the Whiteboys, with or without the involvement of Roger Kelly.

Refocusing on the gallows, he was sickened by the sight of the quartering of the gibbeted bodies of his uncle and cousin. He departed before the grisly process was complete. His father had said that the yeoman soldiers would mount their body parts on stakes on the road between Belclare and Tuam to dissuade others from murder. They would also spike the decapitated head of Shane Hogan on top of the Market House in Tuam, another deterrent to potential murderers.

Before Athenry could organize a search party to arrest him, John tugged at the reins of the grey gelding and rode the six miles to Bermingham House in great haste.

CHAPTER 16

CATHERINE BERMINGHAM WAS FURIOUS that her father had not allowed her to attend the hangings despite the involvement of her betrothed's family. Her aunt, Lady Browne, was no better, following her brother's lead like a sheep. After all, Catherine was twenty and well able to make her own decisions. Perhaps her father was anxious for her safety or her sensibility: if so, he was mistaken on both counts.

After her father had departed, she was tempted to order the saddling of her bay gelding and ride the six miles to Belclare, in spite of the pelting rain. If she stayed on the main road west through Tuam, and on to the gallows, she would be safe. The fascination of the local community with the hangings was such that highwaymen, thieves and beggars were sure to attend along with everyone else. Then, she thought, no! She could not guarantee her safety. It would need only one miscreant to undo her if she travelled alone.

She banished this foolishness from her mind and concentrated instead on her painting. Her pencilled sketches of the prisoners in the dock lay on the white wall of her studio, fastened with fish-glue. These she could paint: but how could she produce authentic portraits of the condemned during hanging unless she were present to sketch their execution? She wondered if Elisabetta Sirani had ever painted a portrait of a condemned man at the gallows in Bologna.

Later that day, she heard the clatter of hooves through the open window of her studio. Who could be visiting at this time, when the world and his wife were attending the hangings? She laid down her paintbrush and pulled aside the silk curtain.

Goodness, it is John! How unlike him to whip the poor horse: what is he doing here? And going round to the rear of the house, too!

Convention demanded that she remain in her studio until he announced himself. Fortunately, Lady Browne had gone to Tuam to shop and gossip. She waited, her painting suspended and her heart beating fast.

Why is he here? Does he wish to elope?

Her father's refusal to name a new date for their wedding had angered him. A knock on the door caused her heart to beat even more strongly.

"A message from Mr John Bodkin for you, Miss," the footman announced.

Catherine put down her palette and covered her unfinished portrait of Shawn Bodkin in the dock. "What is it?"

"He wishes to see you in the stables, Miss." The footman hesitated. "I can act as your escort since the groom is at the hangings."

Catherine was nonplussed. *Something must be wrong.*

Urging the footman to be discreet, she followed him through the long hallway and the servant quarters. The air was chilly outside.

"What's the matter, John?" The darkness in his eyes told her that he was in a state of shock. She appealed to the footman to allow them a few moments of privacy, and he complied.

John hugged and embraced her with an intensity that made her tremble. "Something terrible has happened."

They sat on a mound of straw as his gelding whinnied. John whispered, "Shawn read out a statement from the gallows," he whispered, and then looked cautiously over his shoulder.

"Do not fret, my dear," Catherine said. "The footman will be discreet, and most of the other men are at the gallows. The women are inside the house or in Tuam. Now tell me what Shawn has said."

"He said that I murdered Patrick; that I smothered him to gain his inheritance."

Catherine could feel the colour drain from her face. She fought the urge to faint, and succeeded. "What did you do then?"

"I shouted out that Shawn lied. I denied it more than once, but eyes began to focus accusingly on me. Then I panicked and ran away," John admitted. "I feared your father would order my arrest."

"Goodness me!" Catherine cried. "Who could believe such a thing of you?" She closed her eyes as that awful night came to life again in her mind.

"I must hide until I find a solution to this situation."

"But you are innocent." Catherine lowered her voice. "I shall tell Papa."

"No! I absolutely forbid it," John said with determination.

Catherine realized why John had run away: he had done it to protect her. His flight would lead her father to assume that John was guilty. Why else would he abscond?

"I need time to think," John said.

Catherine's mind worked feverishly on how to gain him some precious time.

"If you can find me some old clothes to wear, I can pass myself off as a casual labourer looking for work."

"The shepherd has some old clothes at the back of the stables. I shall hide your fine hat and jacket under the straw."

John moved out of Catherine's line of sight and donned the rough garments. "Thank you, my darling. I shall return as soon as possible."

"You will need food and money."

"I have ten sovereigns in my purse as well as some small change."

"Permit me to get you some salted meat and fish from the pantry," Catherine said.

"Thank you. Please ask your groom to return the grey gelding to Belclare and allow me to borrow a draught horse."

Catherine threw her arms around her fiancé and hugged him, tears streaming down her face. She was still trembling in shock.

"I love you with all my heart," John said. Then he was gone, looking for all the world like a farm labourer as he rode northwards on a working horse.

Catherine gazed after him in a state of confusion, her thoughts in turmoil. The sudden death of handsome Patrick from reportedly natural causes had been a topic of speculation in Tuam for many weeks. She had wanted to tell her father the truth of the matter, but John forbade it.

She hurried back to her bedroom after cleaning her muddy boots on the foot-scraper and changed her dress that had suffered from contact with John's sodden clothes. After presenting the footman and pantry-maid with a monetary incentive to discretion, she resumed her station in the studio; but no more work was done on her painting that day.

Shortly after the return of Lady Browne from Tuam, Lord Athenry arrived. Having left the library door ajar, Catherine could hear Aunt Bridget demanding a detailed rendition of the day's proceedings.

"I must change my clothes first," Athenry replied. "Where is Catherine?"

"In the studio, I believe," Lady Browne replied.

"I must speak to her."

Those booming words forced Catherine to think quickly. Her father would confirm what John had already told her. She wiped a speck of mud from her boots and prepared herself to feign surprise on hearing the news.

"Catherine, I have sad tidings."

"Tell me, Papa."

"Before he was hanged, the murderer Shawn Bodkin made a dreadful accusation from the gallows."

"What did he say?" cried Catherine.

Her father pursed his lips and hesitated, "I am so sorry, my dear. He accused John of murdering his brother Patrick."

Catherine's eyes glazed over and she collapsed into her father's arms. When the housekeeper had revived her with smelling salts, she cried, "It's not true; I know it is not!" She stumbled to her room to prepare herself for questioning by Lady Browne and by John's parents; she would have to think clearly and say as little as she could within the bounds of acceptable behaviour.

* * * * *

LATER THAT EVENING, CATHERINE held her breath on seeing Counsellor and Mary Bodkin arrive at Bermingham House. She could tell from their ashen faces how shocked they were.

Moving from her bedroom into the staircase above the hall, she heard the Counsellor ask her father if there was any sign of John's whereabouts.

"Not a sign and not a word," replied Athenry.

Catherine joined the group in the drawing room, as did Lady Browne.

"John would not murder his own brother. I simply cannot believe that," Mary cried. "That man is attempting to destroy our entire family, even after his death. John was devoted to Patrick!"

"We must not rush to judgement," Athenry said soothingly. "If he fails to turn up by sunset, I shall arrange for a search party to find him and bring him home. No doubt, he was overcome by panic. You must try not to worry."

Catherine could take it no longer. "Papa, John would never murder anyone, let alone his own brother!"

"Calm yourself, my dear," Athenry responded. "When John returns, he will surely have a satisfactory explanation."

"But suppose he does not return, Papa?" Catherine quivered, fearing that she might have said too much.

"Why should he not?" Athenry inquired.

"I don't know, Papa." Catherine ran out of the drawing room to the hallway, from whence she could still hear her father's words.

"Please excuse Catherine's behaviour. She is overcome with emotion." Athenry apologized. "I shall ride to Carrowbeg in the morning in the hope of a development. Catherine will no doubt accompany me if she has regained command of herself."

Catherine wondered what to do, conscious of a desperate need to talk to someone who would understand her dilemma. She had effectively lied to, or at least misled, the father who loved her so dearly. Apart from him, she could think of no one in the family who might help her. Lady Browne would be appalled at her tale, and she could not talk to the Bodkins in their grief. In desperation, she thought of Dean Bruce who had been so kind to the Bodkins at the removal of their murdered family; perhaps she could talk to him in confidence.

* * * * *

NEXT MORNING, AFTER A hurried breakfast, Catherine rode to Carrowbeg with her father. She had a sinking feeling in her stomach. For how long could she hope to conceal John's rendezvous with her? The footman and pantry-maid might grow loose in the tongue. She hoped and prayed that he would remain free, or reappear with a credible explanation. If John asked her to elope, she would go; but they might not get very far. She would need to prepare herself physically and mentally for such an eventuality. How had they found themselves in such a quandary?

At Carrowbeg, Mary Bodkin told them, "He has not returned. God alone knows where he is, for I do not." She embraced Catherine tearfully.

Athenry replied, "I shall organize a search party."

"I fear that you must." Counsellor Bodkin sighed in desperation.

Catherine knew what a search party meant. If they found John, he would be arrested on suspicion of murder. After incarceration in Galway Gaol, her father would refer the case to the Grand Jury to determine if true bills applied against him. If the evidence was found wanting, the authorities would release him: that would be the best possible outcome. Even so, the extraordinary episode would have tarnished John's reputation. Her father was likely to withdraw his blessing on their marriage, leaving her with the option of elopement and a life of poverty.

Catherine could see that there was now little to discuss. She noted the relief on Counsellor Bodkin's face when she said tersely, "We should return home, Papa," and off they went. Did the clever counsellor suspect that she knew more than she pretended to know? Perhaps they were two kindred souls sharing a secret in order to shield their loved ones from reality.

On arrival home, Catherine retired to her studio. Rather than continue to paint the portrait of the late Shawn Bodkin who had wrongfully accused John of murder, she gazed at the late autumnal landscape. The garden trees, partly shorn of their leaves, reminded her of how bare her life could become if John were indicted for murder.

Later that day, Catherine approached her father. "Papa, could John have left the country?"

Her father replied tersely, "He could not leave without money, especially since I have ordered his arrest."

She had become accustomed to the searching gaze he turned on her, as if he suspected her duplicity.

"I suppose the Bodkins will remain at Carrowbeg until he turns up?"

"I expect so, my dear."

"When John is found, and his innocence established—"

"You must be patient," Athenry interrupted. "I have issued the order. The search for John Bodkin is under way."

* * * * *

THIRTEEN DAYS LATER ON Thursday, 22nd October 1741, Lord Athenry entered the breakfast room in some haste. "Catherine, I want you to ride with me to Carrowbeg."

"For mercy's sake! You have found him?"

"Yes. I wish to inform the Bodkins before the news spreads, so make haste, my dear."

Catherine set aside her porridge. She wondered where they had found John, and what was his state? What would happen next? She retired to her bedroom to prepare for the journey.

Soon they were travelling west to Carrowbeg. As they rode through Tuam, she saw people staring at the top of Market House. Nausea rose in her throat at the sight of the spiked head of Shane Hogan now under attack by a golden eagle. Worse was to follow as they rode westward: dismembered body parts of the executed were staked to trees on the roadside. She shivered. As they approached the village of Belclare, she saw the burnt-out skeleton of Liscarrow House on her right.

When they reached Carrowbeg, Mary Bodkin said, "You have found him? How is he?"

Athenry cleared his throat. "John is in good health. My men found him hiding under a heap of straw in a cornfield on my land some little distance away. He had posed as a farm labourer."

"My poor son!" Mary Bodkin shrieked. "Where is he now?"

Athenry looked grave. "On his way to Galway Gaol, I regret to say."

Counsellor Bodkin's countenance lost what colour it had.

"My boy is innocent!" cried Mary. "John would never have harmed his brother."

Athenry froze. In an expressionless tone, he said, "He has been remanded on suspicion of murder. A Grand Jury will meet to consider the matter. If the accusation is without foundation, he will be released and declared an innocent man."

"Why did he run away?" Mary Bodkin asked. "Why did he pose as a labourer?"-

"What was he doing, hiding in a cornfield?" Counsellor Bodkin added.

Athenry frowned. "That is what I intend to ask my daughter. You must have aided him, Catherine; why did you do so?"

Catherine froze in her turn. She had dreaded that question.

She was relieved when Mrs Bodkin answered for her: "Because she knows he is not guilty."

"We must travel to Galway immediately," Counsellor Bodkin said.

"I shall write a note authorizing you to visit. I regret I can do no more." As Athenry retired to the library to write the note, Catherine moved towards Mary Bodkin who embraced her.

"I shall pray for John every day until his innocence is proven," Catherine said.

Her father returned with a sealed note addressed to The Keeper of Galway Gaol. Handing it to Counsellor Bodkin, he said, "We shall leave you in peace now."

As they left Carrowbeg, now eerily quiet, Catherine determined to visit John as soon as possible. They would yet prevail.

CHAPTER 17

JOHN HAD NEVER IMAGINED himself kicking his heels in gaol. Now here he was—in the basement of the Tholsel in Galway—where he had previously visited those guilty of the massacre at Liscarrow. By coincidence, he found himself in the same cell as that previously occupied by Shawn Bodkin whose statement at the gallows had brought him here. He could almost smell the body odour of his hateful cousin and feel his ghostly presence. If Shawn could see him now, he would surely smirk at the irony of the situation.

He dreaded the thought of having to face his distraught parents who were on their way to visit him. How could he possibly explain Patrick's death?

When they entered his cell, he could see the look of dismay on his mother's face despite her efforts at concealment. "You must be ashamed of me."

"Of course not. We shall always love you," his mother cried. I have brought some food, clothes and blankets, my darling."

"Thank you, Mama," he replied. A tear rippled down his unshaven face. "I feel so guilty for exposing you to this dreadful experience."

Counsellor Bodkin proffered a handkerchief to his son.

"Where have you been for the last two weeks?" Mary inquired. "We were ill with worry."

John ignored his mother's diplomacy and came straight to the point. "I did not kill Patrick," he said. "When Shawn accused me of murder, I denied his dastardly accusation. I was so shocked I did not know what more to say."

"How could he behave so cruelly?" Mary cried. "John, why ever did you run away?"

"I panicked. I was afraid people would believe Shawn, even though what he said was a lie. I needed time to think." John paused. "I disguised myself in shabby old clothes and rode north, past the village of Dunmore."

"Go on," Counsellor Bodkin said.

"I stopped at one of Lord Athenry's estates and sought work on the land."

"Did they not recognize you?" Mary asked.

"No. On my way there, I dragged my fingernails through a patch of exposed soil and rubbed a little mud on my teeth and cheek."

"You poor boy!" Mary said with tears in her eyes.

"I passed myself off as Matt Flaherty from Connemara, looking for work. And there I remained until my accent gave me away."

"What happened?" Counsellor Bodkin asked.

"The foreman said that yeoman soldiers were searching for a young man who had killed his own brother." John stood up and moved about restlessly. "I ran to a nearby cornfield and there I hid under a heap of straw."

His parents were silent.

"What can we do to assist you?" Counsellor Bodkin asked.

"I can think of nothing. I must deal with this myself."

"We know you are innocent." His mother wept.

"It could have been an accident," Counsellor Bodkin said, "in the same way that Oliver accidentally stabbed Dominick in the eye as a child." He moved closer to John and said quietly, "Why not tell us what really happened?"

"Are you sure you want to know?" John replied wearily.

His parents nodded and he began to speak, articulating each word slowly. "Patrick was drunk that night. Catherine asked him about Anna. He told her to look to her own business. I asked him to apologize but he refused and stormed off. Later that night, I heard a scream and rushed to Catherine's room to find Patrick shouting at her. I dragged him away from her. He fell and hit his head off the fender in the fireplace. When I went to tend to him, he was still breathing but concussed."

"So it was indeed an accident," cried Mary.

Counsellor Bodkin remained silent.

John could not halt the welling of tears in his eyes; how could he inflict such pain on his distraught parents. He then thought about his beloved: Catherine would remain loyal to him, he knew, but she would be under strong pressure from her family to abandon him. This thought preyed on his mind as he waited to see her.

* * * * *

MEANWHILE, CATHERINE WAS ON her way to Galway accompanied by her father. Before visiting the gaol, they stopped for luncheon at The King's Head. As they entered, she averted her gaze from the busy dining area, fearful of attracting the attention of scandalmongers. As she lifted her eyes, she saw the Bodkins neatly folding their napkins in preparation for departure.

"Look, Papa," she whispered, drawing his attention to their presence.

Athenry strode quickly towards them. "Counsellor and Mrs Bodkin, I am so glad to see you," he said. "How is John?"

Counsellor Bodkin sighed. "As well as can be expected under the circumstances."

"Catherine wishes to visit him," Athenry said. "Lady Browne refused. I offered to accompany her instead."

Mary Bodkin looked affectionately at Catherine. "I brought him a change of clothes. He should look good now, apart from his beard, which has grown rather wildly."

"Thank you, Mrs Bodkin."

The Bodkins departed and the Berminghams sat down to a lunch of roasted partridge washed down with ale. Catherine savoured the scent of freshly baked bread that contrasted with the anticipated gaol odour, but was determined to bear it if John must. The proprietor insisted that they should try a dessert pie made of Ballyfatten apples from Ulster. By now, Catherine's appetite had diminished, but her father praised the pungent taste of the cooked apple. She thought of bringing her untouched pie to John but feared angering her father, who was less than enthusiastic about the visit. As she sipped the last of her ale, Catherine wondered if John would hate her because her own father had arrested and gaoled him.

Soon they were on their way along the busy High Street towards the Tholsel, paying no heed to the hawkers peddling their wares. Athenry rapped strongly on the entrance door to the basement gaol.

"We were expecting you, Lord Athenry," the cheerful warder said. "Please follow me."

It was Catherine's first time in a gaol. She held a scented handkerchief to her nose to offset the pervasive stench. With her other hand she lifted her cream petticoat above the earthen floor. The muffled sound of prisoners moaning filled her heart with trepidation. She worried for the fate of her beloved John.

Entering the cell, she was shocked at his demeanour despite his fresh clothes. His unkempt appearance did not upset her. What did sadden her was that look of acceptance in his brown eyes for whatever befell him.

"Thank you for coming," John said. "You must be ashamed of me."

"You must not say that, John." She hesitated, trying to find the right words. "I know you are innocent!"

"Thank you, Catherine, but will the Grand Jury agree with you?" John said wryly.

The three stood in silence for a moment until John said, "Patrick died as a result of a regrettable accident." John glanced at Athenry. "It began with an argument that got out of hand."

Catherine had tried to banish the details of the incident from her mind. She was now, forced to recall them. "What a relief!" she exclaimed with forced heartiness. "I knew there must be a good explanation."

After another awkward silence, John looked at her father. "May I have a few moments alone with Catherine, please?" He spoke with a renewed intensity that buoyed her expectation.

"Please, Papa! I will come to no harm here."

"A few minutes only," her father said, leaving to take up a position outside the door.

Catherine whispered, "What is it, John?"

"I love you so much." Placing his hand on hers, his eyes began to darken again. "They are sure to indict me. I should never have run away."

"Patrick's death was an accident," Catherine reminded him reassuringly.

"They will never believe me."

"They will believe you, my dear heart; they must."

John whispered, "I wish you to take off your engagement ring until my future is decided."

"I refuse absolutely. I cannot desert you for a deed you did not commit?"

A loud knock came on the door. "Come now, Catherine, my dear." The booming voice of her father signalled an end to their private conversation.

"I will always love you, Catherine," were his final words.

After departing, she collapsed into her father's arms. She cursed Shawn Bodkin for having cast suspicion on her beloved with that horrid speech from the gallows. Why had he hated her darling John so much?

Not long afterwards, Catherine was distraught to hear that the Grand Jury had found true bills against her beloved. The Crown had charged him with the murder of his brother, Patrick. She was even more upset when the case was deferred to the Assizes at Galway in March.

* * * * *

AS CHRISTMAS APPROACHED, CATHERINE sat in her studio feeling helpless. She had just returned from her weekly visit to John, having persuaded Lady Browne to accompany her. Together they brought food and clothes, and sought to lift John's spirits. His mood vacillated from cheerfulness to despondency during their Saturday visits. Sometimes, he was anxious to hear local news and gossip; at other times, he sat on his straw pallet and said little. Whatever his mood, his eyes always welled with tears when visiting time was up. All she could do was to embrace him tenderly, and promise to return the following week.

Catherine's thoughts turned to the Bodkins. They had remained at Carrowbeg rather than return to Dublin. Contact with them had waned. She saw them at service every Sunday morning in Tuam. Her father had discouraged contact with them because of the sensitivity of the situation. She raised the issue with Lady Browne as they set forth on their next visit to the basement of the Galway Tholsel.

"Aunt Bridget, should we invite the Bodkins for Christmas dinner?"

"The invitations have already been issued as you may recall."

Catherine remained silent. She plucked her handkerchief from her reticule and held it to her eyes.

"Why do you ask?"

"I look at the Bodkins every Sunday at church. They look so forlorn, just as I myself feel. I would like to invite them to share Christmas dinner with us."

"Ah." Lady Browne sat erect in the carriage. "Your poor father is in a dilemma. With your betrothed indicted for murder, he wonders if …"

"… I should break off my engagement." Catherine finished for her. "I shall not do so because I know without question that John is not guilty."

"You cannot know that, Catherine. You believe in his innocence, but you do not know for certain," Lady Browne said gently.

"I know absolutely, Aunt Bridget," Catherine said as a gust of wind almost blew the carriage off the road. "I think Counsellor Bodkin is aware of that."

"I do not quite understand you." Lady Browne looked with puzzlement into the blue eyes of her niece.

"He looks at me in a knowing way in Saint Mary's. We must invite them for Christmas, Aunt Bridget."

"I shall talk to Francis."

Not long after, Catherine told John that Aunt Bridget had worked her magic on her father. Although it was not possible to include the Bodkins for Christmas dinner, an invitation to some festive cheer had been issued to follow morning service. She did not have the heart to tell him that her father had insisted that she remove her engagement ring.

"My parents will be delighted," John said. "Although they are convinced of my innocence, they feel isolated and despondent."

"If only you could be with us," Catherine said.

"I shall be with you in spirit," John replied cheerfully, although he looked pale and cold now that winter had set in.

Catherine waited patiently for the Bodkins to respond to the invitation. As the days passed, she slipped into a mood of despondency. Even though John was innocent of the charge, the court might well find him guilty because he had absconded. She was anxious to meet John's father to gauge his feelings on the matter, and was therefore relieved when a note of acceptance arrived in early December.

At that point, she felt obliged to share her secret with Aunt Bridget. The older lady was distraught as Catherine explained how Patrick Bodkin had died although she concealed his attempt to rape her. She had never before seen her aunt cry. It was almost inevitable that Lady Browne would tell her brother, which relieved Catherine of the necessity, and of this, she was glad.

On Christmas Day, snowflakes drifted through the air as Catherine awaited the arrival of John's parents. She had supervised the decoration of Bermingham House with ivy and mistletoe. A footman escorted the guests to the drawing room where sherry was served against the background of a crackling wood fire.

Athenry said, "May I wish a happy Christmas to one and all—or as happy as possible under the circumstances."

"Thank you, Lord Athenry," replied Counsellor Bodkin. "Mary and I are grateful for your invitation."

"Let us hope that the New Year shall renew our hopes for the future," Athenry said.

An uneasy silence followed.

Catherine roused when Counsellor Bodkin said, "Mary and I intend to visit John tomorrow."

"I saw him recently," Athenry responded. "He is holding up well."

"Aunt Bridget and I visit him every Saturday," Catherine said.

"You are very good," Mary Bodkin replied, a tear trickling down her powdered cheek.

"How are you faring?" Counsellor Bodkin directed his eyes at Catherine.

Athenry said, "Catherine has the advantage of youth. She is expectant that John will be found innocent."

"How do you see it?" Bodkin looked at Athenry.

"Who will defend John?" Athenry responded quietly.

"Mr Staunton has agreed to act for him."

"An excellent choice."

So there it was; her father was not prepared to speculate on John's fate. What would Counsellor Bodkin do now?

"Why, oh why did John run away?" Bodkin said. He caught Catherine's eye and she shivered. "It makes Staunton's task all the more difficult."

Catherine sipped her sherry, unable to answer.

Athenry stretched out his hands to the heat of the fire.

Bodkin tried again. "If he is found guilty of murder—"

"You must stop torturing yourself." Athenry raised his voice. "The trial is months away,"

Both men were silent. Catherine returned Counsellor Bodkin's gaze and hoped he understood her unspoken plea.

"Perhaps Catherine would like to join us tomorrow when we visit John," he suggested.

"I would very much like to do that!" she said. "May I, please, Papa?"

"Very well," Athenry said. "After all, it is Christmas."

Bodkin smiled for the first time that day. "I feel better now. With Catherine present, our visit will be more relaxed and comfortable."

After the Bodkins left, Athenry said, "When you have visited John tomorrow with his parents, you shall visit no more."

Catherine could see from the pain in his eyes that Lady Browne had told him her secret.

"I am so sorry, Papa," she cried and dashed off to her room.

CHAPTER 18

ON SAINT STEPHEN'S DAY, Catherine accompanied Counsellor and Mary Bodkin on their visit to Galway Gaol. Each kept their counsel until Catherine opened her coat to reveal a gold chain carrying an oval locket.

"What a beautiful ornament," Mary said.

"My Christmas present from Aunt Bridget." Catherine smiled. She loosened the lobster clasp and passed it to Mary. "It holds a surprise inside."

Mary glanced at the gold locket as if curious to know what delights such a small object might contain. "How lovely!"

"That is where I keep my miniature paintings." Catherine watched Mary as she opened the ornament. She saw the tear in her eye as she looked at a head-and-shoulder portrait of John gazing out from one side of the locket, and her own face from the other. This was her response to John's parents' dismay at the sight of her unadorned left hand on Christmas morning.

Locket and chain once more around her neck, Catherine opened her reticule, removed her engagement ring and replaced it on the fourth finger of her left hand. She covered it with her kidskin glove and closed her coat.

"John will be happy to see you wearing the ring," Mary said.

Counsellor Bodkin added, "He is a lucky young man to have such a loyal fiancée."

Catherine was unsure how much information Counsellor Bodkin had gleaned from John. She needed to know in order to plan an effective defence for her beloved. Did the Counsellor suspect her of involvement in Patrick's death?

A cry from the groom, urging his horses forward, disturbed Catherine's thoughts. The morning was crisp and dry with a touch of frost. She pulled a rug over her legs ostensibly to keep herself cosy. However, the real purpose of the blanket was to conceal the contours of a knife she had hidden in her petticoat. In a moment of madness, she had thought that John might make good use of it, if she could smuggle it in to him. Being caught in this act was not a possibility that worried her unduly. If suspicion were cast on her as an accomplice, it would deflect attention away from her beloved.

After a period of silence, Counsellor Bodkin inquired of his wife if Patrick's widow, Anna, was well. Would Anna suspect her of complicity, Catherine wondered, even if Bodkin did not?

"Anna is in good health," Mary said. "She is still grieving for Patrick, of course, although little Thomas keeps her busy."

"I'm glad there is no awkwardness between ourselves and Anna since John's indictment," Bodkin observed.

"Had there been animosity, I would have stayed away. My devotion to my only grandchild endears me to her. She trusts me with him."

Summoning up her courage, Catherine asked, "Will Anna attend the trial?"

"I expect so," Counsellor Bodkin said. "The Crown may call her as a witness."

"My goodness!" Mary paled.

"Would Mr Staunton call me as a witness?" Catherine asked.

"He might well do," Bodkin replied cautiously.

"Should I speak to him?"

Bodkin hesitated before eventually saying, "I could have a word with him if you wish."

Catherine nodded and heaved a sigh of relief. She leaned back in her seat and closed her eyes. Her way was now clear: as a witness, she would be in a position to relate the true story of her part in Patrick's death, if it became necessary. John, an innocent man, must walk free. This would be her secret weapon if all else failed.

* * * * *

THE KEEPER WAS ON hand to greet them on their arrival at the Galway Tholsel. "Happy New Year," he gallantly proclaimed against a less than festive background of mould-infested walls.

"Many happy returns," Counsellor Bodkin responded in a restrained voice. After some further pleasantries, a warder escorted them to John's cell.

Although now better fed, John still looked pale behind his full black beard. When Catherine touched him, the coldness of his hand made her heart ache. Little could be done to minimize the influx of cold air through the iron-barred window.

"Happy New Year, my darling son," Mary said.

"And to you all. Thank you for coming," John replied.

"What can we do for you?" Bodkin asked.

"Bring my trial forward as soon as possible. My endurance is coming to an end."

"I shall speak to Staunton. I have briefed him on your situation. Has he been to see you?"

"Not yet." John smiled grimly. "Perhaps I shall escape in the meantime."

"How might you do that?" Catherine asked excitedly, keeping her voice low.

"I could exchange clothes with papa, then he could stay and I could leave."

They laughed, but their humour was without mirth. Catherine noticed that the security arrangements were quite lax, no doubt due to the festive season. She had spotted a half-empty bottle of whiskey in the warder's stall as they passed by. The man himself was in jolly humour and bore the scent of alcohol.

"It is so good to see you laugh, my dear," Mary said.

"I plan my escape in earnest, just to keep me occupied. Time passes so slowly here; it is cold, dark and malodorous, with rats and mice running about the cells. The trial cannot come too soon, whatever its outcome."

"You will be found not guilty," Catherine declared, "because Patrick's death was an accident."

John nodded. "That is what I hope for, if only we can prove it."

"We shall continue to pray for you, my darling. We shall …" The words got stuck in Mary Bodkin's gullet.

Catherine understood her turmoil. Mary Bodkin must fear that John was heading for the gallows although persuaded of his innocence. At that moment, Catherine almost confessed the true story to the Bodkins in the hope of easing their burden; however, she wished to discuss the matter with John first.

Before they left, Catherine asked if she might have a private word with her betrothed.

"Of course," Counsellor Bodkin said.

When they were alone, Catherine blurted out, "I told Aunt Bridget that Patrick's death was an accident." John paled as Catherine asked, "What have you told Counsellor Bodkin?"

John took a deep breath. "I told him that a drunken Patrick fell on to the fireplace in your room, and never woke up. Do not tell him more than that; it is my dearest wish."

"I know not what may happen now. Perhaps we should see what Mr Staunton thinks," Catherine said. "In the meantime, close your eyes. I wish to give you your Christmas present." She lifted her petticoat to retrieve the knife and passed it to John.

"Thank you, my darling." John, almost in tears, put the knife into an inside pocket of his plate-buttoned jacket.

"If your escape fails, I have another plan."

"What do you mean?"

As she opened her mouth to answer, a loud knocking signalled the end of their visiting time.

"I shall tell you when I can." Catherine hugged him and flashed her engagement ring at him, having removed her glove. She knew by the sparkle in his eyes how much it meant to him to see her wear it.

On the journey home, she wondered how John might plan an escape and how he might use the knife. He could bribe the warder with the ten sovereigns he had carried when he went on the run. The money, stitched into the waistband of his old breeches, which he had retained, had not yet been discovered. If the warder baulked at accepting the fortune, John could threaten him with the knife and nick his throat ever so slightly to protect the man from dismissal.

"You're deep in thought." Counsellor Bodkin observed, disturbing her daydream.

"I was just imagining that John had escaped," Catherine replied. "What would happen if he did?"

Bodkin furrowed his brow. "He could go to the docks and try to get on a ship to America."

"I could follow him there."

"Or he could seize a horse and ride to Bermingham House." Bodkin looked intently into her eyes.

Catherine blushed. She believed that Bodkin now knew of her collusion in John's flight after the hangings in Belclare. Hoping that she had not been careless with her words, she was relieved when Mary broke into the exchange.

"This kind of thinking will do us no good," she said, raising her voice, as their journey concluded.

Back at Bermingham House, Catherine was restless throughout January and February, her mind bubbling over with a multitude of plans to secure John's acquittal. Her father had refused permission for her to visit John again. If he had attempted to escape, she was unaware of it; all she could do was sit, and wait. She prayed to the Almighty for guidance but received none. Unless John was sure to be acquitted or escaped in the meantime, she would have to use her plan of last resort at the trial. She quivered at the thought.

AS THE TRIAL DATE approached, Catherine moved into the Bermingham townhouse in Galway along with Lord Athenry and Lady Browne. The Bodkins moved to Lynch's Castle in Galway. The invitation had come from the widow of the misfortunate Marcus Lynch who had been slain at Liscarrow.

Finally, the day of reckoning arrived. Sitting on a bench in the second row of the courtroom, Catherine saw the arrival of her beloved John from the basement of the Tholsel. Dressed in mourning black, his face brightened when she signalled her love for him with her fan. Wearing a black hat and jacket, Catherine sat between her own family and the Bodkins, directly behind the front row accommodation for the gentlemen of the law. Other dignitaries present included the Blakes of Oranmore and Mrs Lynch. They still wore black out of respect for their murdered relatives. The intense interest in the case led to the occupation of every available seat in the compact chamber, including those in the gallery. To maximize attendance, women were instructed to leave their hoops and panniers at home while men divested themselves of their swords in a reception room.

The clerk of the court opened the proceedings. Then Mr Justice Rose spoke. "It is a matter of great sadness that I have been called upon to preside over yet another case involving the misfortunate Bodkins of Carrowbeg. I apologize for the delay in hearing the case caused by a complication in scheduling the locations of the Galway Assizes. You are all aware that the Crown has charged the prisoner in the dock, John Bodkin, with the murder of his brother, Patrick. The Grand Jury has indicted him. I shall now ask the clerk of the court to read the charge against John Bodkin."

The shackled prisoner in the dock was sworn-in. The clerk of the court said: "John Bodkin of Dublin and Carrowbeg, you are charged with the murder of your brother, Patrick Bodkin, at Carrowbeg on 3rd May 1739. How do you plead?"

Catherine watched as John peered into the middle distance, composed, although still pale and thin. His mother had insisted on trimming his black beard to acceptable proportions. Much to the amazement of the assembled multitude, he remained silent. Catherine understood: it was all part of his decision to conceal the truth of the matter.

Justice Rose looked at Staunton who replied, "I hereby enter a plea of *Not guilty* on behalf of my client."

Rose said, "I shall now ask the Solicitor-General, The Honourable St George Caulfeild, to present the case against John Bodkin on behalf of the Crown."

"Thank you, my lord." Caulfeild rose and glanced around the chamber, paying particular attention to members of the jury. "John Bodkin, you may recall that the late Shawn Bodkin read a statement from the gallows, on Thursday, 8ᵗʰ October 1741, in which he said that you had murdered your elder brother, Patrick. Is this true?"

"It is not true."

"Would you say that the late Shawn Bodkin lied in his statement from the gallows?"

"It is not for me to speak ill of the dead."

Catherine saw a tinge of redness rising in the cheeks of the prestigious prosecutor just above his flap collar. She was pleased that her beloved was equal to the challenge of interrogation.

"Can you think of any reason why Shawn Bodkin would lie as he prepared to depart from this earthly world?" Caulfeild asked, having recovered his normal cheek colour.

"I object, my lord," Staunton cried. "The defendant has already responded to that question."

Rose directed his eyes at Caulfeild. "My lord, a statement made by a convicted man is generally accepted as truthful provided that he has confessed his guilt in public. By so doing, he has cleansed his soul before meeting his Creator. Therefore Shawn Bodkin's statement at the gallows cannot be disregarded." Caulfeild glowered at John. "Perhaps I should move on."

After Rose nodded, Caulfeild resumed, "John Bodkin, would I be correct in assuming that the murder—"

"I object again, my lord!" Staunton exclaimed loudly. "It has not been established that the death of Patrick Bodkin was in fact murder."

"Sustained," Justice Rose responded.

"My apologies, my lord. I shall approach the matter from another angle." Caulfeild peered around the silent courtroom. "Is it true that you are now the heir apparent to the estate of Carrowbeg, worth £800 a year, following the demise of your brother, Patrick Bodkin?"

"That is a matter for my father, Counsellor Bodkin, to decide."

Catherine's mood lifted as she noted John's composure under cross-examination and the robustness of Staunton's defence.

"My understanding is that the estate is entailed in such a manner that you are now the rightful heir to Counsellor Bodkin." Caulfeild walked towards John.

John remained silent, as did Staunton.

"Would you agree that the situation provided you with a motive to murder your brother, Patrick? A simple yes or no will suffice."

John remained silent again.

"Shawn Bodkin said that you rose in the middle of the night and left your room. Is that true?"

"Yes."

"Shawn Bodkin said that you carried a pillow with you. Is that true?"

"That is not true,"

"Why is it not true?" Caulfeild asked.

"I quietly left the room because Shawn was snoring loudly. He could not have seen me or heard me because he continued to snore loudly."

"Why did you leave the room?"

"I could not sleep. I sat down on the sofa in front of the dying embers of the fire in the parlour."

"And sometime after you sat by the fire, you rose and proceeded to the room of Patrick Bodkin. There you murdered him by suffocation with a pillow as Shawn Bodkin has stated."

Catherine held her breath in the silent chamber waiting for her beloved to answer.

"I did not enter the room of Patrick Bodkin," John said.

Caulfeild leaned towards John. "If you did not kill Patrick Bodkin, why did you run away when Shawn Bodkin accused you of murdering your brother? Why else would you flee, given that you had means, motive and opportunity to commit this heinous crime?"

"I panicked," John said.

"When your panic had subsided, why did you not then return home?"

"I feared that people would believe Shawn's accusation, although it was not true; so I passed myself off as a potato picker."

"Why did you later hide in a cornfield under a heap of straw as recorded by Lord Athenry?" Caulfeild caught the eyes of the gentlemen of the jury.

"I was afraid that people would think the worst of me."

"You hid, John Bodkin, because your deceit had been exposed. Your disguise had failed. By running away, you admitted your guilt. That is why Lord Athenry arrested you on suspicion of murder. That is why the Grand Jury found true bills against you."

"Thank you, Mr Caulfeild," Justice Rose said. "We shall now recess for lunch."

CHAPTER 19

CATHERINE WAS APPREHENSIVE ABOUT the forthcoming luncheon in The King's Head. It would be the first time she had met Anna Bodkin since the funeral of her late husband, Patrick. Prior to that, she had met her briefly at her marriage ceremony earlier that year in Saint Mary's Cathedral. On each occasion, her contact with Anna had been minimal.

Catherine remembered how strangely Patrick had looked at her on the day of his wedding. Afterwards, John explained that Patrick had become madly jealous when his younger brother paid successful court to the beautiful Miss Catherine, a lady above his station in life.

"But Mrs Bodkin is also beautiful," Catherine had countered.

John smiled. "Not as beautiful as you."

Catherine had been flattered by John's response; it made her forget that expression on Patrick's face until the night he assaulted her, when she felt the full force of his jealousy and resentment. Yet how friendly he had appeared early on that evening: memory rushed in upon her...

"You look as beautiful as ever," Patrick said.

Catherine blushed. She wore a low-cut pink dress with a cream petticoat. "Thank you. You look very well yourself. Your waistcoat is so elegant."

Patrick gulped down another draught of whiskey. "I hope John is treating you well."

"Very well, thank you," Catherine sipped her lemonade. "Anna is looking lovely tonight."

"Anna! She told me not to drink whiskey." Patrick moved closer to her. "Would you tell John not to drink?" He cast a lascivious eye on her bosom.

Catherine remained silent as Patrick demanded another whiskey. She shook involuntarily when he brandished his pistol. He was one of those drinkers who became morose rather than cheerful as the night progressed. She prayed that someone would intervene as his mood deteriorated. As she backed away from him ever so slightly, he staggered and spilled some of his drink on her petticoat.

Anna intervened. Conservatively dressed, she kissed Patrick lightly on the cheek. "My dear, let us retire."

"You go. I'm talking to.... Catherine." Patrick slurred his words.

"Please, Patrick," Anna implored. "You've just soiled Catherine's petticoat."

"No!"

Catherine caught John's eye.

*John strolled over leaving Dominick and Shawn to their own devices.
"How is my dear brother?" He wrapped his arm around Patrick's shoulder
and winked at Catherine.*

"Mind your own business," Patrick growled.

*Catherine took the opportunity to make her departure with Anna.
"Please excuse me, gentlemen. It is past my bedtime." She touched John
gently on the arm. As she left the room, she heard John invite Patrick to put
his pistol away and Patrick's rough refusal. Poor John, it looked likely to
be a difficult night. She prayed for her beloved before undressing with the
help of her maid, and donned her nightgown. Soon she was fast asleep.*

Later that night, the sound of her door opening awoke her.

"John?" she whispered.

"John is ... asleep."

She recognized the refined but slurred voice of Patrick.

"Anna is at the far end of the corridor."

*"I still think you're gorgeous." Patrick leaned over her and caressed
her posterior.*

*Screaming as loud as she could, she then grabbed the pistol from under
her pillow that John had returned to her for protection. It was the small
flintlock pistol, which she had given him as a Christmas present.*

*Patrick smashed the pistol out of her trembling hand. "You slut!
Flaunting yourself in public." He covered her mouth with one hand and
pulled the bedclothes off her with the other hand. She screamed again,
when he released his grip on her mouth to rip off her nightgown.*

Suddenly there were footsteps, just as Patrick loosened his breeches.

*John burst into the room. "You scoundrel!" he cried. He pulled
Patrick away and threw him to the floor. Catherine hastily seized her robe
and donned it. Turning, she saw Patrick regain his stance, draw his pistol
and point the gun at John.*

"Patrick, put that pistol down and have sense," John pleaded.

"Your Miss Catherine needs some manners put on her."

"For Christ's sake ..."

*Patrick staggered. "My pistol is primed and loaded. You ... get out of
here while I finish with your whore."*

*Catherine quietly lifted a poker from the fireplace and tiptoed towards
Patrick from behind.*

"Go now before I blow your head off, you pup."

"Calm down, Patrick." John raised his arms.

*"You fancy yourself a ladies' man, but you have no fortune." Patrick
raised the pistol.*

Catherine heard the pistol click from half to full-cock, ready for firing. She saw the colour drain out of John's face. Just as she raised the poker, Patrick sensed something and spun around, catching a blow to the side of his head just above his ear. He fell to the ground, and remained there, motionless, apparently unconscious.

"Dear Lord! What have I done?" Catherine cried.

"Do not fret, my darling. He is merely concussed and still breathing." John was on his knees with his ear close to Patrick's mouth. "He'll be as good as new in the morning, though I warrant he will have a sore head."

"Look at the bruise!" Catherine paled as she uncovered his long brown hair.

"That will have subsided by the morning."

"I must tend to him first." Catherine poured some cold water from her pitcher into the washbasin. She dipped her towel into the water and held it against the wound for a few minutes until the flow of blood stopped. Then she cleaned his head before brushing his hair gently into its natural position, thus concealing the wound. "You must turn him over on his side away from the bruise."

"Well done, my darling." John was still pale. "I shall drag Patrick into my bedroom and let him rest till morn. I should not disturb Anna at such a late hour."

"I shall help you." She placed a pillow on Patrick's chest. "In case you need it," she said.

When John opened the door wider, Catherine heard footsteps on the stairs.

John placed his index-finger to his lips, "Hush! Some one is coming. Stay here and tidy up."

As John departed, Catherine heard Julia Kelly offer to help. She quietly closed her door, hid Patrick's pistol away, hung the towel by the fire and returned the poker that remained untainted to the fireplace. How serious was Patrick's wound? Should she have asked John to call a surgeon? Had Julia seen the pillow on Patrick's chest? She would also have to conceal her torn nightgown and clean up any traces of the struggle.

The memory slowly faded and Catherine returned to reality, sitting beside Patrick's widow, Anna, eating soup in The King's Head.

There was a glint of tears in Anna's eyes but she blinked them away. "When my beloved Patrick died, I was distraught and mystified. I had never heard of the natural death of a healthy young man." Turning to Catherine, she gazed steadily at her. "I was astounded when John was accused."

Catherine was quick to respond. "I too was devastated when my father arrested John." She felt guilty, watching the heartbroken Anna struggling with the possibility that someone had murdered her husband.

Catherine was relieved when Counsellor Bodkin said, "The truth of the matter is that we are all victims of the recent horrific events."

"I simply do not understand," Anna cried. She wept inconsolably as Mary Bodkin tried to comfort her. "Why would John have murdered Patrick? Was it for money? And if he did, surely Lord Athenry or someone would have seen evidence of it?"

Catherine felt deeply uncomfortable, and set aside her food that she had scarcely touched. She feared what might emerge during the trial. Butterflies fluttered in her belly as she realized that she might have to confess in court.

*   *   *   *   *

IN A STRANGE WAY, John was relieved to stand in the dock surrounded by the palatial architecture of the Tholsel courtroom with its sweeping arches and dome. His long period of incarceration, more than four months, had taken its toll. The never-ending days of loneliness and coldness were surely a worse punishment than the ultimate sanction. The weekly visits of his parents temporarily alleviated his despondency; they did their best to raise his spirits, but he knew only too well, how low was their own morale.

He cursed Lord Athenry for having forbidden Catherine to visit him even though he was trying to protect her. How he missed her cheerful disposition and her mad plans for escape. He still had the sovereigns that he had stitched into his waistband when he ran away, and the knife that Catherine had smuggled into his cell, although he had not yet tried to use them. Scanning the crowded courtroom from the dock, he saw her flashing smile and the sparkle in her eyes. How he longed to hug and kiss her!

Then he saw Anna, also sitting with the Bodkins, staring at him with unblinking eyes. She looked perplexed but determined: poor Anna!

His thoughts returned to his trial when the clerk of the court cried, "All rise."

"Please call your first witness, Mr Caulfeild," Justice Rose said.

"Thank you, my lord," Caulfeild rose. "I wish to call Lord Athenry."

John watched as the tall immaculately-dressed aristocrat from Bermingham Demense took the stand. Would Athenry change his verdict of natural death in the light of Shawn Bodkin's accusation of murder?

After the swearing-in, Caulfeild commenced his examination: "Lord Athenry, I understand that you rode to Carrowbeg shortly after receiving the news that Patrick Bodkin had died. Is that correct?"

Athenry nodded. "Yes."

"Why did you go there?" Caulfeild asked.

"I was summoned there in my capacity as a Justice of the Peace."

"Can you tell this court what you found when you entered the house?"

Athenry stood erect. "The coroner was already there. The housekeeper escorted me to a room where the shutters were drawn. Patrick Bodkin lay semi-clothed on a high pillow in bed, lying on his back. His body was cold and stiff. Neither the coroner nor I could see any evidence of foul play."

"A young man in the prime of his life lying dead—did it not strike you as strange?"

Athenry nodded without comment. Caulfeild continued, "Was there any evidence to suggest that he had been suffocated, poisoned or assaulted?"

"Neither the coroner nor I could find any such evidence although he stank of whiskey. We concluded that Patrick Bodkin had died of natural causes possibly resulting wholly or in part from alcohol poisoning."

John could not believe his ears. Had the leading pillar of society perjured himself? Only yesterday, Athenry had visited him in gaol to tell him that Catherine had admitted her involvement in Patrick's death. Given that no new witnesses had come forward, Athenry declared himself confident that John would be found innocent. John hoped that he was not being asked to accept acquittal provided he broke his engagement to Catherine. He would never accept such a price.

Meanwhile Caulfeild persisted. "Could Patrick Bodkin have been suffocated with a pillow in the manner that Shawn Bodkin indicated?"

Athenry leaned forward. "We saw no evidence to suggest that to be the case."

"However, it is possible that Patrick Bodkin was suffocated with a pillow without leaving any evidence to the fact, is it not?"

"That would have required the presence of another man to hold Bodkin still while his accomplice held the pillow steady."

"Unless Patrick Bodkin was so inebriated, that a second man would not have been necessary?"

Athenry merely nodded.

"Lord Athenry, did you meet the defendant, John Bodkin, during your visit to Carrowbeg?"

"Yes."

"What was his demeanour then?"

"He was in a state of shock. He said he could not believe that Patrick was dead."

Caulfeild dusted his gown. "And yet, more than two years later, you arrested him on suspicion of murder—"

"Murderer!" cried a voice from the gallery. John clenched the rail on the dock in order to steady himself.

Caulfeild resumed, "May I ask, if you had any qualms about this arrest?"

John could see Athenry's cold eyes darkening.

"My function as Justice of the Peace is to ensure that anyone suspected of murder is detained to allow a Grand Jury to determine if an indictment should be served. After Shawn Bodkin made an allegation of murder against John Bodkin, I had no alternative other than to arrest him."

Caulfeild sat down.

Justice Rose adjusted his wig. "Your witness, Mr Staunton."

"Lord Athenry, can you confirm that the late Patrick Bodkin died of natural causes?"

"When the coroner and I examined the body of Patrick Bodkin, we concluded that he had died of natural causes possibly aggravated by excessive alcohol."

"Why so?" Staunton continued.

"There were no marks on the body consistent with either strangulation or suffocation, nor had there been any evidence of ill-health that might have suggested the gradual application of poison."

Staunton walked towards the jury and then turned to face Athenry. "Was there any evidence of physical attack?"

Athenry coughed. "I saw none."

"Can you confirm that the late Patrick Bodkin was not murdered?"

"That was our conclusion at that time."

The phrase *at that time* dismayed John. It implied that Athenry was open to the possibility of having been mistaken. Was it possible that the blow to the head delivered by Catherine had been noticed by Athenry at the time, but ignored?

"Thank you, Lord Athenry." Staunton returned to his seat. "No further questions, my lord."

Apart from Athenry's ambiguous answer, John was pleased that Staunton had started well. He stole a glance at Catherine, who closed her fan so that it touched her right eye. He understood the signal: she wished to see him but could not do so until the trial was over. He wondered what was in her mind; an escape plan, possibly. The question was; would Staunton call her as a character witness? And if so, would she override his wishes and confess her complicity? All he could do was stand in the dock, and bask in the warmth that he could see in her eyes.

* * * * *

JUSTICE ROSE MOTIONED TO Caulfeild who rose from the front bench. "I wish to call my next witness, Counsellor Bodkin."

After swearing-in, Caulfeild said, "Counsellor Bodkin, can you confirm that the late Patrick Bodkin was heir to your estate until his demise?"

"My son, Patrick, was the heir to my estate."

"Who is the new heir to your estate, Counsellor?"

"My younger son, John Bodkin."

"Thus the defendant, John Bodkin, had motive to murder his elder brother, Patrick."

"Any second son would have been in the same position; it does not turn them into murderers. My son John is not a murderer." Bodkin held himself erect and remained calm as he answered.

Caulfeild continued, "Your late nephew, Shawn Bodkin, alleged from the gallows that your son John murdered his elder brother, Patrick. What say you to that?"

"Leave Counsellor Bodkin alone," a man shouted from the gallery, accompanied by the stamping of feet.

Bodkin winced. "Shawn Bodkin was a disturbed young man who conspired with others to brutally murder three members of my family as well as another seven. His allegation should be regarded as unreliable."

Caulfeild approached the witness. "I understand your anger and your grief. I also understand the sympathetic response of those present, some of whom have also suffered. However, it is my duty to prosecute this case on behalf of the Crown." The prosecutor regarded the counsellor speculatively. "I understand that Patrick Bodkin and his brother, John, were accustomed to spending their summers at Carrowbeg rather than at their home in Dublin."

"Once they had turned seventeen," Bodkin replied.

"With whom did they live?"

"My late brother, Dominick, and my late nephew, Shawn."

"Both of whom were conspirators in the Bodkin massacre." Caulfeild adjusted his gown. "Shawn Bodkin claimed that he was encouraged by the example of the undetected murder of Patrick——"

"My lord," Staunton cried. "I must object to the use of the word murder when this crime has not been established."

"Mr Caulfeild?" Justice Rose glanced at the prosecutor.

"I am aware that this is very painful for Counsellor Bodkin," Caulfeild said. "However, the statement of the late Shawn Bodkin is in the public domain and needs to be examined."

"I shall allow it for the moment." Justice Rose ruled.

Caulfeild stood erect. "Counsellor Bodkin, why would the late Shawn Bodkin accuse the defendant of murder unless it were true?"

"Because of jealousy and hatred: the oldest motives known to man." A round of applause rippled through the crowd.

Justice Rose glared and said, "I will clear the courtroom unless you behave yourselves: no shouting, no clapping and no stamping! Your witness, Mr Staunton."

"Counsellor Bodkin, like my learned friend, I too am sensitive of the difficult situation you find yourself in as a witness." Staunton paused. "Do you believe that the demise of your son, Patrick, arose from natural causes?"

"That was my understanding."

Staunton coughed. "Do you believe that your son, John, was jealous of Patrick's inheritance?'

"I do not." Bodkin directed his eyes at John.

"Have you changed your will since John's arrest?"

"No, John is my heir as my only remaining son alive."

Staunton walked towards Bodkin. "Because you believe he is not guilty of the charge of murder?"

Bodkin looked in the direction of the jury. "I know that my son, John, is not guilty of the charge of murder."

A round of supportive whispering followed as Staunton concluded his cross-examination.

Judge Rose tapped his gavel. "Since there are no more witnesses at this time, we shall recess for twenty minutes; after which Mr Caulfeild and Mr Staunton shall make their concluding remarks."

John was confused. Neither Athenry nor his father had been completely frank in their evidence. They had not perjured themselves, but had crafted their answers to conceal what each presumably believed had happened. As things stood, he felt he had a chance of acquittal if there was no one to provide corroborative evidence for the prosecution.

Then he looked at Catherine and saw tears in her eyes as the warder escorted him from the dock back to his cell.

CHAPTER 20

JOHN WAS SHOCKED TO see Julia Kelly enter the witness box when the court reconvened. Wearing a dark dress and red petticoat, her hands shook when she was sworn-in.

Caulfeild rose. "My lord, a late witness has come forward, Miss Julia Kelly. I request permission to have her testimony heard."

"I must object, my lord," Staunton said. "I have only just received notification of this additional testimony."

Caulfeild retorted, "I advised Mr Staunton as soon as I myself found out. The witness was a housemaid at Carrowbeg on the night Patrick Bodkin died. Her testimony may be crucial to this case."

Justice Rose stared at the prosecutor. "Very well. Tread carefully, Mr Caulfeild."

John remembered the maid. She had offered to assist him in his effort to carry Patrick to bed. A sister of Roger Kelly, she had been dismissed some months later when found to be pregnant. It was rumoured at the time that one of the Bodkins was the father. If she bore a grudge against his family, his chance of acquittal was rapidly diminishing.

"Miss Kelly, please tell the court of your connection with Carrowbeg House," Caulfeild asked, his voice ringing out in the eerily silent courtroom.

"I was a housemaid there."

"Were you present on the night that Patrick Bodkin died?"

"I was, Your Honour."

Temporarily nonplussed at the appellation more appropriate to the presiding judge, Caulfeild blushed ever so slightly but quickly recovered his composure. "Please describe the events of that night."

"There was a lot of drinking that evening." Julia looked at the prisoner in the dock. "Then a row broke out between Mister Patrick and Mister John."

"What were they rowing about?"

"It was something to do with Miss Catherine."

"What happened next?"

"Later that night, I heard a bit of a commotion upstairs. I went up. As I came to the landing …"

John watched Julia Kelly in trepidation. Her forehead was swathed in perspiration. Caulfeild plucked a handkerchief from his breeches and handed it to the girl.

"Take your time, Miss Kelly. As you came to the landing …"

"I seen John Bodkin dragging Mister Patrick out of Miss Catherine's room … and along the corridor into his own room."

"Murderer," a man shouted from the gallery as Justice Rose called for order.

"I asked if I could help. He told me to pull the blanket off his bed and take the pillow off Mister Patrick's chest and place it on the bed."

"Please continue, Miss Kelly."

"He laid Mister Patrick down on his bed, gentle-like," Julia said. She wiped her brow with Caulfeild's handkerchief. "He said he would be grand in the morning. Too much drink, he said, and you could smell it off him, right enough."

"Was Patrick Bodkin alive or dead, Miss Kelly?"

"I thought he was alive until I heard a cry the next morning. I rushed upstairs to find Mister John with his hand on his brother's forehead. Mister Patrick was cold and stiff; he was stone dead."

Julia Kelly spoke with such intensity that silence pervaded the court chamber. John clenched his fists in frustration, realizing that this testimony was damaging to him.

"Blind Dominick told the groom to ride over to Lord Athenry, and you know the rest, Your Honour."

"Your witness, Mr Staunton."

Staunton walked towards the jurors before turning to the witness. "Miss Kelly, when you saw John Bodkin that morning with his hand on the forehead of Patrick Bodkin, did he look bewildered? Surprised?"

"He looked like that, Your Honour."

John heaved a sigh of relief. His life was now in the hands of his defence counsel.

Staunton continued, "Miss Kelly, were you the source of the story that Patrick Bodkin was strangled by John Bodkin, as reported in *Pue's Occurrences*?"

"A gentleman from the newspaper spoke to me and Roger in Canavan's shebeen after the hangings."

"That would be your brother, Roger Kelly?"

Caulfeild rose. "I must object, my lord!"

"Sustained, Mr Staunton," Justice Rose responded. "I must remind the gentlemen of the jury that any relationship between Julia Kelly and Roger Kelly is not relevant to this court."

"My apologies, my lord," Staunton said, his point made.

John understood. Roger Kelly, the Whiteboy, had been a co-conspirator in the Bodkin massacre until turning informer and had since absconded. By associating Julia Kelly with her infamous brother, John hoped that the jury would question her reliability as a witness.

"Did you tell the journalist that John Bodkin strangled his brother Patrick Bodkin?"

"I did not."

"Did the gentleman from the newspaper make up the story himself?"

"I don't know, Your Honour." Julia Kelly had started to perspire again.

"Miss Kelly, did John Bodkin kill his brother Patrick Bodkin?" Staunton walked towards the witness box.

"I don't know."

"Miss Kelly, did Patrick Bodkin die of natural causes as attested to by Lord Athenry?"

"Everybody thought so at the time."

"Miss Kelly, you were dismissed from your post at Carrowbeg by Counsellor Bodkin when you became with child. Were you upset by this dismissal? Remember you are under oath."

"I was … torn asunder."

"Thank you, Miss Kelly."

John breathed a sigh of relief. Staunton had done well to demonstrate that Julia Kelly had not witnessed the death of Patrick Bodkin, and to sow some doubt in the minds of the jurors as to her reliability as a witness.

"We shall now take a short recess to allow Mr Caulfeild and Mr Staunton to finalize their closing statements to the jury." With these words, Justice Rose left the bench.

*　*　*　*　*

CATHERINE WAS NOT THE only person shocked by the afternoon's proceedings as an animated discussion broke out among the people. She therefore avoided the Bodkins and joined Lady Browne in a small room in the dome of the Tholsel in the hope of meeting her father.

"Aunt Bridget, I must speak to Papa."

Lady Browne removed her plumed hat. "I believe I hear his step even now."

Athenry entered. "That was quite a surprise."

"Was it? Papa, how did Mr Caulfeild find Julia Kelly?" Catherine looked squarely at her father.

"I expect she was approached by one of his lawyers." Athenry sat down on a mahogany chair with cabriole legs and claw feet.

"Why has Mr Staunton not approached me to testify?"

"Hush, my dear!" Lady Browne whispered. "You must keep your voice down."

"Staunton did approach Counsellor Bodkin, who referred him to me." Athenry stood up and looked out the window at the busy intercourse on High Street.

Lady Browne added, "We could not permit you to testify; you would have been in danger of the gallows."

"And so an innocent man will die," Catherine cried. She opened her mouth to accuse her father of corrupting the course of justice but realized in time that both she and John were also guilty of this, and perhaps even Counsellor Bodkin.

"Staunton is doing very well." Athenry countered. "You must not give up hope yet."

"After Julia Kelly's testimony, the jury will find John guilty." Catherine clenched her hands at the thought.

Athenry did not deny it. He paced the floor while Lady Browne put on her hat and then took it off again.

"I know what you can do, Papa," Catherine said. Her blue eyes blazed with intensity.

"I know, my dear," Athenry leaned forward and looked straight at Catherine. "I can ask you to remain silent."

"Papa!" Catherine cried.

"Francis, let the poor girl say what she wants to say," Lady Browne said. "Then she must remain silent."

When Athenry removed his wig, his hair appeared to bristle. "Let us hear it!"

Catherine fought back tears. "If John is found guilty, you must appeal the decision to the Chief Secretary."

"I could not possibly approach Viscount Duncannon at such short notice."

Catherine knitted her brow but held her tongue. She told herself that if he did not agree, she would admit her complicity from the floor of the courtroom. But she also knew that nothing would please her father more than to have good reason to approach the Chief Secretary.

"Well!" Athenry fingered his chin. He paced through the room again and then gazed into the middle distance. After an agonizing delay, he said, "Should I do so, I would have to draft a letter for immediate delivery to Duncannon this evening."

"But what would you say, Francis?" Lady Browne wondered.

Athenry sat down. "I would have to say that special circumstances unknown to the court have rendered their guilty verdict unsafe."

Lady Browne leaned forward. "How would Duncannon react?"

"He would want to know the nature of the *special circumstances*, I expect," Athenry replied.

Catherine was satisfied with the direction of the conversation. Now that her father had sufficient time to draft the letter, with the help of his big sister, she knew he would send it. Inwardly she urged her aunt to help her father phrase the *special circumstances*.

"Hmm!" Lady Browne wrinkled her brow in thought. "You could perhaps say that the *special circumstances* are too sensitive to write in a letter, and that you will explain the situation to him privately when you attend Parliament next week."

"Very well!" Athenry said, dabbing his quill in the inkwell.

"Goodness!" said Lady Browne. "What is that I hear?"

"The crier," Catherine said. "Court is about to reconvene."

Catherine departed with Lady Browne, leaving her father to draft his letter to the Chief Secretary.

By the time the Bermingham ladies had resumed their seats, Caulfeild was on his feet. "Gentlemen of the jury, I have demonstrated that the defendant, John Bodkin, had the means, motive and opportunity to murder his brother Patrick Bodkin in Carrowbeg House on the night of Thursday, 3rd May 1739. Whether he murdered him by suffocation with a pillow, or by strangulation, or by physical assault is no longer relevant."

"We now know from the evidence of Julia Kelly, the former housemaid at Carrowbeg, that John Bodkin dragged the quiescent body of his brother, Patrick Bodkin, along the corridor to the very room where Lord Athenry discovered him dead on the following morning, a fact carefully concealed in the evidence of the defendant."

Catherine watched the jurors, some of whom nodded as Caulfeild paused. She cursed herself for not having anticipated the evidence of the servant. Despite the agreement of her father to intercede on behalf of John with the Chief Secretary, she had a sinking feeling in her belly.

Caulfeild continued, "Gentlemen of the jury, you will recall that John Bodkin absconded after the late Shawn Bodkin accused him of murder. Was this the action of an innocent man overcome by panic? I do not think so. If John Bodkin were not guilty, he would have presented himself to Lord Athenry after he had calmed down. Instead, the authorities had to hunt him down, discovering him under a heap of straw in a cornfield thirteen days later."

"Gentlemen of the jury, you have before you a man who had the means, motive and opportunity to murder his brother, Patrick. His motive was personal gain: the inheritance of Carrowbeg. When his cousin exposed the foul deed on the gallows, the defendant ran away and remained at large, thus confirming his guilt. Even more incriminating was his concealment of the fact that he had dragged the quiescent body of his brother along the corridor on the night Patrick died."

Caulfeild stared deep into the eyes of the jurors and then—pointing to the prisoner in the dock—and raising his voice, concluded, "You have no option other than to find this man guilty of murder!"

Catherine trembled. Her heart went out to John. Should she intervene now or wait to see how Staunton would respond?

* * * * *

JOHN WAS IN LITTLE doubt that the mood had shifted against him. He felt his life drawing to a close as he waited for Staunton to respond. Even though Catherine smiled at him, he had seen her lips tighten when Caulfeild concluded. He saw Athenry returning and wondered what had delayed him.

Silence descended on the courtroom as Staunton commenced, "Gentlemen of the jury, may I take this opportunity to congratulate my learned friend, The Honourable St George Caulfeild, on his recent elevation to the post of Attorney-General for Ireland. I wish him every success in the execution of this prestigious appointment. However, despite the elevated status of the prosecutor, my duty must remain to defend my client without fear or favour."

Turning to the jury, he said, "Gentlemen, you must look at the facts in a cool and dispassionate manner to ensure that your verdict is consistent with the principles of natural justice. Many young men of good families in Ireland have the means, motive and opportunity to murder an elder brother who is heir to the family fortune. They do not engage in such criminality because it is immoral to do so, and because other opportunities for advancement present themselves. Indeed, sometimes the elder brother can feel jealous of the success built by a younger sibling in Dublin or London. In fact, I had never heard of such an outrage except in the unusual case of disinheritance that led to the tragic Bodkin killings at Liscarrow."

John felt the colour flow back into his cheeks. Staunton had started well. Maybe there was hope for him yet.

"I accept that means, motive and opportunity are crucial components of any investigation of murder. However, the prosecution must present evidence of perpetration of the crime itself to ensure the reliability of the charge. Therein, lies my difficulty. Apart from the report of the incident in *Pue's Occurrences*, the only indication we have is that of the late Shawn Bodkin who charged my client with the murder of Patrick Bodkin. Like the defendant, I am reluctant to speak ill of the dead. However, I have to remind you that Shawn Bodkin was the prime mover in the Bodkin massacre, resulting in the death of ten innocent people including his pregnant stepmother and his seven-year-old half-brother. At—"

An outburst of animated conversation forced Staunton to pause. The memory of that heinous deed had sent a shiver through them all. John appreciated the sensitivity of Justice Rose, who allowed the busy whispering to dissipate of its own volition. Staunton's energetic defence continued to buoy his hope of acquittal.

"At the very least, you must treat the testimony of Shawn Bodkin with caution. Most importantly, there was no indication in his statement from the gallows that he actually saw the murder being committed, if murder it was. What he might have seen was the same thing that Miss Kelly saw: namely, the quiescent body of Patrick Bodkin being dragged into the room where Shawn Bodkin slept and the removal of a pillow from Patrick's chest to bolster his head on the bed."

John could see some jurors nodding as Staunton gazed confidently around the chamber.

"There is a perfectly reasonable explanation for that incident. We know that Patrick Bodkin drank heavily that night—that he had rowed successively with Miss Catherine, his wife and the defendant while continuing to drink whiskey—that a commotion occurred later that night, overheard by Miss Kelly—that the quiescent body of Patrick Bodkin was dragged along the corridor by the defendant towards the room where both he and Shawn Bodkin slept that night."

Staunton had completely silenced the courtroom with each person hanging on to his every word. John was impressed. He could yet walk out of this court a free man.

"If Patrick Bodkin was murdered during a commotion in Miss Catherine's room, we have no evidence of it. In fact, the defendant, a young man with an unblemished record, has sworn under oath that he did not kill his brother. So what really happened? We may never know. But I concur with the speculation of Miss Kelly: that Patrick had passed out from having taken so much drink, and that John Bodkin was helping him to bed to sleep it off."

Staunton walked around the area in front of the jury. "The prosecution has based its case largely around the behaviour of the defendant after the accusation was made against him from the gallows. Had I been in John

Bodkin's shoes, unfairly accused of murder in a volatile situation, I too would have lain low fearful of the vengeance of an angry mob. In these circumstances, it is not surprising that the defendant panicked. Less easy to understand was the decision to disguise himself as a farm labourer ..." Staunton paused to clear his throat.

John's heart began to beat faster and blood accelerated into his cheeks. He wished he could hide so that no one could observe his momentary embarrassment. If the jury spotted his involuntary reaction, they would surely convict him. He hoped Staunton would retain their attention.

"John Bodkin disguised himself as a potato picker and obtained work on a nearby farm. Torn between the choice of returning home in humiliation—weighted against discovery by a search party—he panicked again, hoping that his nightmare would simply vanish. Had I been his father, I would have punished him severely for behaving in such an immature fashion."

John was not the only person to glance at Counsellor Bodkin, who bowed his head.

"I have no desire to forgive the accused for absconding. It forced Lord Athenry to harness scarce resources to hunt him down. If the Crown had laid a charge of abscondment against John Bodkin, I would have supported such an action. However, neither immaturity nor abscondment is murder and, as such, gentlemen of the jury, you have no option other than to find John Bodkin innocent of the charge of murder. You must find him not guilty because no reliable evidence has been laid before you to indicate that Patrick Bodkin was murdered by John Bodkin, if indeed he was murdered at all."

Staunton sat down amidst a silenced gathering. John saw a juror turn to a colleague who nodded his head, suggesting that the defence had performed with distinction. He prayed to the Almighty for acquittal.

"Thank you, Mr Caulfeild and Mr Staunton. Gentlemen of the jury, John Bodkin has been charged with the murder of his brother, Patrick Bodkin, on Thursday, 3rd May 1739. If you are satisfied beyond a reasonable doubt that the accused is guilty of the charge, you must report a *Guilty* verdict. If you are not satisfied beyond a reasonable doubt of the guilt of the accused, you must return a verdict of *Not guilty* to the charge. This court is now in recess to allow the jury to consider their verdict."

CHAPTER 21

THE PERFORMANCE OF THE defence counsellor had enhanced the prospects of a *Not guilty* verdict. Catherine felt a cautious optimism, and would have spoken more openly about it were it not for the presence of Anna Bodkin at their family meeting. She bit into her scone and took a sip of ale as they passed time in the dome of the Tholsel, awaiting the announcement of the verdict.

Catherine wondered who would open the conversation.

"I was pleasantly surprised at Caulfeild's restraint," Mary said.

"So was I, my dear," Counsellor Bodkin replied. "As Staunton hinted, his mind is elsewhere since his recent appointment as Attorney-General."

Catherine added, "Papa said that Justice Rose persuaded Mr Caulfeild to take the case. He was reluctant ..."

"Please excuse me," Anna interrupted. "I find it hard to express any opinion on the situation. No matter what happens, my beloved Patrick is dead. All I can do is pray for him and concentrate on raising little Thomas."

"Well spoken, Anna," Mary said.

Anna continued, "This is difficult for all of us. I can understand why you wish for a not guilty verdict for your beloved."

Catherine turned away as blood rushed to her cheeks. What would John's parents and Anna think if they knew that she was the killer, albeit inadvertently? She could only hope and pray that John would be found innocent. Even if he were found guilty, there was still hope that the Chief Secretary might declare the verdict unsafe, but only if her father submitted such a request in time. To whom could she speak about her torment? No one would understand except John, and he was suffering because of her.

In a sense, Catherine understood that Anna might secretly hope for a guilty verdict so that she could grieve properly; such a verdict would quash the vile rumour that Patrick had committed suicide. But did Anna appreciate the blow that a guilty verdict would deal to John's parents? Another stab of apprehension fluttered in her stomach. She could not banish the vision of John swinging from the hangman's noose with the light fading in his eyes.

On returning to the chamber, Catherine was shocked to find that Dean Bruce and the Vicar of Belclare had arrived from Tuam for the conclusion of the trial. It was almost like a signal from heaven that God had decided to welcome his son into eternity. Her worst fears were intensified when the foreman of the jury avoided her gaze.

"All rise," cried the clerk of the court.

Justice Rose returned. He allowed the crowd to settle. Catherine fixed her eyes on the austere black hat beside him. "Gentlemen of the jury, have you reached a verdict."

"We have, my lord." The foreman coughed.

A bout of whispering erupted in the courtroom as Justice Rose banged his gavel. As a deathly silence descended, the judge raised his voice. "Do you find the defendant, John Bodkin, guilty or not guilty of the murder of his brother, Patrick Bodkin?"

The foreman took a deep breath before responding, "Guilty, my lord."

"No!" cried Catherine who buried her head in her hands.

John's equally distraught parents were in tears.

Justice Rose paused. "Is your verdict unanimous and without call for clemency?"

"It is, Your Honour."

The trial that had lasted from nine of the clock in the morning until ten at night had reached its grim conclusion.

.   Having recovered her composure, Catherine knew she must intervene when she saw Justice Rose donning the dreaded black cap. She rose to her feet; but then she froze and the words got stuck in her throat. People looked at her in wonder. Before she could compose herself, Justice Rose began to speak.

"First, I want to extend my sympathy to the Bodkin family who have suffered so much in recent times, and also to Miss Catherine, the fiancée of the defendant. Unfortunately, I have no option other than to sentence John Bodkin to hang by the neck in Galway tomorrow morning at noon. This court is now in recess."

* * * * *

JOHN WAS NUMB WITH defeat as he slumped on to his straw bed in the Tholsel basement. He wondering how much the hanging would hurt. Would it break his neck instantly, or would he suffocate slowly? How could he console his parents when their only remaining child would hang like a common criminal? He regretted not telling them more about Patrick's death when it had happened; not that he would have revealed Catherine's part in it, but he could have emphasized more clearly that it was an accident arising from a row. In that way, Cousin Shawn could never have used the death as an incentive to plan the subsequent Bodkin murders. He grimaced with anger and frustration. How could he have allowed jealousy and greed to fester within the family to the extent that Cousin Shawn and Uncle Dominick would tarnish the good name of the Bodkins?

The sound of a key turning in his cell door roused him from his torment. Catherine burst through the open door and stood before him trembling, guilt in her eyes. John wept as he saw his beautiful teary-eyed fiancée, a sodden handkerchief in her gloved hand. His ashen-faced parents followed her. A shout of *Murderer* came from an adjoining chamber, muffled calls of *Hang the scoundrel* from others. What had he done to deserve such hatred? He felt the urge to defend his name and locked his jaw, resolving not to be intimidated by incitement.

"Order!" shouted the warder as he banged a cell door with his truncheon. Turning to the visitors, he said quietly, "I will leave this lantern with you for the duration of your visit."

Mary, Counsellor Bodkin and Catherine took it in turn to embrace John when he rose from his straw pallet.

"Thank you so much for coming to see me on this, my darkest day," John said, gladdened by the company of the people who loved him so much.

"Oh, John, my darling, what have you done?" Mary cried inconsolably.

"Whatever I have done is done. Now I must prepare myself for eternity."

"Dean Bruce and the Vicar of Belclare are available if you wish to speak privately to them," Counsellor Bodkin said in a quivering voice.

"Be easy, Father," John soothed. Although he had mentally prepared himself for a visit from the Church of Ireland dignitaries, their presence reminded him of the immense interest his trial had generated. "I would like you to stay while I confess my sins."

His wish for openness would impress Dean Bruce, given the Protestant suspicion of private confessions. The advice of his church in relation to confessing came to mind: *All may* (confess), *some should, none must.*

Bruce entered the cell with the Vicar of Belclare.

John stood erect. "Bless me, Father, for I have sinned." He used the Catholic salutation, following the example of his formerly Catholic mother, despite the conformance of his family to the religion of the ruling classes.

"I have brought shame and disgrace on my family. I beg the forgiveness of my mother, my father and my betrothed, Catherine; all of whom I love so dearly … all of whom have loved me so dearly."

Mary and Catherine shed tears as Bruce responded, "Thank you, John." The dean hesitated. "Is there any sin in particular you wish to mention?"

John felt a momentary flicker of anger that he quickly concealed. "I have confessed all my sins to God. I hope he will forgive me."

"I hope and pray that he shall forgive you, as I do now." Bruce joined his hands in prayer, as did the Vicar of Belclare, followed by the Bodkins and Catherine. "May I wish you a safe journey to eternity."

John understood what Bruce had implied. Unless he admitted his guilt, he would go to hell; yet how could he confess to a crime he had not committed? He looked at Catherine, whose eyes reflected her dilemma. He would have to talk to her privately.

Dean Bruce extended the hand of forgiveness, which John shook firmly. "Until tomorrow morning, we shall leave you in peace."

After the reverend gentlemen had departed, John said, "I am at peace now and ready to meet my Maker." But this was untrue: he had lied to protect the feelings of those he loved.

His parents and Catherine wept inconsolably.

"Please do not weep on my behalf." John felt that the time had come to bid farewell to his beloved parents.

"Mama, please take this gold band, handed down to me by my grandfather. You must give it to little Thomas when he is grown enough to wear it."

"May God bless you, my darling son." Mary hugged him and wept. "You will be in my prayers until I join you in heaven."

"Father, please take this watch and chain which was handed down to me. You must pass it on to Thomas also."

"That I will, John." Counsellor Bodkin embraced his son and held on to him for an age. "May the Lord have mercy on your soul."

"I would like to speak to Catherine alone for a few moments, please."

His parents nodded sadly and departed. He would see them once more, at the gallows in the morning.

* * * * *

JOHN OPENED HIS ARMS and held Catherine close to him. "My dear Catherine, you did your best to help me escape but I failed. The challenge of trying to escape kept me occupied over the dreary months of winter and early spring. My plans were interrupted more than once when I had to wash and change with little forewarning, necessitating the burial of my knife and money." John rummaged in his jacket and produced a slim parcel.

"Please keep it until tonight, when I shall return," Catherine said.

"How can you do that?"

"Our townhouse is close by, as you know. When the footman dozes off, I shall slip out."

Though facing the hangman's noose in the morning, John felt a warm rush of emotion when Catherine gazed at him with tears in her eyes.

"You could be attacked in the dark of night." John warned.

"Papa said the oil lanterns work in the street throughout the night."

John changed tack. "Why did you stand up in court?"

"I intended to confess my crime." Catherine sighed. "It would have been the first time I ever spoke in public."

"You were going to disobey me." John frowned, realizing how close she had been to danger.

"I thought my courage equal to the task, but the words got stuck in my gullet." Catherine paused. "I had rehearsed what I was going to say so many times, and when I needed to, I could not say it."

"Thank God you failed," John said. "What were you thinking of?"

"Perhaps I was thinking of Duncannon."

"Not the Chief Secretary?" John could see that Catherine was yet plotting on his behalf.

"Indeed! Papa has sent a letter to Dublin Castle, asking him to find the verdict unsafe." Catherine waved her fan in the air in a vain attempt to disperse the odour.

"I cannot believe that Athenry would do such a thing." John stared straight into Catherine's eyes.

"He is afraid that I will confess."

John stepped forward and embraced the love of his life. "Thank you, my darling."

A loud knock on the door betokened an end to their conversation.

"When I return tonight, you could try once more to escape. I shall do whatever I can to help," Catherine whispered. "If that is not possible, I will confess tomorrow morning unless a favourable reply arrives from Duncannon. Good night, my darling."

John hugged her again. "You must not confess! I forbid it." He held on to her until the warder had to tear them apart.

When Catherine had left with tears glistening on her cheeks, John found himself in a state of confusion. He had begun to prepare himself for execution, but Catherine had indicated three other options still open to him: escape, pardon through the Chief Secretary or pardon through her confession. John still had the ten sovereigns as well as Catherine's knife. When the warder was on his nightly rounds, he could offer him five sovereigns. He could nick his throat with the knife to feign duress, for the sake of the man's livelihood. Having left him bound and gagged in his cell, he would make haste to the quays no more than two hundred yards away. With his remaining five sovereigns, he would purchase a passage on any boat ready to sail.

Escape was the only realistic option, he thought, recalling his first attempt of abscondment. That had ended in humiliation when a yeoman soldier prodded him with a hayfork underneath a heap of straw. This time, he would exercise more cunning.

On the other hand, if Duncannon replied favourably he would be a free man: better then not to hazard an escape. A botched escape, or even a successful one, would almost certainly complete the destruction of his reputation. Would the clever Miss Catherine come to the same conclusion, now that she had some time to reflect on the options?

If Duncannon delayed his reply, would Athenry flex his local muscle and insist on a deferral of execution? If he failed to act, his feisty daughter might confess her complicity at the gallows. The resulting mayhem might delay John's execution, but it would also destroy Catherine's reputation.

Why had he not considered the implications of all these possibilities throughout his long internment? At this point, he was so confused that he lay down on his straw bed and tried to sleep: but slumber was elusive. He could not banish the vision of a noose tightening around his neck. Unsure of what best to do, John decided to do nothing as yet and let events take their course.

CHAPTER 22

Catherine RETIRED TO HER bedroom only too aware that her beloved John lay in a prison cell awaiting execution in the morning. She lay down on the bed fully clothed and closed her eyes, her mind a riot of conflicting emotions. One decision she was sure of—if John was not reprieved in the morning, she would confess. This time, the words would not stick in her throat.

In the meantime, she must wait and be patient. How soon would her father's letter reach Duncannon in Dublin, a distance of about 140 miles? A series of horses galloping at 20 miles per hour would take seven hours, arriving at five in the morning, she reasoned. If the Chief Secretary read it and replied promptly, his letter would arrive at about one hour after noon on the morrow at the earliest. Her father must surely have thus calculated, and come to the same conclusion; perhaps he had already arranged to have the hanging deferred until the afternoon. She would ask him at breakfast.

Her greatest desire now was to speak privately with John. Determined to achieve it, she waited until her father and aunt had settled for the night and then tiptoed down the stairs. The footman dozed in his chair in the entrance hall. She quietly drew the bolt on the front door and, wearing a light cloak, hurried towards the nearby gaol. Her father had warned her never to walk alone at night, and now her heart raced as a man approached her from the shadows.

"A penny for a poor old man, Miss," he beseeched her as he staggered across her path.

"I have no money with me." Catherine told a white lie as she had brought ten sovereigns in her reticule in case it might be necessary to bribe the gaoler. She neatly stepped around the drunkard and soon reached the gaol.

The warder opened the door in response to her repeated knocking.

"Good evening, kind sir. My name is Miss Catherine Bermingham." She smiled. "I am here to visit my fiancé, Mr Bodkin."

"Two ladies in one night!" The young man whistled. "The visiting hours is over."

She opened her reticule and pressed one of her five sovereigns into his hand.

He closed his fist and said, "Follow me, Miss."

Catherine followed the warder to the keeper's office where Anna Bodkin was seated on a bare wooden bench.

"My goodness, Mrs Bodkin—what are you doing here?"

Anna said, "I came here to confront the man who murdered my husband." She stood up and faced Catherine. "For more than two years, I have mourned Patrick in the belief that his death was from natural causes. My world has been turned upside down by the revelation that he was murdered."

"John did not murder him," Catherine told her firmly. "After the trial, Dean Bruce visited John in gaol in the company of John's parents and myself. He refused to acknowledge his guilt. This is a miscarriage of justice: John is not guilty!"

"I cannot go on like this," Anna cried. "How can I grieve for the man I loved so dearly unless I know what befell him?"

Catherine paled. "How can I begin to grieve for my fiancé, whom I believe to be innocent?" She kept her passion in check, not wishing to speak freely to Anna as yet.

"All the more reason for you to talk to him alone, if they will allow it."

Catherine concluded that the warder had refused Anna permission to visit John. He would probably deny her also. Her plan to bribe the warder to release John no longer seemed a viable option.

The warder returned. "Miss Catherine, I cannot allow you into the cells tonight. Perhaps in the morning—"

Turning away from Anna, Catherine opened her reticule and extracted four gold sovereigns. Placing them on the palm of her gloved hand, she extended the coins towards the warder. She stared pleadingly into the flickering eyes of the young man, who blushed and then sadly shook his head.

"Could I have a word with the keeper, please?" Catherine implored.

"He's not here, Miss, but he will be, in the morning."

Catherine gritted her teeth. "Thank you for your kind consideration." She moved towards the exit, anxious now to return home before the footman noticed the bolt drawn in the front door. "Please tell Mr Bodkin that I shall visit in the morning." That was a coded message to John; perhaps he should defer an escape attempt in the hope of a favourable response from Dublin Castle.

As the ladies departed, Catherine started, as the silhouette of a man emerged from the shadows.

Anna said, "This is my brother, here to escort me home." She looked around, as if searching for Catherine's escort. "You came here alone?" Patrick's widow pursed her lips. "What a brave woman you are."

"I am well able to look after myself," Catherine snapped.

"We shall nevertheless escort you home, my dear," Anna replied.

Catherine noted the softening in tone. These extraordinary circumstances had created a bond of sorts between the two women, united by their love of the Bodkin brothers. That fragile bond would be broken tomorrow by her public confession at the gallows if John had not been pardoned in the meantime.

When Catherine opened the front door of the Bermingham townhouse, the creaking noise woke the dozing footman.

"Where have you been, Miss? If I had known you was out, I would have called his lordship."

"There was no need. All is well and I am safely returned." Catherine raised a finger to her lips as the footman rebolted the door. "I shall away to bed—not a word to anyone, if you please." She handed him one of the sovereigns that had proved so useless in the gaol.

Catherine lay on the bed in her nightgown and attempted to prepare herself for the horror of the morrow. This time she would stand at the gallows, no matter what her father or aunt said. She would look into John's eyes and express her everlasting love for him. Stepping forward, she would then admit her guilt.

* * * * *

AFTER A NIGHT OF fitful sleep, thoughts of being drawn and quartered had convinced John that escape was the only option. He was grateful that Catherine had attempted to visit him. Despite her coded message, relayed to him by the warder, he held out little hope of a pardon from Dublin Castle.

If Catherine did not come soon, he would try to bribe the warder, change clothes with him, nick his throat with a blade, and gag and bind him. Dressed in the warder's clothes, he would hurry to the nearby docks. If he avoided detection, he would procure a passage on the next boat to leave Galway presuming the captain would overlook his prison uniform. It would not be possible for Catherine to join him there, of course; he must travel alone to the New World. After a year had passed, he would invite her to join him there if she would still have him; by then she would have attained her majority and could make her own choices in life.

Preparing for action, he dug up the knife from the earthen floor where he had hidden it. Hearing the insertion of the key into his cell door, he held the knife behind his back and prepared to pounce.

Then he heard the warder say, "Miss Catherine to see Mr Bodkin. You have ten minutes."

When the door closed, John dropped the knife and opened his arms wide to hold Catherine close. He would have held her forever if it were possible. "I was on the point of attempting to bribe the warder when you came," John said, kissing her.

"I feared Aunt Bridget would not allow me from her sight. She agreed to walk around the town with me after an early breakfast. Then I persuaded her to allow me to visit, for a few minutes only, to say goodbye ..." She choked on the words as her eyes welled with tears.

John hugged her again. "Do not weep, my darling. We may yet survive this."

Wiping her tears, she lifted her petticoat and retrieved a small band with five sovereigns stitched into it. "Here is a little gift for you. I have another five sovereigns in my reticule if you should need them."

"I shall delay my escape attempt for five minutes after you leave." John placed the money band in the inside pocket of his jacket. "Then I must move. It's my only chance."

"Unless Duncannon pardons you," Catherine responded. "Papa said at breakfast that the hanging has been postponed until the decision of the Chief Secretary has been received."

Now John was confused again. The decision to postpone the hanging confirmed that Athenry had indeed petitioned Dublin Castle. Should a pardon result, it would be counterproductive to attempt an escape.

"I know what you are thinking," Catherine said.

"Zounds!" John exclaimed.

"It would be difficult for the Chief Secretary to grant a pardon unless he understood the special circumstances. He might postpone the hanging for some days to allow Papa to travel to Dublin."

"What have I ever done to deserve such a wonderful girl?" John held her close again. "Even if I am pardoned, Catherine, your father will never permit our marriage."

"I have thought of that also." Catherine kissed him. "I shall remain loyal to you. We will bide our time and marry next autumn, when I am of age. Aunt Bridget will help us."

"But life here would be very difficult. People would continue to regard me with suspicion." John paused.

Catherine hesitated. "We could elope to the New World."

A loud knock reminded him that ten minutes had passed. John held her close for one last time. He had a premonition that he would never hold her again. Catherine clung to him as if sharing his fear: the warder had difficulty in separating them.

"Lady Browne says you must come at once," the young man said.

Alone again, John understood that his final hour was approaching and he could no longer delay his escape attempt. Catherine had moved heaven and earth to protect him from the gallows. If he failed to escape and no pardon was granted, she would step forward at Gallows Green. She would then proclaim her participation in Patrick's manslaughter. If her public confession led to his freedom, she could be imprisoned or transported. He could not allow that to happen.

He extracted five sovereigns from his waistband and another five from Catherine's gift. Placing the ten sovereigns on a stone slab, he waited for the warder to enter. He heard the key turn and clasped the knife behind his back. The door opened and the warder walked in, accompanied by a colleague. John silently swore because the enhanced security arrangement had made his escape plan more difficult if not untenable.

Noticing the ten gold sovereigns, the eyes of the leading warder bulged. He reluctantly shook his head. "They have sent extra men to ensure that nothing goes wrong, Mr Bodkin."

"Of course." John was dismayed. He sat down on the straw pallet to hide the knife with his body. "You have looked after me well." He saw little option other than to leave the money there in the hope that the warder might reconsider his position.

* * * * *

JOHN'S DISMAY DEEPENED WHEN the warder returned some time later to shackle his feet.

"Is this really necessary?" he asked.

"Keeper's orders, Mr Bodkin."

John glanced toward the ten gold sovereigns neatly laid out on the stone, but the young man ignored the gesture.

"What will happen next?" John asked, feeling the coldness of the iron chain on his ankles.

"You will be brought on a cart to Gallows Green."

John shivered at the mention of the words. "What time is it?"

"Twelve of the clock." The warder shook his head sadly.

"When will I go there?"

"The hanging has been postponed for a short time. Sometime this afternoon, I believe."

"Unless there is a stay of execution?" John said hopefully.

"Stranger things have happened, I suppose. I will leave you be for the moment."

"You must not forget the money!"

The warder made no comment but departed without touching the coins.

John checked the chains: the warder had locked them securely. Escape was no longer an option. The postponement of his hanging confirmed that the authorities were awaiting a response from the Chief Secretary, so there was still hope. He put his hands on his head. Had he been Catholic, he would have prayed on a rosary as he had seen the servants pray after the massacre at Liscarrow.

If the Chief Secretary responded positively, his decision should arrive sometime in the afternoon and John's freedom would follow. If the response were negative, he would be transported through the city for immediate execution. One way or another, he felt a need to pray. He knelt down on the earthen floor and prayed for Catherine, for his parents, and for Anna and little Thomas. A strange but pleasant sensation of spirituality surged through him; it dawned on him that he had never before prayed with real emotion. Prepared for what now seemed inevitable, he still clung to the slim possibility of redemption. He wondered if Shawn Bodkin had thought him in truth a murderer … this was something he would never know.

John lay down on his bed of straw. A range of emotions surged through him as he sought vainly to make sense of his fractured life. He dozed off from time to time and then awoke. It was still daylight. He was still chained and the ten gold sovereigns remained untouched.

Then he heard the key turn in his cell door. The warder entered, accompanied by his colleague. They were unsmiling and did not meet his eyes. There was to be no stay of execution.

"Your time has come, Mr Bodkin. Please place your arms around our shoulders."

As they escorted him up the stairs and into the fresh air of Galway City, he glimpsed the distraught faces of his parents and Catherine, as well as Lady Browne. The warders raised him on to a cart and stood on either side of the horse-drawn vehicle. John knew he was about to be transported along Shop Street and through the great gates to Gallows Green. People watched in silence as the modest cavalcade moved forward over a distance of about two hundred yards. Some people crossed themselves with a blessing. Aside from the trial, it was the first time in his life that he had been the centre of such attention—such a strange sensation.

Poor Catherine! All her plans had come to naught. John hoped she would think better of confessing her complicity at the gallows. How could he prevent it? Perhaps even now he could admit his guilt: but if he lied in the face of eternity, it would surely rouse her into action with a greater determination.

They passed through the city gates. He could now see the inverted U-shaped timber frame from which the noose hanged. The city dignitaries stood silently as they observed his arrival. Lord Athenry, who had been chatting animatedly with Dean Bruce, avoided his gaze. The reporter from *Pue's Occurrences*, who had attended the earlier Bodkin trial in Tuam, pointed him out to a colleague. John had attended hangings before but never as the main protagonist. He thought of Shawn Bodkin, understandably abused by victims of his heinous crime before his hanging. Had that abuse persuaded Shawn to launch the vindictive outburst that had led John to the gallows?

The two warders stepped down from the cart and moved it forward under the gibbet until the noose dangled alongside John's head. He stood there, watching the hangman light a wood fire, the purpose of which made him tremble. The final drama in his life was about to commence.

CHAPTER 23

AS JOHN WAITED AT the gallows, a roar went up from the large crowd. He craned his neck and saw Catherine standing between Lord Athenry and Lady Browne. He saw the tears in her eyes, the words *I love you*, forming on her lips. He directed one last look of love and longing towards her and his parents, his heart breaking at the sight of their grief-stricken faces. He stumbled but quickly regained his feet.

The hangman instructed him to stand erect whereupon he felt the noose swaying gently against his head. The horror was about to commence.

At that point, Dean Bruce and Thomas Shaw, High Sheriff of Galway City, approached him along with the Gentlemen of the City.

"Before you depart from this earthly world," Shaw said, "may I humbly request you to declare your guilt and make your peace with God?"

There was a deathly silence; John felt faint and doubted the ability of his legs to support him for much longer. This was the moment he had dreaded ever since Shawn Bodkin had accused him of murder six months ago. Shawn had publicly admitted his guilt on that occasion. John considered admitting guilt as a public duty, but could not bring himself to do so. He was innocent; but he could not openly declare it for the sake of his beloved Catherine. Looking at her, he saw she was holding her hand to her mouth.

"Mr Bodkin, please answer," Sheriff Shaw cried.

John gazed into the earnest eyes of the Gentlemen of the City. He opened his lips, as if to reply, but then closed them and remained silent. Catherine would understand, but his parents would not. Neither would Anna. His faintness had worn off. He now stood erect and composed, though pale and unshaven. The palpable tension was broken by a shout from the crowd, "Speak up, you murderer!"

John remained silent. He looked again at his beloved Catherine and formed the words *I love you* on his lips. He saw her moving towards the front of the crowd to join his parents. Staring at her, he shook his head vigorously and shouted, "No!"

He pulled the hangman's cap down over his head. The noose that lay around his neck was slowly tightened. With his eyes shut, he waited for the warder to move the cart away. His falling body would further tighten the rough-textured rope.

Instead, he heard the booming voice of Dean Bruce:

"As Jeremiah saith,
Only acknowledge thine iniquity,
that thou hast transgressed against the LORD thy God ...

... or otherwise, if you are not guilty,
please acknowledge your innocence."

While he was repelled by the patronizing bombast of the Dean of Tuam, John was nonetheless grateful for the opportunity to bid a final farewell. Although public speaking was an ordeal to which he was unaccustomed, he steadied his nerve, pushed back his cap and focused his brown eyes on Catherine and his parents.

"I wish to beg your forgiveness for any action that may have given offence to any member of my family or to the community at large. Having confessed my sins to the Lord, I now beg you to allow me to die in peace. I forgive mankind."

Astonishment and confusion were visible on many faces in the vast crowd. What did his final three words mean? Was he declaring his innocence? John had indeed declared his freedom of guilt, but in a coded manner that few would understand. He heard a busy whisper circulating through the crowd as people tried to make sense of his extraordinary statement.

Then Catherine stepped forward.

My God! He screamed "No!" but he was powerless to stop her. If she confessed, it would save him but it would destroy her own reputation, if not her life. How could she perform such a desperate act? Yet that was why he loved her so much; her strength of character and independence of thought, allied to a natural beauty and charm, made her the joy of his heart. Both of them were now centre-stage in a drama that would reverberate in Galway society and beyond for generations.

* * * * *

JOHN WATCHED IN MORBID fascination as Catherine looked at him, then at Dean Bruce and the Gentlemen of the City. She turned towards the crowd and said, "Ladies and gentlemen, my name is Catherine Bermingham. I am the daughter of Lord Athenry and the betrothed of John Bodkin."

Athenry looked aghast. Lady Browne made an effort to break through the throng but her panniers impeded her progress.

Catherine continued, "I feel obliged to make a public statement because this hanging must be prevented." The whispering stopped and silence reigned. She now had the undivided attention of the assembled multitude.

"I must speak out," she cried. "I tried to do so at the trial, but my throat dried up."

John paled. He was astonished, not so much that Catherine had sought to address the gathering but that she had succeeded in holding their attention. Her intrusion into the proceedings had caused a sensation and nothing could stop her now.

"I know John is not guilty," she said, her voice quavering. People gasped.

"That is what he meant by the words, *I forgive mankind*." Catherine brushed away a tear from her cheek. "It recalled to me the words of Dean Bruce, *Why did Jesus have to die on the cross?* Why could not God simply forgive mankind? Those three words, *I forgive mankind*, mean one thing and one thing only." She turned around and pointed to John. "That man on the gallows is not guilty."

"Not according to the court!" a man shouted from the crowd.

John suspected that Catherine would now lose the argument. He saw her frown as the whispering gathered momentum.

"The court was in error." Catherine raised her voice. "John Bodkin did not kill his brother, Patrick."

"Prove it!" a woman screamed.

"I can vouch for his innocence. I was in the room when Patrick was killed."

"Who killed my husband?" This cry from Anna Bodkin silenced the crowd.

"I can swear on the bible that John did not."

John looked at Lord Athenry, who remained impassive. That man knew the truth: he had notified the Chief Secretary that the verdict reached by the court was unsafe. Presumably, Duncannon was unconvinced and had accepted the guilty verdict; otherwise, John would not be standing there with a cord around his neck.

Catherine's cheeks flushed as she nerved herself to admit her guilt. "It was—"

"I have heard enough," Sheriff Shaw interrupted. "I appreciate that Miss Catherine has sought to perform a public duty; however, the time for evidence to be admitted is past and the verdict of His Majesty's court of law must stand. Miss Catherine, I insist that you immediately rejoin your family and allow us to proceed with the business of the day."

Catherine bristled as two soldiers escorted her back to the side of Lady Browne.

"Draw away the cart!" shouted a man in the crowd.

John looked around in despair. His last sight was of Catherine looking at him with love and tears in her eyes, then he slowly pulled the cap over his head once more. All fear was displaced by the love and pride he felt coursing through him. She had demonstrated the extent of her love for him by her courageous public pronouncement; had it not been for the interruption of Sheriff Shaw, she would have admitted her complicity.

He could now face his Maker content in the knowledge of her love for him, his only regret that she and his parents had to bear the horror of his execution.

* * * * *

JOHN FELT THE ROPE tighten around his neck until it began to cut into his skin. The cart began to move. He kept adjusting his feet to support his body until finally the vehicle was gone from under him. His body dropped, jerking the noose taut underneath his chin. He tried to scream but his compressed windpipe made it impossible. Legs flailing in the air, he gasped for breath. He could still hear the roar of the crowd and the bleating of Dean Bruce.

It was like being held underwater, lungs bursting, struggling to obtain air. He tried again to scream but the cord only dug deeper into his neck. All he could do was whimper. The pain was unbearable. He prayed to be spared and to die quickly; then he lost consciousness.

After a short interval, John woke again: for a moment, he thought he had reached heaven. The tension in the noose had relaxed. Then he felt his arms and legs being tied with cords. The hangman had cut him down and he now lay on the cart, his clothes ripped open to expose his privy parts. Unable to move, he watched a hot knife plunge into his belly. *Please spare an innocent man,* he tried to shout but his windpipe was crushed. *My dear Catherine, please turn your eyes away!* He heard her scream. The pain was indescribable as he was disembowelled, and then his innards scooped out of his body. *Christ!* He heard the crackle as the flames engulfed his body parts. This surely was hell on earth, he thought, before once more losing consciousness.

He roused again, feeling that he had been raped by the devil. Silently he pleaded with God to spare him and let him go now; but the Good Lord did not listen to his plea.

Now came the swish of a sword: suddenly he was in a basket, and from thence raised on to a spike. From that elevation, he had one last sight of the huge crowd but saw only the distraught face of his beloved Catherine. Then he knew no more.

CHAPTER 24

WHEN CATHERINE SAW THE hangman brandishing the red-hot knife over the body of her beloved, she fainted into the arms of her father. He escorted her to the Bermingham carriage where she lay on the back seat. As she recovered, the roar of the crowd turned her stomach.

"Sheriff Shaw should not have interrupted me," she cried.

"It is over, my dear; you must think of it no more," Lady Browne said firmly.

"Why will no one believe that John is innocent?" Catherine sobbed.

"I believe you and so does your father."

"But not Viscount Duncannon."

"Your father did his best to persuade him but sadly did not succeed."

A louder roar came from the crowd. Catherine looked out through the window of the carriage. Some people began to depart. She moved towards the door, but felt the arm of her aunt restraining her.

"You must not go out there," Lady Browne said. "Close your eyes, please do!"

"Oh, no!" Catherine screamed hysterically at the sight of John's head raised on to a spike. She threw open the door of the carriage for one last glimpse of her beloved. Catherine saw his lips move in what seemed to her a last declaration of love. In the hope that she was not deluding herself, her lips responded silently with those same words until the hangman closed John's eyes.

"Did you see, Aunt Bridget?" Catherine gasped, her senses now fully aware. "John looked at me. I saw his lips move with words of love. I shall love him until the day I die."

* * * * *

SINCE THE DAY OF John's execution, Catherine had dressed in mourning black. On the following Sunday morning on the way to service, she stopped the Bermingham carriage at the site of his remains. Despite her father's objection, she dismounted from the carriage and stood on the pavement with her hands joined together in prayer. She was only vaguely conscious of the curiosity of pedestrians as she bowed before her beloved: his spiked head was on public display, in a cage in the Market House in Tuam.

During the subsequent service, she stared at Dean Bruce when he rose in the pulpit to deliver his homily. He avoided her eyes. She had sent him a note on the previous Friday, asking him to pray for the soul of John Bodkin. He had not replied nor had he mentioned the matter.

Catherine's gaze fixed on Counsellor and Mary Bodkin, also in mourning black. What a disconsolate couple they were, and little wonder. They had lost not only their extended family but their only two children, Patrick and John, to violent deaths. Little Thomas, seated there between his mother and his grandmother, was all that the Bodkins had left. Poor Anna! She must now grieve for Patrick all over again.

All that Catherine had was the memory of her darling John: his love for her and his insistence on shielding her from the guilt she now bore. She had killed Patrick and failed to protect her beloved John from the gibbet. Despite her despondency, she had to restrain herself from smiling at Thomas as he fidgeted with a ribbon on his dress. He was the Bodkin's only hope for the future. All their plans and dreams for their sons now lay with him: a heavy burden for a little boy to bear.

After the service, Catherine stood in the churchyard with Lord Athenry and Lady Browne. She looked imploringly towards the Bodkins but they avoided her gaze. Would they ever understand that she had no option other than to defend John when Patrick threatened to kill him? Patrick had cocked his pistol and his finger was on the trigger. A vivid memory of his attempt to rape her flashed through her mind. When she had lifted the poker she had not consciously meant to kill him, but her anger had led her to strike him with all the energy she could muster. As she relived the events of that night, Lady Browne touched her gently on the arm.

"Catherine, my dear," she said. "We must go now."

"I must speak to the Bodkins, Aunt Bridget."

"Of course you must," Lady Browne replied, "but not here and now."

Catherine collapsed in tears at the situation that now confronted her. She had to make her peace with the Bodkins. Surely, they must know by now that she had killed Patrick, even though Sheriff Shaw had cut short her confession. John had already told his parents that the killing was an accident. It would not be difficult to deduce that if John had not killed Patrick, she must have done so. No doubt, that was why they had averted their gaze from her.

"What can I do to improve matters?" Catherine implored.

"That you must answer yourself." Lady Browne replied. "Are you thinking of anything in particular?"

Catherine had thought about the options available. "Should John's remains be buried at Carrowbeg?"

"It will only be possible to bury his head," Athenry reminded her.

Catherine was aware that John's torso, arms and legs had been buried in a shallow grave close to the gallows. Had there been a medical school in Galway at that time, his body parts would have ended up there as an educational aid to the students. She remained silent in the hope that Aunt Bridget might intercede.

"Burying his head is what she has in mind." Lady Browne opened her fan.

Catherine nodded. Athenry said, "Apart from that, the issue is a matter for John's parents in the first instance. However, I shall consult with Sheriff Shaw and the Gentlemen of the Town to see if they will release the head."

Catherine was surprised at the accommodating attitude of her father. She reasoned that Duncannon's negative response to his request for a pardon for John Bodkin must have dismayed him. He could reassert his local authority to some degree by having the remains of her beloved released after an appropriate interval.

"Should I succeed in my request," Athenry said, "how do you think the Bodkins will respond?"

Catherine thought furiously as Lady Browne fanned herself; the reputation of her family was at stake. Her proposal would require delicate choreography. Counsellor Bodkin would surely be amenable, but the reactions of John's mother and Patrick's widow were more difficult to gauge. Then a thought struck her.

"Papa, is it quite possible that the Bodkins are thinking along similar lines?"

"What a clever daughter you have, Francis." Lady Browne smiled.

"Quite so!" The wrinkles on her father's brow melted away. "How shall we find out?"

"I could draft a note to the Bodkins," Catherine suggested. "Perhaps we could discuss it over dinner."

"I do not consider that a good notion, my dear," Athenry said as the carriage drew up on the gravelled forecourt of Bermingham House. "The initiative must come from the Bodkins."

That decision made her realize why Dean Bruce had ignored her request to pray for her beloved. He would not have done so if accompanied by a similar request from the Bodkins. Instead of brandishing her quill, she prayed every day for an intercession from John's parents. Would they write, or visit, or just ignore her?

She understood that she would have to control her impulsiveness. But how could she grieve properly for John when she was forced to see his handsome face deteriorate every day on that dreadful spike.

* * * * *

ON THE FOLLOWING DAY, Catherine kept vigil near the front door hoping for a letter or message from the Bodkins. As darkness fell with no word, she surmised that they needed time to craft an approach, if they were indeed of the same mind. Mrs Bodkin might well baulk at the prospect of inviting her son's killer into her home. Even more understandable, perhaps, would be a reluctance on Anna's part to meet with her late husband's killer.

The days slipped by one by one. The tick-tock of the great clock in the hallway drove Catherine demented as she waited for the Bodkins to make a move. Despite her father's objections, she insisted on visiting the Market House every day with Aunt Bridget or Miss Blake to pray for John. His face was at peace, but the tissue of his handsome cheeks had begun to sag. She had hoped to meet one of the Bodkins at their son's remains in Tuam but they did not appear while she was in attendance there.

As she prepared for dinner on that Friday evening, she had given up watching for a communication from the Bodkins although she had prayed for that cause at Saint Mary's Cathedral. Seated at her dressing table, Catherine's ears picked up the sound of hooves galloping towards the house. She set aside her toilette and rushed downstairs. The footman accepted the message from the rider and walked towards the library with the sealed letter on a silver salver.

Entering the library on his heels, she waited impatiently while her father scanned the message.

"You may prepare to visit Carrowbeg next Sunday," he said, handing the letter to her. She rushed towards him and hugged him. "Thank you, Papa. That is a great relief to me." She dashed off to her room and read the letter, not once but three times.

Private and Confidential.

Carrowbeg House,
Belclare,
Tuam,
County Galway.

Friday, 19th March 1742,

Dear Lord Athenry,

Mary and I are naturally heartbroken by the recent loss of our only remaining son, John. The public display of his remains in the Market House in Tuam is extremely upsetting to us, and that feeling is accentuated by our belief that John was innocent of the crime for which he was hanged.

We are anxious to commemorate the memory of our son in an appropriate fashion. Despite normally being of a decisive nature, I find myself unsure of how precisely to do this despite lengthy discussions with Mary on the subject.

In the hope that you might be able to assist us to come to a decision, and bearing in mind the devotion and love of Miss Catherine for John and he for her, we would like to invite yourself, Lady Browne and your daughter to visit us here next Sunday after service if that should prove agreeable to you.

Yours faithfully

Counsellor Bodkin.

After dinner that evening, she knelt by her bed and thanked the good Lord for his intercession.

CHAPTER 25

CATHERINE QUIVERED WITH TREPIDATION as the Bermingham carriage approached Carrowbeg House on the following Sunday morning. Absentmindedly, she watched the faces of passing walkers —were they wondering what new trouble faced the Bodkins? It was the first time that Athenry's carriage had traversed that route since the night Patrick had died. She dreaded the thought of meeting the eyes of Patrick's grieving widow, Anna, and hoped she might not be present. She could not defend her actions without exposing Patrick's attempt to dishonour her, yet to do that would cause even more anguish to Anna and to Patrick's parents. She longed for the presence of little Thomas at their meeting to lighten the mood, but thought it unlikely.

As the house came into view, Catherine noted the drawn shutters on the front windows. When they entered the long narrow stone building, the great clock was silent and a mirror was covered in the hallway. The sombre atmosphere was somewhat alleviated by a blazing fire of wood in the drawing room, and more so by the sight of little Thomas playing with a toy soldier on a rug.

"You are most welcome, Lord Athenry, Lady Browne and Catherine," Counsellor Bodkin proclaimed. "Please take a seat."

"Thank you, Counsellor." Athenry sat down.

The housekeeper served the tea for Mary Bodkin to pour and passed around sweet cakes.

Catherine sat between Lady Browne and Mary, with Anna further to the left. Little Thomas dropped his toy soldier at her feet. She picked it up and returned it to him, registering the coldness in Anna's face. How would Thomas react in the future, were he to find out that she had killed his father? She pushed away the thought.

Bodkin cleared his throat as the housekeeper left the room. "Thank you for visiting us today. It is necessary to discuss the issue that I raised in my letter to Lord Athenry. Mary and I have lost two sons, two brothers, two nephews, and a sister-in-law …"

A tear rolled down his cheek and his voice wavered. "A veritable roll-call of misery for the Bodkin family. May I ask for a minute's silence to honour the memory of our dearly departed?"

Catherine joined her hands and prayed, her admiration for Counsellor Bodkin unbounded. His words suggested that he had forgiven his brother and his nephew for their dastardly crimes against his family. The lawyer had aged since his collapse at the funeral of his slain relatives and since John's indictment for fratricide. John's subsequent hanging was an added affliction too hard for him to bear. His hair was a lighter shade of grey and his hands shook slightly. Mary also had also suffered, her face pale and more wrinkled.

"Now we have a decision to make." Bodkin gazed into the fireplace which crackled with the sound of burning wood. "What shall we do with … John's remains, if we can persuade the authorities to release them to us?"

"Before we discuss that, may I ask a question?" said Anna.

Catherine closed her eyes as Bodkin nodded assent.

"I apologize for asking but I must know," Anna said. A tear escaped from her eye. "Who killed my Patrick?"

"Good heavens!" Lady Browne shook her head.

An awkward pause followed as Catherine gathered herself to respond. The world shrank to just herself and Patrick's widow, and everyone else seemed to fade into the background. Heart pounding, she replied, "Anna has every right to ask that question."

"Ladies …" Athenry began but the great man was powerless to halt the flow.

Catherine laid down her cup. The sound of it clinking against the saucer made her jump. "When I rose in court to profess John's innocence, the words got stuck in my throat." She took a deep breath. "Because I expected a guilty judgment, I persuaded my father that such a verdict would be unsafe, but the pardon was refused. When that intervention failed, I spoke at the gallows in an attempt to save John's life—the life of an innocent man— until Sheriff Shaw cut me short."

"We know that already," Anna snapped.

Lady Browne waved her fan frantically. "Is this really the time …"

Catherine looked at her father, who remained impassive. "Allow me, then, to finish what I tried to say at the gallows," she pleaded, looking at the tear-streaked faces of Anna and Mary Bodkin beside her. "Please forgive me. It was I who killed Patrick, though I never intended his death." Catherine buried her face in her hands and cried inconsolably alongside the stunned silence that followed.

"Catherine, my dear," Lady Browne whispered. "May I have a word in private, please?"

Catherine followed her aunt into the hallway.

"What have I done, Aunt Bridget?" she cried.

"Wipe your tears, my brave young girl." Lady Browne proffered a handkerchief.

"Anna will never forgive me."

"That we shall see. We must return to the drawing room," Lady Browne said. "You must explain your actions more fully to the Bodkins."

"But what will I say, Aunt Bridget?" cried the distraught girl.

"Speak from the heart, my dear."

Catherine hesitated. "Should I tell them that Patrick tried to dishonour me?"

"Goodness me!" For once in her life, Lady Browne was speechless.

"That is why John was so angry, you see. When Patrick attempted to kill John, I could not merely stand by and watch him do it."

Catherine saw her father standing at the drawing-room door. He opened his arms and Catherine rushed into them.

"Catherine wishes to explain," Lady Browne said.

"Of course," Athenry replied. Anna felt his strong arms around her, holding her safe.

*　*　*　*　*

WHEN SHE RETURNED TO the drawing room, the Bodkins were standing around in shocked silence. Mary Bodkin ordered some fresh tea and sought to console her daughter-in-law while little Thomas clung to his mother. Lady Browne whispered to Counsellor Bodkin. Catherine understood that it was now her task to make peace with John's parents and with Anna.

Mary Bodkin poured tea for them with a shaking hand. Catherine sipped the fragrant potation. She then put her cup and saucer down decisively, pleading in her head for guidance.

"I wish to beg forgiveness from all of you," Catherine began, hoping that Mary or Anna would respond.

Anna raised her tear-filled eyes. "I have never been able to grieve properly for Patrick. It seemed unlikely that my husband had died from natural causes, but I could not see what else might have occurred."

"I felt the same," Mary Bodkin said. "But I never had the courage to raise the matter with Lord Athenry."

Athenry remained silent but Catherine saw the colour rising in his cheeks. She did not know how to continue, and sought inspiration but found none. The initiative now rested with the Bodkin women.

"Now that I know that Patrick was killed," Mary said, "it will be easier to mourn his loss."

"But why did you kill him?" Anna asked the question in all of their minds.

Catherine paled as all eyes focused on her. "A drunken row broke out between Patrick and John. Patrick cocked his pistol and aimed it at John. His finger was on the trigger. I hit Patrick on the head with a poker ..."

After a long silence broken only by the inconsolable sobbing of Catherine and the Bodkin women, Counsellor Bodkin intervened. "Thank you, Catherine. As John told us after his trial, it was an accident."

"I cannot credit this," Mary said. "Patrick never drank to excess, merely a little wine at dinner."

"That is true as a general rule," Anna said. "However, on that night Patrick did drink too much whiskey. I do not understand what came over him, but he did not deserve to be killed for it."

"I never meant to kill him, only to prevent him from shooting John," Catherine said shakily. "John put him to bed, thinking that he would merely suffer from a sore head in the morning. We could not believe it when we found that he had passed away."

"Why did you lie to your father at the time?" Anna asked.

"John and I were afraid. He made me promise to say nothing." Catherine took a deep breath. "I should have told my father there and then."

"But you have told us now," Counsellor Bodkin said.

"Can you ever forgive me?" Catherine asked tentatively.

After what seemed like an eternity, he said kindly, "I forgive you. You acted in John's defence and did not intend to kill Patrick. Now that we know the truth, we can all start to grieve properly for both Patrick and John."

Catherine heaved a heartfelt sigh of relief, and thanked the Lord that she had at least managed to spare Anna the knowledge of Patrick's assault on her person.

Counsellor Bodkin continued, "I want to thank Lord Athenry for offering to co-operate with us in commemorating John appropriately."

"That is the least I can do," Athenry said.

"But how should we do it?" Bodkin wondered.

After they had all bent their minds to the problem, Lady Browne spoke up, "Catherine has a suggestion."

As all eyes turned to her again, Catherine steeled herself. "I think that John would have liked to be buried here at Carrowbeg." There, she had said it.

"But where at Carrowbeg?" Mary Bodkin raised her eyebrows.

"I know just the place," Bodkin interjected. "At the Mary Skerrett Mount, just north of the house."

Catherine was not surprised. John had told her about his grandmother, Mary Skerrett, a devout Catholic. She had refused to conform to Protestantism although her husband had done so to protect their property.

Before she died, she instructed her young cousin, Friar Skerrett, to bury her at Carrowbeg rather than at the Bodkin plot, within the ruins of the old church at Belclare. Local people claimed that the widow Skerrett, as she was known, had put a curse upon the Bodkins. Nobody knew why she had laid the imprecation, or if they did, they kept quiet about it. Some people used the reputed curse to explain the Bodkin massacre, the death of Patrick, and lately, the execution of his reputedly innocent brother.

"Friar Skerrett told me that Mary Skerrett was a distant relative of mine," Anna said.

Catherine held her breath. When she saw Mary Bodkin nodding, she knew her mission was accomplished.

＊　＊　＊　＊　＊

SOME DAYS LATER, LADY Browne spoke to John's parents, and Lord Athenry addressed the Gentlemen of the City; Catherine was authorized to preserve the remains of her beloved. Having researched the requirements, she assisted the local doctor to dry out the severed head using a salt called natron. Once it had dried out, she watched it being wrapped in strips of white linen in the Egyptian manner. What a strange, sad experience it was to hold thus the ravaged head of her betrothed. When John had been replaced in his display cage, she watched the astonished faces of onlookers as they stared at the mummified head.

Lord Athenry persuaded Sheriff Shaw and the Gentlemen of the Town to release the remains one month after the execution. Catherine was present when the preserved head of John was released to the Bodkins. She travelled with them to Carrowbeg on the appointed day: Sunday, 11th April 1742, and was pleased to find that Anna and little Thomas were present. Athenry and Lady Browne had sent their apologies on the basis that it was a private ceremony, knowing that their presence would have brought it to a more formal level.

Friar Skerrett and the Vicar of Belclare had agreed to officiate at the simple ceremony. Together with the Bodkins, Catherine placed John's remains into an oak coffin. The lightweight chest was carried on the shoulders of Counsellor Bodkin, Mr Joyce, the groom and the shepherd. How tragic it was, thought Catherine, that only one Bodkin male remained to carry the coffin.

At noon, the funeral cortege moved north towards the Mary Skerrett Mount. Catherine followed with Mary Bodkin.

Anna halted. "I am so sorry, please excuse me, but I cannot do it."

Little Thomas cried, "I want to go, Mama."

Anna replied. "No, Thomas! We must stay."

As they walked northward to the grave, Catherine could still hear the childish shrieks of little Thomas who wanted to follow the cortege. Then the shrieking stopped. Catherine glanced anxiously over her shoulder: Thomas was dragging his reluctant mother towards them.

As they made their slow progress along the muddy boreen, people gradually joined the cortege, appearing from behind walls and hedges. At the sacred burial place, Catherine was overwhelmed to find a large crowd of estate workers and tenants in attendance. It made her happy when Counsellor Bodkin, relieved of the burden of the coffin by a footman, threw his arms around both herself and Mary. Anna maintained a discreet distance from the grave but Thomas kept pulling her towards it.

As the wind whipped up dark clouds and sent them scudding across the spring sky, Bodkin spoke, "We are gathered here today to honour the memory of my son, John. I am happy to say that Friar Skerrett and the Vicar of Belclare have kindly agreed to witness the burial."

"Thank you, Counsellor Bodkin," Friar Skerrett said. "It is a great privilege for me to be here today at a ceremony attended by Catholics and Protestants together. I am a Catholic friar and a nephew of Mary Skerrett, a Catholic and the grandmother of the late John Bodkin, a Protestant, who is about to join her in heaven. Counsellor Bodkin and his family have endured a series of events that would have torn asunder a lesser family. Miss Catherine is grieving the departure of her fiancé from this earthly world. So too, is my cousin, Anna, who is still grieving the loss of her husband, John's brother, Patrick. Both young women have shown remarkable fortitude in the face of the deaths of their loved ones."

Catherine gave silent thanks that Friar Skerrett was such a master of diplomacy.

"I now call on Counsellor Bodkin and Mr Joyce to lower the coffin into the grave." Skerrett intoned:

> *May his soul and the souls of all the faithful departed*
> *through the mercy of God rest in peace. Amen*

The sky darkened even more. Catherine followed Mary Bodkin, each dropping a daffodil on to the coffin. Little Thomas dragged his mother forward. Catherine, holding the last daffodil, glanced at Anna and indicated the flower, but Patrick's widow shook her head. Thomas stretched out his arm to snatch the daffodil so that he could follow his grandmother's lead. Catherine directed her eyes at Anna again; this time she nodded.

Catherine watched as Counsellor Bodkin led his heir to the grave. Thomas dropped the daffodil on to the coffin of the uncle falsely convicted of murdering his father. Catherine hoped and prayed that the long journey towards reconciliation had finally begun.

James Joyce and his assistants quickly filled in the grave. As people began to disperse, the heavens opened. Catherine scurried through the rain into the house, there to partake of refreshments with family and friends. She heard the rumble of thunder, quickly followed by the flash of lightning. The gods were angry. Catherine's spirits lifted when Anna approached her with open arms, and they both wept with the emotion of their restoration to favour. Catherine felt that the curse of the widow Skerrett had been lifted.

Counsellor and Mary Bodkin joined in the embrace, encircling little Thomas. Through her tears, Catherine rejoiced at the wonderful innocence of the little boy. She fervently hoped that Thomas, present heir to Liscarrow and Carrowbeg, would lead them all to a better place.

AUTHOR'S NOTE

In 1742, John Bodkin of Belclare Co. Galway was hanged drawn and quartered having been found guilty of the murder of his brother Patrick in 1739. On the gallows in Galway, he refused to acknowledge his innocence or guilt of this crime as recorded in *Pue's Occurrences,* a primary source. Instead, as the noose tightened around his neck, he proclaimed *I forgive Mankind* implying that he was not guilty.

I have investigated the possibility of his innocence through the medium of a historical novel in which John Bodkin and Catherine Bermingham, the third daughter of Lord Athenry, are the principal characters. Both are real people but their romance is fictional.

The delay in John Bodkin's trial was occasioned by the belief of the local Justice of the Peace, Lord Athenry, that Patrick Bodkin had died of natural causes. It was not until the aftermath of the Bodkin murders in 1741 that John Bodkin was accused of fratricide. These events have been described in a primary source, *Pue's Occurrences* in 1741, later amplified by Oliver J Burke in his 1885 *Anecdotes of the Connaught Circuit...,* a secondary source. Three members of the Bodkin family, Oliver Bodkin (John Bodkin's uncle), Oliver's pregnant wife, Margery, his son, Oliver, a visitor, Marcus Lynch of Galway and a number of unnamed servants were murdered in a family feud.

The Bodkin massacre occurred in Carrowbaun House, Belclare, a village, about four miles west of Tuam in County Galway. I have fictionalized Carrowbaun House as Liscarrow House to avoid confusion with the other Bodkin residence of nearby Carrowbeg House. Recent reports of the murders include those by Jarlath O'Connell, Martin Dolan and William Henry, all secondary sources. These adhere closely to Burke's version.

Burke took some licence with the primary source, a practise I have accepted in the interests of clarity. The most obvious licence is that John Bodkin had three brothers rather than one, namely, Dominick, the aforesaid Patrick and Frank. It was Dominick rather than Patrick who was reputedly murdered by John. I presume that Burke substituted Patrick for Dominick as the eldest son to avoid confusion with his Uncle Dominick, a convicted participant in the Bodkin massacre. Burke removed the youngest son, Frank from his narrative because he had passed away by the time the Bodkin murders had occurred.

Six servants have been chosen to represent the other unnamed victims whose number varies from four to seven in the various sources. These are fictionally named as Henry Burke, Mrs Agnes Burke, James Fallon, Michael MacDonagh, Thaddeus MacHugh and Nora O'Brien.

ABOUT THE AUTHOR

PAUL McNULTY

Paul is a Fulbright Scholar and Alumnus of University College Dublin, Ohio State and MIT. He served on the academic staff at UCD from 1972-2005. His writing credentials include editorship of a student magazine, *The Anvil*, followed by publication of scientific and popular papers during a career in Biosystems Engineering.

After retirement, he studied Genealogy/Family History and Creative Writing. His diploma project, "The Genealogy of the Anglo-Norman Lynches who Settled in Galway," was published in the *Journal of the Galway Archaeological and Historical Society* in 2010. The discovery of a treasure trove of fascinating stories linked to the Lynches inspired the author to write historical novels and plays based on real events in 18th century Ireland.

Paul has written two historical novels, *Spellbound by Sibella*, and *The Abduction of Anne O'Donel*. Both have been finalists in the William Faulkner Novel Competitions in 2012 and 2013 respectively, and have been published by Club Lighthouse CLP, Edmonton, Alberta, Canada.

He has also self-published *The Genealogy of the Anglo-Norman Lynches who Settled in Galway* in 2013 and a novella, *A Rebel Romance* in 2014, both with CreateSpace Independent Publishing Platform. More recently, he has written the first draft of a play, *Spellbound by Sibella*, based on an extract from his novel of the same name.

Paul lives in Dublin with his wife, three children and two granddaughters. The wild splendour of Mayo and Connemara inspires his writing. Links to social media include Facebook and Twitter. His website address is:

http://paul-mcnulty.com.

OTHER CLUB LIGHTHOUSE PUBLISHING BOOKS BY THIS AUTHOR

Spellbound by Sibella
The Abduction of Anne O'Donel

Made in the USA
Charleston, SC
25 May 2015